Books by Belinda Burke

Eight Kingdoms

Dark Side of the Sun
The Circle Unbroken
The Burning Season
The Shadow Road
A Harvest of Dreams and Embers

Single Titles

Wolf of the West
Undone
Deathless

I0542393

A Harvest of Dreams and Embers

ISBN # 978-1-78686-114-6

©Copyright Belinda Burke 2017

Cover Art by Posh Gosh ©Copyright 2017

Interior text design by Claire Siemaszkiewicz

Pride Publishing

This is a work of fiction. All characters, places and events are from the author's imagination and should not be confused with fact. Any resemblance to persons, living or dead, events or places is purely coincidental.

All rights reserved. No part of this publication may be reproduced in any material form, whether by printing, photocopying, scanning or otherwise without the written permission of the publisher, Pride Publishing.

Applications should be addressed in the first instance, in writing, to Pride Publishing. Unauthorised or restricted acts in relation to this publication may result in civil proceedings and/or criminal prosecution.

The author and illustrator have asserted their respective rights under the Copyright Designs and Patents Acts 1988 (as amended) to be identified as the author of this book and illustrator of the artwork.

Published in 2017 by Pride Publishing, Newland House, The Point, Weaver Road, Lincoln, LN6 3QN, United Kingdom.

No part of this book may be reproduced, scanned, or distributed in any printed or electronic form without permission. Please do not participate in or encourage piracy of copyrighted materials in violation of the authors' rights. Purchase only authorised copies.

Pride Publishing is a subsidiary of Totally Entwined Group Limited.

If you purchased this book without a cover you should be aware that this book is stolen property. It was reported as "unsold and destroyed" to the publisher and neither the author nor the publisher has received any payment for this "stripped book".

Eight Kingdoms

A HARVEST OF DREAMS AND EMBERS

BELINDA BURKE

Dedication

For Stella

"Things fall apart; the center cannot hold;
Mere anarchy is loosed upon the world,
The blood-dimmed tide is loosed, and everywhere
The ceremony of innocence is drowned."

— W. B. Yeats

Chapter One

Sleep had come to Spring, though it did not belong there.

Myrddin advanced alone through the stillness of the Wyrdwood and found even the birds sunk into slumber. Drowsiness had descended, and with it a sacred silence that brought disharmony, reducing the promise of the branches to the ghost of leaves. There had never been such lethargy in immortal Spring before, but the season had traded away its show of splendor for somnolence.

King though he was, even Myrddin was tangled in threads of torpor and his own sudden awareness of the presence that incited them. Why here, why now? *Father?*

Yes.

With the feeling of acknowledgment came a summons Myrddin could not deny, though he wanted to. No other being was so perilous to him, had ever cost him so much, as his own father. And now, now that he finally had Kas for his own…

Neither the time nor the place of the visit pleased him, but Myrddin could no more deny the summons of the one who had sired him than the buds could refuse the spring.

His heart clenched. Had he regained what he'd lost only to have it taken away? *Kas.* All his desires were bound up in the single syllable of that name. He would not give his lover up again, no matter what demand the god of the wild had for him.

Myrddin found his father at the heart of the forest, wrapped around its most ancient oak. He *knew* it was his father, but Myrddin had never seen him like this. As the Stag of the wood, yes, carrying the moon in the spaces between his antlers. As a mist, or in a man's shape, but like this?

The god of the wood had come to him as a dragon. His father was a moss-backed beast with leafed and feathered wings whose span stretched beyond Myrddin's sight. He was the wildest and most beautiful of his kind Myrddin had ever seen, but he was a dragon all the same.

Did that mean...he was no longer a god?

There was a shiver in the branching pinions, a sibilant trembling of feathers. A sound like silk being stretched too tight and too quickly snapped through the air as the great wings beat once then settled.

"Father..." The dragon opened his mouth and breathed out the scent of somnolent blossoms, but not a single word in answer. "Father?"

He resisted the urge to go to one knee as he resisted the drowsy pressure of the air, a sudden urge to yawn. Silence greeted him. More than before, stronger the closer he came to the unsteady orb of his father's eye. He recognized the source of the unnatural sleep with a familiarity that reminded him of his own long-vanished past.

'My little shoot.'

Not his father's voice, but the memory of his mother's, brushed Myrddin with a faint prickling of dread. This sleep was akin to his own lost winter slumber. The sleep that had taken him at Samhain each year, before Spring had had a rite, or a kingdom... When winter had come to him as to the blossoms and dropped him down the well of the sleeping season.

His father blinked one enormous eye, and the flickering facets drew Myrddin in. The eye became a world, a universe in the shape of an ochre orb. *"I forget who I was before the birth of this moment."*

Understanding came to Myrddin not in words but image-emotions. Foreign thoughts expanded across his consciousness in a blur that was reminiscent of his Spring vision and the madness that had brought it.

"I have lost the way and from the hollow places of the world, the languor and silence of the sacred spaces, I hear fear and fever, and ever fewer the voices that once were mine.

"Where are the new peoples? Where is the new god who is only a new name, given to what I am and always have been? The land where first I was worshiped has gone under the sea, and now what remains of the old ways has become overgrown in the minds and memories of men.

"The Spring is a harbor of whispers. I hear rumor from the root of the world. I see the shadow of the future casting its long fingers through time, but it is all silence to me."

Myrddin experienced his father's awareness in the inner sharing, a hush of rites that quickened the speed at which many things hurtled toward nonexistence. The offerings that remained did not belong to his father under any name. Sacrifice had turned to prayer. The old accords with the land and its gods had become a plea for intercession with foreign power, the Christian God.

"I don't understand. Why now? Why would you come to me now, when it's too late for anything to be done?"

The dragon opened his mouth, but this time it was for a panting rumble of laughter.

"You don't even have speech left, do you? How is that amusing?"

The whole of his father's presence spoke to one reality, one truth.

Sleep.

The great jaws parted and the flower-scented breath came tinged with iron. "Boy. Must be born. *Must be.*"

It was a terrifying confirmation of all Myrddin's hopes and fears. Jade leaves lashed at him. The billion facets of his father's eyes glinted with immutable silence.

Wild god, dragon, he curled again around the primeval oak. As he did so, Myrddin's own shape shifted, not under his will but his father's. Spring stag, Spring son, he went closer and caught a breath of beast-language, neither divine nor mortal, but in between.

"It is in your hands now."

In the moment after, the silence of the Wyrdwood was returned to its usual chatter. The birds made their endless music, and Myrddin wondered if the stillness had been for him alone.

Already his father was fading into echoes, the shape of him subsiding, feathers into leaves and grass. The roots of the tree were become like the subtle magnificence of his flesh – or was it his flesh, which shared the gnarled grain of the living wood?

Myrddin wanted... He didn't know what he wanted. To be free of the oppressive suspicion that his whole world was already only a memory. A dead thing. He needed to be anywhere but where he was, feeling his own heartbeat struggle against the pressure of sleep. He hadn't experienced anything like it since – when had it been?

When mother died. When my mother –

Myrddin turned and ran as the thought came to him, ran like a child from the serpentine whisper coiled in his mind. He ran straight out of Spring and into the soft warmth of Britain's summer, then over the water toward the wide, dark wood where Autumn waited its turn.

The warmth of his lover's kingdom embraced Myrddin pleasantly for the first time he could remember. He swept through it in a rush, his thoughts too distracted to appreciate the ease of his passage.

"Kas, where are you?"

The Autumn wood liked to make its roads spiral, lead away from where one wanted to go instead of toward it, but the moment he said Kas' name Myrddin felt hands on his shoulders and turned into an unexpected embrace.

"*Kas*. Always sneaking up on me. I missed you, so I came to find you for myself."

If Kas was startled by his urgency he didn't show it, only slid his hands up into Myrddin's hair and pulled his head back so he had no choice but to lift his mouth for Kas' kiss.

Even that was enough to soothe Myrddin, for the first time since…their golden age. Their summer. But the autumn had already come. They'd had their spring, their strawberry time, and now the summer was past, and the sweet taste that had lingered with it.

His lover bent to scrutinize him as Myrddin dropped his head to Kas' chest. "Something wrong, Merlin?"

He shook his head, rubbing his cheek on Kas' chest. "Just looking at you. Remembering. You haven't changed."

Kas lifted an eyebrow. "No. Nor you. Even if you might like to."

Myrddin traced the line of Kas' torso with his fingertips and watched the muscles contract beneath his skin. "I don't want to change. I want to be what I am, that's all. Whatever that is. When I was a child I wanted to grow up, so I did. But all at once, not like boys do, or should. It taught me a lesson."

The hint of a frown bent the corners of Kas' lips downward. "I do not like the sound of your sadness. Is it nostalgia that moves you? The way we are together after so long? Is it *me*?"

Again, Myrddin shook his head. "All those things. None of them. I…was just thinking of what it was like when things began between us. You were innocent then." He followed the 'V' of Kas' pelvis with his fingers, down to the smooth, soft skin of his inner thigh. "Innocent of pleasure, innocent of pain."

Warm hands tightened at Myrddin's hips. "Never that. I was only without words for what I was feeling. To know the name of things, or not to know them, neither changes the things themselves."

Myrddin traced the curve of Kas' cock and it stiffened under his touch as Kas reached up and brushed his index finger over one of Myrddin's nipples. "Even so. I still think you were innocent. The way death is supposed to be."

"Is that what you think?" Kas closed his fingers around the dark, tight peak he had teased into stiffness, tugged, then rolled it back and forth.

"Yes—*oh.*"

"But you are wrong. About me and about death. There is no innocence in the ending of things. Only in their beginnings." He slid the tingling warmth of his hands down, down, down, then stopped. "That is the truth, my hawk. *You* are the innocent one. So much so that you gaze at me and see what you cannot interpret in yourself."

"Kas..."

"Perhaps that is why I wanted you the moment we met. Why I was so drawn to you—why I have always been, will always be unable to resist you." He bent closer so that his breath brushed Myrddin's ear. "My only selfishness. The one desire I cannot put aside."

"*Kas.*" The beat of his heart sped faster, a pounding he could feel in his throat, behind his eyes, in his fingertips.

"Look at you, even now. *Innocent.* You make work for yourself in the name of your own conscience, but my own duty is only the existence I cannot escape. The being that I am, which is Death."

'*Cannot. Escape.*' Myrddin shivered then nudged him away, pushed him down to the ground and straddled him. He pressed his mouth against the smooth dip in Kas' collarbone. "But you can't escape me, either."

"Nor do I want to."

"I can guess what you want." He slid off to one side and lay flat. The moss was cool and damp beneath the ancient fall of leaves. "You want...strawberries."

Kas leaned over him, a darting movement. "*Strawberries.* You know better than that—" But Myrddin sat up, his fingers over Kas' lips, and only smiled, distracted, when Kas licked at them, sucked the tips into his mouth. "My hawk. Where do you think you are flying away this time?"

"Something...someone is calling for me." And he frowned. "That Pendragon, I expect. It's in the wind, can you hear—?"

"Yes." And though the lust was not disturbed from Kas'

expression, there was a sudden, uncertain sadness behind it. "Is it not what I said? You make work for yourself. Why would you do that, when it wasn't so long ago that you chided me for my own duty? When you would have refused even the weight of your own power and its consequences?"

Myrddin pulled his fingers away from Kas' mouth and kissed him instead. "Because I meant it when I said I wanted you forever. And I've been bored, and missing something to do in the mortal world. It's the timing that's inconvenient, I thought I would have longer, especially since…"

He smiled to himself and shook his head, hearing the memory of Uther's words. '*I have no need for sorcerers or omens, boy!*' Not really a lie, but not really the truth, either. The wind brought Myrddin another echo of the summons. Uther, the High King he'd given a red dragon omen and left behind, was not a patient man.

Though Myrddin was not bound to obey instantly, the call came too close on the heels of his worry about which direction the future would take. Was this one of the choices that would change his course, his purpose? He turned his head on Kas' chest, restless, unwilling to move and uncertain of whether he should.

But this is connected to that earlier thing. My father, the dragon, lost in his own wild. And the memory…of the Spring vision. The tower. The Sword. A meeting – and those words. What else, after those words?

'*Son of no man.*'

They had been a summons too, in their own way…but not like this. Eager memories tangled his thoughts in sticky intentions. What did he want, this Pendragon? Why now, so soon?

"This someone who is calling for you, you really must listen?" Kas' words flowed warm across his shoulders. Myrddin turned and found himself caught in his lover's arms.

"Yes. This time it's my turn to go." He paused, confused by the humor he found in the moment even now. "My turn to be summoned away."

"I hear it. Did I not say? But I am surprised to find you giving such power to a mortal."

"No lesser man than the High King of Britain." He grinned as he said it, but the smile faded quickly as Kas stroked his hair.

"Why?"

"For the sake of peace, and my own conscience, and maybe…"

Kas gave a little tug to the strands still in his grasp. "You cannot stop what is coming. Not even you."

Myrddin scowled and pressed his face against his lover's chest. "Don't pull my hair."

"No? But that is not what you say when I take you." And he stopped, ran his hands over the curve of Myrddin's buttocks. "You have time before you leave me, do you not?"

"Always time for you." He slipped out of Kas' grasp and dropped onto his hands and knees. "Do what you want with me."

Kas took Myrddin's hips in his hands, bent over him and kissed the ridges of his spine. "What I want? That could take a while. This mortal king, he will have to wait his turn."

Wait his – ? Myrddin made a face. "No, thank you. I'll have only you."

"What a fool, to think that was what I meant. Even in jest, you would say that? As if I would let you, as if I would share you ever again." The words were scalding, almost angry, but Kas' hands were gentle, easy and eager both as he slipped them down to open him up.

"*Kas.* I don't deserve – *oh!*" Kas crooked his fingers inside, stroked just the right spot, and Myrddin gasped out the rest of his words. "I don't deserve you. I don't – deserve – *ohhh.*"

Kas slid one hand up Myrddin's spine and into his hair again, tugged his head back and bent by his ear. "No. You probably do not. No more than I deserve you."

There was a hint of subtle humor in his voice, the suggestion that he meant his words both ways that they could be taken. Myrddin opened his mouth to protest, but Kas kissed him and suddenly he was groaning instead.

"It does not mean anything, Merlin. *Deserve*. You should know that better than I."

"Ka-a-ahhh-*ahh*—" Slow, deep penetration. Cock, not fingers. Then slower. *Deeper*. Each thrust dragged out almost past bearing. But the sensation was intertwined irresistibly with Myrddin's memories of every other time Kas had touched him, and with the fear of the future that went on compelling him.

Incongruous, and yet not so, Myrddin suddenly craved the taste of the strawberries he had teased Kas about. The taste of Kas, of his kiss…and strawberries. "Kas, let me— *kiss* me." Myrddin glanced over his shoulder, twisted and met his lover's lips as Kas leaned in, devouring his mouth with the intensity of the moment.

Kas sucked on his tongue and Myrddin bucked his hips forward, cock twitching in sympathetic sensation. He moaned against Kas' lips, lifting himself to the slow, deep thrusts as he tried to keep his impatience contained. It wouldn't do him any good, never did him any good, unless…

There was one word that always seemed to slip right past Kas' defenses and get Myrddin what he wanted. "*Please*."

Kas slid his hands up Myrddin's sides in response, threaded one into his hair and dragged him near enough to kiss again.

Yes. "Please, *please*."

He dragged the word out as long as he had breath. Kas licked at his lips, kissed the corner of his mouth, then a hot line from that kiss to a spot on his neck that made him shudder all over.

"Harder?" Kas slammed into him and his lips slipped down Myrddin's neck. "More?" But Myrddin could barely breathe, gasped in air and let out a keening wail.

Kas laughed at him, not out of breath at all. His voice came soft and taunting, but only in play. "I should bring you just like this, before your British king. 'Summoned him?', I will say. '*Summoned* him? He is *mine*.' And who would deny it, with you on your knees for me? What would he think of you then?"

Myrddin shook his head, gasped out the only other word he could think of. "Love…"

"Yes. My hawk, my love." Kas gripped his thighs and lifted without pulling out of him, turning him onto his side.

Myrddin clutched his lover's hip and held him close while Kas caught one of his legs and pulled it over his shoulder.

"*Please.*" One pale hand and its slender fingers held Myrddin pinned, splayed over his ribs. He let his head drop to the ground and moaned. "*Kas.* Want you to—"

Something amused flickered in Kas' face, in his eyes, and he let Myrddin writhe as he chose, onto his erection then up again, only so he could push himself down onto it. As if Kas would ever—as if he could—but the thought of being taken like that, shown off before a whole court of mortals, that red-faced king…

A burst of laughter was caught in Myrddin's throat, trapped behind a moan. He tossed his head against the grass, wrapped his free leg around Kas and reached for his own cock. Kas let him, but the faster he stroked himself the slower his lover thrust into him. Counterpoint and tension, the pleasure spread into a tangled blossom of heat somewhere between Myrddin's cock and the base of his spine.

He lifted his hips and Kas caressed him, his fingers a whisper over his nipples, down his sides. Myrddin arched and Kas let his leg down, leaned over him and mouthed his way from nipples to collarbone, from collarbone to the curve of his ear.

"Mine, you are. My hawk, my spring. I will not share you. I will leave my mark on you. On your throat and your red lips, and where else, love? Where else should I kiss you?"

"Ka…*ahh.* Ahh, ah—*ah!*"

"Here?" His tongue came wet and sudden against

Myrddin's chest, a lick of heat followed by teeth.

"Ohhh..."

"Or here?" Kas fastened his mouth around one nipple, sucked and bit gently.

"Kas! Please, I can't, *please*." Sensation separated Myrddin from everything but his own body, the pressure of Kas' fingertips and the thick, full feeling of his cock stretching him as he thrust inside.

"If it was up to me I would kill you and keep you with me forever. Kill you and..."

"Do it, I – do it and – *Kas*." The word came from him rich with pleasure, elongated by heat. Time had turned thin and insubstantial.

Kas' mouth was hot as those unexpected summer days that come mid-autumn, and his pace was increasing, his fingers tight as talons around Myrddin's wrists.

"Can't wait for... Want our...*rite*. Our..."

"Yes. Just like this. Now, and always. *Always*, Merlin."

Shuddering tension came into Kas' thighs, his erection somehow bigger, harder, opening Myrddin up even more. The inevitable peak rushed toward him as Kas hitched him up and surged over him, drove into him more fiercely with every thrust.

His whole body tingled, every muscle clenched. Myrddin locked his legs around Kas' hips and held him deep while his climax overwhelmed him. It was a lightning spike of pleasure that dragged a hoarse cry out of his throat, then another when Kas gave in to his own release.

Myrddin was still panting when he pushed his hair out of his eyes and grinned up at his lover. "Kas, I really do have to go – "

"'Have to'. I do not like you talking this way. You have only talked this way...then."

He dropped his eyes from Kas' stare, the questions in it that he didn't want to answer. "It's not like you don't leave me all the time because of – "

"*My* responsibilities are a part of my existence. The essence of it." Kas chided him gently. "I could no more deny those duties, keep from passing the dead into the other world, than you could drain the Spring from your own blood."

"I wish I…" But Myrddin smiled, wan and thin, and wrapped his arms around Kas, pressing his cheek to the soundless warmth of his chest. No heartbeat now. Just the silence that he had grown to love. "No. Never mind. How could I keep you then?"

"I will remember this moment." Kas' hands slid off his body like reluctant oil. "I will remember, and when he dies, this mortal—"

"Kas. You wouldn't." But he was both touched and amused by the possessive, serious way Kas stared at him.

"You think so? Perhaps I will not do to him the worst of it. Perhaps I will save that for…" He fell silent, and the black power rose thick and choking as smoke. "But I will not make his passing pleasant. He *dared* to summon you from me." Myrddin disentangled himself from Kas' fingers and started to dress himself, but Kas was not through. "If you are too long away from me, too long among mortals, I will come for you. I will take you away and then I truly will not share."

Suddenly, Myrddin knew that Kas was just as afraid as he was, just as aware of the ominous cloud that seemed to thicken daily. Of the sense of danger to all that was most precious to both of them. "I love you. And when I'm through with Uther, with his court…when I know what he needs, and I've made the place *I* need, I'll come find you. I don't want to be away from you, Kas. I don't want…"

He stared at the sky, couldn't focus on the blistering stars. "My father came to Spring. To me. Before I came to you. He's *sleeping*, Kas. The god of the wood is sleeping." He turned then, and what he saw on his lover's face almost broke his heart. Still the same shadows but no surprise.

"It is beginning."

Myrddin clenched his fists until his nails bit into his palms. "Then I will make it *stop*." He suffered Kas' goodbye kiss, the cold, heavy heat of it, then turned and raced away.

* * * *

The forest was silent and too dark for the end of summer, but Aisling had grown used to that. How many months had it been since the world had followed its usual cycle? Since the seasons had progressed one after another as they should? More than a year now, since Dealla had slain the Spring Maiden and started a new cycle.

Death, instead of life.

Here, where the green border of the last living grove gave way to the gray that had overwhelmed the rest of Ireland, the difference drew her eye. But it wasn't what she was supposed to be observing.

The hand that closed on her shoulder drew her attention where it belonged. "Princess. *Carefully*."

Her companion was still, the muscles of his body taut with waiting. Cathán was the only one of those Lughaid had found to teach her how to hunt who'd had the patience to do the job. She was grateful for that, but she almost sighed at his address. 'Princess', still. After so many weeks. But the sigh wasn't permitted, might scare away their quarry, so she restrained it.

She followed the line of Cathán's gaze with her own stare. In the tangled branches across the empty clearing they had come to, a pair of bright eyes gleamed. A head became visible as Aisling watched.

It was a doe, lean with the long season of hunger, nibbling at the tips of the bare branches and the black bark.

She pitied the beast, but pity wouldn't feed her people. She tightened her fingers on the spear in her hand, nodded when Cathán gestured with his own. Around from the sides? *Yes*. They'd have a better chance of a successful strike without the thorns in the way, and the branches around the doe, though bare of new leaves, were still thick enough to present a problem.

She obeyed the lessons she'd learned in practice. *Listen to the messages of your body, the messages of the ground.* Where were the safe spaces around her to tread? What did the breeze have to tell her as she stalked forward?

A step, then another. Aisling followed the curve of the thicket to the north and the west, watching Cathán make his way around the other side. One step at a time. She must remember to beware the rustling leaves and the shapes under them, roots waiting to snarl her feet, twigs that might crack and give away her intent.

Their prey lifted her head. The brown eyes of the doe focused on the distance while her ears twitched.

Aisling held her breath.

The deer lowered her head again, nibbled on the raw end of a stripped branch, and Aisling slid another step forward, then another. She was close now. The spear was heavy in her hand but she refused to shift its weight out of this best position. Sweat prickled her brow, but she ignored it for the sake of the kill.

Cathán stepped forward across from her. They locked eyes for an instant. He nodded, and Aisling thought a prayer at the same moment she skipped forward and flung her spear. There was a high-pitched squeal, loud as the heartbeat screaming in Aisling's throat.

Cathán was waiting when she paced through the thicket, already crouched by the doe's head with a knife in his hand. "Well done, princess."

She laid her hand on the butt of the spear, then pulled it free and stared down as a jet of warm blood painted her hands with red. "How many times do I have to tell you? My name is Aisling. Use it."

"It's not my place."

"No? What is your place, then? You're the only one who had the patience to aid me, to deal with the weakness that was all the years of my life before now. The only one. Call me by my name. If anyone deserves to, you do." Aisling saw how little impression she was making on him, and this time allowed herself the sigh.

Weeks of the same argument. Since Lughaid had demanded that *someone* help her feed the people. Feed them, before she asked of them…anything.

The children were as lean as the deer she'd slain, and their parents approaching skeletal. They had come in families, sometimes whole villages, all without hope. The refugees were *still* coming, swelling the encampment around the one green grove, though the flood had been reduced to a slow trickle.

Cathán met her eyes, defiant, then lowered his gaze and shrugged. "Princess, it's because of you that there's a people left to help. The Druids are content with their fires and their councils and their talk. Now that you feed them —"

"Now that I feed them, I'm expected to ask them to fight. Before my sister gets us all killed." She thumbed the wet point of her spear. "Perhaps it wouldn't be so bad if she was the one who would die first."

"You wish this for her?" She saw a black spark in his eyes when she turned to peer up at his face.

"Wish it? I would kill her myself if I could."

"Princess —"

"*Aisling*, Cathán." She tightened her fist on the spear in her hand then shook her head and tried to loosen her shoulders. "We've work to do. You said it would make it easier if we left the offal here."

"Yes. And it's a fine beast for your first kill, prin — my lady." He lifted an eyebrow at her.

Aisling only shrugged. "Better. I suppose we'll just have to work on that along with everything else. Now. Give me your knife and show me what to do."

The smell of blood grew heavy in the thicket while they worked. It attracted unruly attention out of the afternoon as the day darkened around them, skipping dusk and heading for the night.

"We should leave soon, my lady. Unless whatever protects you is something that does not need the light."

She turned and scanned the wood behind them. There was nothing there that she could see, but that didn't mean anything. The *presence* of someone or something watching was thick, almost oppressive. "I don't know. I really don't, it hasn't been tested. Lughaid told me—"

There was a rustle as Cathán stirred beside her, shifting the doe. "Lughaid told *everyone*. You were marked by the Spring, and by the Summer before it. You were touched by the Green King himself. But I know something of the eight kingdoms, and it is Winter that hunts Ireland now."

She turned, startled, so much so that the knife slipped and cut her thumb. "Ah!"

"Princess! Carefully. You are not to be hurt, that was not our arrangement." He took her hand and wiped away the deer's blood with the tunic let down around his hips.

Flushing, she looked away. "It was just an accident." He was suddenly too close, and his skin radiated heat. But she couldn't say that. He would never call her by name if she said that.

Cathan wiped away the blood spilling from her finger, too, then brought it to his mouth and sucked on it. Something in his face changed, something in his eyes, but Aisling didn't move. He was…so close.

Too close.

The tip of his tongue moved over the stinging wound, but she didn't feel pain. *Something in his eyes…* His mouth, his tongue, were making her hot inside. Then he let her go, and she blinked at where the cut on her finger had been—and now wasn't.

"Cathán, you…" She reached up, touched his lips and stood frozen that way for a long moment, until she caught his gaze again, saw an amused sparkle in it and jerked her hand away. "You aren't…you can't be *human*."

He blinked at her almost lazily then returned to gutting the deer with swift, clean movements. "Is that a problem, my lady?"

"N-No…I suppose not. But no one mentioned—doesn't

anyone *know*?"

A certain stiffness came into his shoulders. "The people of my village. We lived by the sea, and my mother came from the sea, and when I was old enough to understand she told my father and I it was time for her to go home."

Cathán paused, elbows balanced on his thighs, and stared into the trees. "She asked if I would go with her. To dark Winter, the Red Kingdom. But my home was with my father. I live for the hunt, yes, but with a spear in my hand, not in a seal's shape."

Surprised, Aisling took a step forward then stopped. "Your mother was a selkie?"

"And my father was a man, and I have chosen his way of life. Yes."

She eyed him silently then got to her knees and started to help him again with the carcass. "Not many would do that."

"You think not?"

Shrugging, she wiped blood off her palms and onto the grass. "The lure of an immortal life is strong. Even my sister…"

"Dealla desires—"

Aisling laughed, shook her head and accepted the liver into her hands while he hauled out the steaming guts. "Not Dealla. Saoirse Saorla. My little sister… Dealla found her helping the *sidhe*. She was beaten, whipped. But the Red King came for her, freed her, took her away and now she is…"

"Unchanged, isn't she? But not the same."

It wasn't a question, and Aisling shrugged helplessly. "I don't know how to answer that. Changed? Not her face, not the shape of her. But she wore the thinnest dress, though it was Samhain and chill. She rode a horse that was more smoke than flesh. And the way she regarded me, the way her teeth flashed in her mouth…"

Cathán darted a glance in her direction. "Did she recognize you?"

Aisling hesitated. "Yes, but not at first."

He shrugged. "So, you see? That enviable immortal life, it has its price. Maybe she was willing to pay it. I am not."

Something like anger flashed through her, a sense of loss, magnified. "She's just a child! She was only eight years old."

"You should forget about her as she was, my lady. It might be better to forget she even exists."

She shook her head as he strode away from the deer and crossed to the edge of the grove. Cathán cut down a few dead vines, testing them with a strong pull. He bound the legs of the doe to their spears, made sure the edible organs were secure in the carcass, and Aisling hefted her end without being asked.

"I can't do that. Just forget her. I don't *want* to forget her."

Cathán shrugged, and her gaze lingered more on the lines of his shoulders as he did so than it should have. "I said it would be better, my lady. Not that I thought you would, or could."

Chapter Two

Saoirse watched the Red King stride down frosted dunes and into the darkness that reflected off the water. Without ripples, without waves, it lapped at the motionless shore. The sea was black and still, but as the Red King approached, the surface was broken by small, dark heads.

Selkies.

She had playmates and companions among their number, had been warned in the days just past that this moment was coming, but she hadn't quite believed. Now they were here, at this shore, staining the sand with tracks as they went to sea.

Without a splash, her special friend among them was out of the water and by her side. Saoirse watched the selkie come closer without allowing any expression on her own face. "Hello, Líadan."

"Saoirse, you shouldn't have come."

Now, she frowned, more than a little annoyed. "You did intend to leave without goodbye, then? I thought you were my friend!"

The edges of Líadan's soft, sable body went stiff. "Your friend. Yes, I am that. But this is my family, and all of my kin, and I will not be the one who is left behind."

"I didn't ask for that, did I? Only for goodbye. Which is polite, if you cared." Saoirse squinted and peered through only one eye, but her *friend* didn't seem bothered in the least by her frustrated tone. "The Red King—"

"Will let us go. Will see through excuses and promises, then talk of fear. Of how little it should matter to those such as us. Perhaps he will be right, too."

Saoirse blinked at her friend, both understanding and confused. She remembered fear from her time in the human world and from those first hours, alone here, wondering if she would be safe. But the sting of the emotion, the feel of it, was all but lost to her now.

"Líadan, I don't understand. You're Hunters. What *does* it matter?"

The selkie had only black laughter to offer, a sound as shadowed as the matte surface of her eyes. "We are dark Summer's people. Our time here is over, that is all. You do not understand, but then, you aren't one thing or another." Her smile showed pointed teeth. "Not yet."

Saoirse made a despairing sound and shook her head at Líadan's continued laughter. "It's not fair. I learn so much, but it's never enough."

"Something will call you eventually, meaning or madness. You will find your way."

"But I'm tired of waiting." She was grumbling and she knew it, but she didn't care. "Time is different here and still, I'm tired of it."

Líadan swished her tail through the water, stirring white foam on the surface. "The mortal in you is murmuring. Haven't you felt your soul slipping away? A little longer, and the space that is left will have to be filled by something else. What have you chosen?"

Saoirse blinked, confused. That was an obvious question. "Blood, of course. The Hunt and its power."

"Oh?" The smile on Líadan's face stretched wide, then wider. "Saoirse, I think you will surprise yourself with how much emptiness will be left behind when you lose your human self for the last time. With how little *blood* will fill the space inside you."

Saoirse frowned as her reflection in the black eyes distorted, changing shape, size…something. "You are not the Red King. You may walk in shadow, but I do not think it will be his."

Crouching, the girl reached forward and petted the flat,

smooth space between Líadan's ears. "What, then? *Whose*? I've been hunting without knowing. Tell me!"

The selkie closed her eyes to slits. "A pale shade. Not red but stripped of all color."

Saoirse contemplated this, but she had never heard of a person or a place to fit that description. Nowhere in the Red Kingdom, nowhere in the mortal world. Not in bright Winter, which she had been told was white radiance and ice. Not in Summer, where she had been bathed in sunlight. "When I find it, will I know what I've been seeking?"

"Perhaps." She paused and squinted over her shoulder, then along the line of the coast. "Saoirse Saorla, it is nearly time."

"Time?"

"For us to go."

The girl stared across the surface of the water, then, turning, behind her over the dunes. The last of the selkies were entering the deep. Black heads, bobbing on the surface of the sea, were vanishing into the distance, and she sensed Líadan's impatience. "You will be safe, won't you?"

"These are dangerous times, and there may be no safety for anyone, anywhere." The selkie's body could not shrug, but Saoirse sensed one in the sound of her voice. "Still, we will make the attempt. If things change, perhaps we will even return. I will find you then, and be, even as I will be far from you, your friend."

"As I'll be yours. I promise." The selkie slipped into the water, following her kin.

Saoirse stepped back from the tideline, thinned to a shadow and sped over the frosted dunes. She could hear the Red King's voice, and she wanted to know if Líadan had been right.

Would he let them go? She was curious but not concerned. There was no violence, not even the anticipation of it, in the taste of the wind tonight.

Macsen stood with his feet in the cold, foaming rush of

the waves, staring at the selkies who had come to petition him. He wanted to hunt in the mortal world, wanted to kill that woman…Dealla. The taste of her name twisted his thoughts to viciousness…yet here he was, dealing with minutiae.

He wanted to spend all his time with Bran at his side, but here he stayed. In the wild of the Red Kingdom. Because of duties like this one, the requirements of his position… *No.* That was a lie. He stayed because he had made Bran a promise. He stayed *here*, away from his lover, because the promise grew dangerous when he was too long without distraction from it.

"My king…"

Macsen stood straighter, glaring at the selkie floating on the surface of the sea. "What do you want of me?" He growled the words. All he could taste was fear, and there was no excuse for that, not in the Red Kingdom.

"We want only your permission to leave and not be pursued." Inky eyes blinked at him, then opened wide. "Something is coming. We have felt it in the waters of the world. Now we taste it even here, in this dark kingdom beyond the touch of mortal sun. We do not know why, but we do not wish to linger in the hope of finding out."

Snarling, Macsen showed his teeth. He was not angry, but he wished he was. Better that than the tremor of loss sending out its shivers through the fabric of Winter. Something *was* coming. Something had changed and was still changing.

He had already been warned. Kas had come to him, Black King that he was, and had told him that the world and its cycles were coming undone. Was that warning come to fruition?

Undone. According to Kas. According to Death.

But what he had told the Black King remained just as true now as it had been then. For Bran, he would sustain the world himself if it was needed. For Bran, he would hold up the burning sun.

The incongruity of his lover's presence was all Macsen

needed now, more than any prey he could stalk through the snow. More than his kingdom—more than to be king. Bran, who was a blaze in his arms, on his tongue, in his thoughts. The fire of Summer and the thousand reflections that were the moon's dilution of that same flame.

Macsen glowered down again, but despite the writhing blister of his aura, its predator intentions, what fear there was in the selkie's eyes wasn't because of him. The taste of it, floating into the salt-scent of the sea, was bitter because of that.

"I give you my permission. I wouldn't chase you even if you had left without it. Go if you want to, go if you can. You are afraid, and what is fear to those who live in the blood of Winter?"

Selkies began to slip away, disturbing the frozen blank of the water's surface. Macsen watched them go while the elders remained, staring at the sea and at the shore, one eye for the past and one for the unknown future. It was only when few were left and he made to turn away that another voice addressed him, answered him.

"Once more I call you *my king* and then never again. You've done well by us, and we by you, for all the time that was ours to share. But I cannot go and let this pass, what you've said to us. What you've implied. Even you fear. We know it, as you know it—that to love is to fear. And you love, Macsen Cadoc. *You love*."

Macsen stared into black eyes in a frost-marked face, into pupils the shape of snowflakes, the two unalike. "Fear is to follow the instinct of flight. That's all. I have nothing more to say about it."

The last of them slipped away, ripples of darker black in the ebon water, singing now as the horizon ate their shapes.

"Are they all gone, then? Are there no more left?"

He whipped around, but there was nothing on the shore. Then—Saoirse. The girl stepped out of the shadow with an expression on her face that told him she had been listening.

"They've gone."

She took a step closer to him, staring not at him but at the waves coming in. "Will they return?"

"Foresight is not my talent, and they are following fear." Macsen repeated the words he'd given the elders, but they slipped dead and toneless from his mouth. "Fear is to follow the instinct of flight."

The girl turned and cast her glance at him, curious. "Then you think that in a world without wings we wouldn't dream of it?"

"It."

She held her arms out at her sides, stood on tiptoe, then crunched onto the frosted sand. "Flight. And so, falling. And so, being afraid."

He shook his head at her, scowling. Twisting his words like that. But how many years had it been now? Two... three...four? A little more than that? Yes. She had not grown, had not aged, but she was no longer the child she had been. The wild of Winter had refined her, altered the structure of her being in a fundamental way.

Changeling child. But he had taken her too late. A little girl, but neither her mind nor her heart would stay that way forever, even if her body was unchanged. "Saoirse Saorla, what are you becoming?"

A smile stretched her face. "Something like you. I will never *be* like you, but something close. A drinker of blood, of silences... I, too, am hunting."

"Even now?"

"Always. I think the difference between us is power and that you always know your prey. I'm always hunting, Red King. I don't yet know what."

The sadness of her smile interested him. "Soon enough you will be hunting for your own nature. You will need a name for your new self and a way to bind that self to this world or the other. You have choices to make, Saoirse. Before you are left in a flesh that denies all your facets."

She knelt in the sand and picked out patterns through the icy surface with a fingertip. "Ffion showed me how to make the wind of winter follow me, how to fix the frost. From you I learned the taste of blood and all its power, and from Bran the proof of a promise and loyalty…and love."

And love.

Her voice caressed the words and her lips curved up, up, wider than a mortal smile. "Red King, if not for Bran it would be you who was my prey. But it can't be you, and so I don't know who I am hunting."

Macsen tilted his head, peered more closely at her face. "One day soon, you will return to the mortal world."

"I have already returned."

"For the Samhain hunt. Yes." He remembered. A little figure astride a black horse of Winter, bare, tiny legs gripping the skeletal sides of a beast that should have sought the sweetness of her flesh, not to be her steed. "But you have not set foot on mortal ground. One day soon, you will do so. You will become more fully who you are then. You will begin to grow up and to understand who it is you're hunting."

Saoirse pushed herself to her feet. "I already know, at least a little. Or how else would I know that it *isn't* you? My prey, my prey, I wonder who it is? Couldn't you tell me?"

Macsen understood what she was saying, but he had no answers she would appreciate. He could not hunt her future for her, could not bring down prey she had yet to name even to herself. "Saoirse, even if you called from me the promise I made of my power, the boon I owe you, there is nothing for me to say. You were listening. You know the truth."

"You…have no foresight." She was silent for a moment, almost downcast, but when she spoke again there was predatory eagerness in her voice that he could appreciate. "How will I know? I don't want to just be patient. I want to chase it down."

Chuckling, he shook his head and patted her hair fondly. "Chase down the future? Ambitious little thing. You should know better. Even I do not do that, and I am the Hunter

King."

She laughed, and it was still the laughter of the girl he'd stolen. That one thing was utterly unchanged. "I know. Red King I call you, and you are. More than anything else to me, more than *sidhe* or *vampire* or Macsen Cadoc."

It was an odd statement, but he ignored it as he turned away from the shore. The selkies were long vanished and he had left someone waiting behind him. But her voice held him for a moment more.

"I came today not just because of the selkies, Red King, though I heard the rumor and I did want to say goodbye. You should go home. Bran is waiting."

He lifted an eyebrow as he inspected her, amused despite himself. "Do you read my mind, Saoirse? Is that also a power you've gained?"

"Not yet. No, not yet." She shrugged, careless and unconcerned. "But one day I'll anticipate you. I'll know what you need before you do, and prove myself."

"Oh? And leave me the day after, following your prey, I'm sure." He tossed the words over his shoulder as he strode away from the water and didn't check to see if she was following. Strange. In some ways, the girl was more like his own child than the daughter he'd sired.

Morgan. Foolish creature. Orchards and blossoms, flowering and fading. Even though Saoirse had once been human, she was easier to understand.

* * * *

Time in the Red Kingdom had not condensed for Bran as he had been told it would. Instead, the longer Macsen was away, the more Bran became aware of each long, cold minute. He hadn't complained—not out loud, anyway. Better for Macsen to be distracted with work and the needs of his people.

There had been whispers and more since Dealla had slain Talaith, set fire to Macsen's palace and bloodied the dancing ground. Though it had affected Macsen worst of all, Talaith's vanishing had spread a pall of concern over his whole kingdom. She had been slain. She had been stolen, and all Macsen's vassals were still caught up in the moment Macsen had said, "Wait with me."

They were impatient, as Macsen was impatient, but they were waiting. Yet since Macsen had returned with Bran from their visit with Bran's father, weeks had become months, nearly a year, slow and dark in its passing.

Most days, Bran tried to distract himself with his own work, making pretty bits of nothing in the forge Macsen had given to him. When he grew tired of that, there was the game he had invented for himself.

Lines of night had grown through the fire that sustained him, not Macsen's darkness but his own. A consequence, he thought, of the moonlight moving within him. The moon needed the night. It could be the brightness of a moon shrunk to its thinnest sliver, and that was enough for dark purposes.

He'd suffered enough, and so had Macsen. His father had taught him how to use the moonlight, and in the Red Kingdom there was only one hour each day in which that light was dark.

When he closed his eyes, he could choose to walk that shining road of power into Dealla's mind. One such venture at a time, he stirred her toward madness. Bran had begun with her dreams. It had, at first, been easier while she was sleeping. The unconscious defenses of her mind were negligible and he had free rein. Words, images, memories, both his and hers were Bran's to use as he pleased.

His own happiness was one of the worst things he could share with her. The golden world of Summer and its dance. The Red Kingdom's night. Macsen's kiss. The heat of the coldest thing in the world, burning in the terrible way only ice could burn.

Bran shivered just thinking of it. There was no surer way to wake Dealla's fear, to enrage her, than to wash the suffocating tension of Macsen's aura over her mind. Remind her that he would soon come hunting. That it was only Bran who restrained him, and only as long as he chose. That perhaps he was tiring of waiting and watching Macsen's predator nature chafe.

Even if it is to torment you. Woman. This game I can't share with him. This he takes no pleasure in. Not as he will from the spilling of your blood.

The flow of words and power came easily now as he reached out along the thread of moonlight and his own strength. It was far swifter and more certain than the first time he'd tried it. Bran laughed and the sound bubbled into Dealla's thoughts. Shifting movement greeted him, her awareness of his presence.

Wrath echoed at him, impotent curses thrown across the narrow space that divided him from her mind. It didn't matter. Dealla's fury was all he required to infiltrate her thoughts further.

She was awake, sitting alone in some quiet place that irritated her with its discomforts. Damp. Dark. But it had promise, too, because her focus on her current location was thick with a smug aura of satisfaction.

The thing that was sharpest in her awareness confused him. Swords? Yes, and not only. Many weapons, all of them bright gold and each one familiar. How could he not remember? His shame. His pain. All those things he had been forced to forge while he'd been kept captive, knowing so little that it might as well have been nothing.

Were these thoughts her attempt at defending herself, or something else? Her rage hadn't abated in the slightest, and when Dealla was enraged, she wasn't thinking. The cunning that was so vicious when she had turned her full attention to her enemy's destruction was a thousand times more dangerous than her fury, which precluded plotting.

Still.

The images floated over her consciousness in a golden web. Each point of connection was another weapon, another memory, and he raced through them with the speed of mind and magic. Only a few were missing, and he wondered why that was, if her thoughts were so caught up in his creations.

One staff—the one he had made for her sister. One sword—the sword that Macsen had stolen from Noirine, and her dagger, which he had also taken.

It made sense that Dealla, terrified of Macsen as she was, would never think of weapons that had fallen into his hands. That would require thinking of him. But the staff? Perhaps she did not like to think of her sister, either. But none of that explained why the image of every other weapon he'd forged was so fresh in her mind.

Wary, Bran withdrew from those thoughts and prodded Dealla with smiles. Saoirse's, and his own, and Macsen's. Terror filtered through to him, and he caught the tone of it and smiled more truly. Behind his closed eyelids, he could see her now, broken thing that she was. On her knees, pushing him off though he existed only in her mind.

The connection was growing stronger the more he used it to torture her. They had already begun to notice—her women, and her priests. The way she feared the dark, the way she stayed up now, restless, and slept only to wake screaming.

The head priest lingered most firmly in her consciousness under Bran's prodding. Her thoughts of him included memories of pain, and the desire for that which she still wanted to inflict. Bars. Bones. Blackness.

Bran shied away from that. He knew enough of cages and of *sidhe*. Much as it amused him to play games with the tangled threads of her mind, he wanted her done with— now more than ever.

The time in which he could keep this wolf of his on a leash was coming to a close.

Dealla's denial was not in words. Bran didn't know if that was because he didn't want to hear them, or because she didn't have his power. *"Deny what you want. He will come for you. He has been asking me what I want for a Midsummer gift.*" There was a physical intensity to the shudder that convulsed her awareness. "*Shall I tell him to give me your life? Shall I tell him that?*"

The woman's thoughts cowered away from him and Bran felt his power increasing. Moonlight and its madness. Enough to peer at every secret, enough…to possess. If he were to send but a little more of himself along that thread, he would see through her eyes. He would taste her air, have the use of her hands and legs. He would be able to kill her any way he chose.

But it was the last thing he wanted. To become closer to her? See what she saw, the way she saw it?

No.

Never.

He couldn't even think of a thing that would make him want to do that.

* * * *

Early in the evening, one of Dealla's women came to report on the progress of the only work that interested her these days. Chains to bind the Red King. Chains to keep her foe imprisoned, if he could not be defeated or destroyed.

It had been Marcus Pontius' idea, and a good one, but the Priest had not stayed to see the work completed. "Tell me you have good news, Braith."

Her visitor bowed. "Yes, my lady. The chains you ordered forged out of the Summer weapons are finished. The last link was being closed as I left."

A slow, cold smile poured itself across Dealla's face. "Have them made ready to move. We'll find a better place to lay a trap than my own house."

"Yes, my lady."

"But before that, I want you to take two score of women north, to this grove I keep hearing of." Dealla clenched her good hand into a fist and glared at the scarred palm of the other. "This…green place where all my people have fled. Aisling is there. I know it. She is the only one with a claim who could challenge me, the only one with a reason."

There was a pause, a confused hesitation, in Braith's voice. "A…reason, my lady?"

"She betrayed us!" Turning her back, Dealla watched the slate edge of the horizon through the window. "Betrayed us, when we are still at war." She grimaced over her shoulder and held Braith's gaze with a fervent glare. "The chains may be ready, but we must take care of *her* before we attempt the Red King's capture."

Braith stood straight, and the torchlight flickered her shadow into a trio of selves as she moved. "What shall I do with her, my queen? And, for that matter, what shall be done with those accompanying her?"

Dealla scowled, the burned side of her face twitching painfully as the expression stretched her skin. "Kill Aisling. She has no place left here. The druids may be left to flee, but that old man they all rely on, the one who protested. Lughaid. If he is there, if he still lives, make sure it is not for long."

There was a twinge of heat in the empty socket of her eye. A flicker of laughter in her mind. Inhuman noise. She blinked and it passed, but she wouldn't be free of it for long. Dealla curled her fingers, testing the painful tension of her scars, a gesture that was fast becoming a nervous habit.

"The rest, my lady?"

"The rest…"

Braith blinked at her. "Of the people with your sister."

Swallowing, Dealla licked her lips and waved a hand at the woman. "They are peasants. They don't matter. Burn the green and they will flee where they may. Go now. If the Red King is coming the trap must be set in time, and somehow I think our time grows short."

Braith bowed and left, but Dealla was on one knee the moment the door closed, heaving in breath as fire exploded in her brain. It turned to light and the shape of someone who could not be there.

Bran Fionnan.

The hazy image of him intersected her table, on the other side of which Braith had been standing. That was a real thing. He could not be, was not there, but when he reached out for her she fell and scrabbled across the floor until her spine was straight against the wall.

Dreams again? Even while she was waking, he could draw her into the darkness behind her eyelids that was no longer dark.

Dealla burned, feeling the pain of old wounds anew. Fire flowed over her fingers, blistered her eyelid, the side of her face, her eye. Then it was gone, replaced by laughter and visions of things she had never seen, did not want to see. The Summer wood, lit with golden light and music. Winter and the black tide of the Red King's aura, overflowing. Endless. Nothing should go on forever and yet it went on forever, inflicting itself on her.

In her tormentor, she sensed only pleasure.

Damn him. No matter what she thought, what she tried to hold on to, she found herself giving in to the power he had over her.

The pain was a little less each time he reached out and touched her, but her internal turmoil grew greater. She had no defense. No spell, no structure of mind or thought, no chant, not even the priestly interference of Marcus Pontius and his men had been any help.

The druids remained out of reach, but their magic was her magic, their gods her gods. She had avoided that worship. There was a chance it could do more harm than good. An indefinable connection existed between the *sidhe* and the gods that had spawned them, that bred with them. They were not the same type of being, but the *sidhe* had a closer tie with that other world, and her aims…

My aims might not be supported by the gods to whom I am sworn. But the gods are not human. The gods do not always know what is best for us, or we would not be in this position.

Laughter again. It echoed between her ears and Dealla squeezed her eyes shut. *Ignore it. Just ignore it.* He wasn't here and it wasn't real. She couldn't let herself be shifted off her course. "You won't turn me aside! Do you hear?"

He did not answer her.

Sooner or later, probably sooner, the Red King would come for her. Dealla had dreamed the deaths of her mother and huntress-sisters a thousand times, thinking of how he must have taken their lives. About how each one of them, sharing her power, her strengths, had still never had enough of either to vanquish him.

She defied her own pride to confront the truth, because she wanted victory more than pride and glory both. *To destroy you I will sacrifice it all.* Already, her people were dying. Winter was eating away at the soul of her kingdom, but she would not give it up.

It had been proven to her enough times that trying to kill the Red King with a frontal attack would be pointless. But the gold she had acquired and the Summer power with which it was infused were a weakness of his, as of all his blood-drinking kin. The chains would be enough, *had* to be enough, to hold him.

"And you won't know what to do then, will you? *Bran Fionnan*. Without your protector, without the Red King standing between you and me. Will you come to your death?" Dealla wondered if he could hear her. He had more control over her dreams than she did, could send her sounds and images. He could touch on memories that she wished would stay buried forever.

But her thoughts weren't open to him in the most basic sense. Her plans and intentions were safe, even when she was holding the chains she had made for his damned lover in her hands. Still. It was a concern. If there was only someone, some thing, that might help her.

Marcus Pontius knew only that a troublesome secondary pain had come of the wounds they had both believed already healed. She hadn't dared reveal more, though it was likely the priest was the only one she could trust with anything near the truth.

Dealla pushed herself to her feet, wary of the sudden silence in her mind. She turned to the window and stared out at snow-blasted fields that should have been gleaming with grain. Perhaps, when they had subdued Winter's King, they would be able to subdue winter. "But at least we will have vengeance for our dead. I will see to that."

Sudden internal laughter beat her down to her knees, and Dealla's hands snapped up over her ears. Her body's reaction was not to be denied, even if the sound came from inside herself.

If he hadn't burned it out of her, she would have torn her own eye from its socket in the hope of tearing out the connection between them. As it was, she hunched over and didn't feel that she'd fallen to the floor again until the cold of it seeped through her clothes and numbed her skin.

There was a knock at the door and she whipped around. A real sound or – but no. It was her own door. She took a moment to compose herself then called out. "Enter."

"My queen." Subservient as he had been since she had forced him behind her into Summer, Marcus Pontius stood at the threshold, waiting for her further permission to approach.

His eyes settled at her knees, then on her arms before moving to her face, and she knew he had been eyeing the dust there. She ignored the question in his eyes to ask her own. "Marcus. What brings you here?"

Something slithering was in his stare as it shifted around her face, settling nowhere. *Not good news, then.* "A messenger has finally come from Uther Pendragon."

"And?" She lifted her eyebrow, impatient, but the priest wet his lips, was not quick to give her the message he had received.

"The High King says only, 'Take your trouble elsewhere. Do not return here.' Britain is closed to us, my Queen."

Dealla clenched her fists and turned to face the window.

That was it, then. It had all begun for Britain, for Vortigern…
but obviously those who had inherited his throne did not
feel they had inherited his debts. "So, it is victory or death.
No matter. I knew that already. Tell me, what do you know
of *sidhe* magic? What do you know of protecting yourself
from such things?"

"No more than I have learned from you, my queen, and in
your service. Hallowed ground is some defense. Weapons
of the right construction will harm the creatures, depending
on their form and allegiance."

She stood straight. "Hallowed ground. Of course. I hadn't
considered…but then, your god has not been mine."

She did not miss the greedy flicker in his eye at those
words. She was a queen. She couldn't blame him for
wanting to claim responsibility for converting her — if she
were to allow such a thing.

"Has not been, my queen? Your words suggest you have
second thoughts."

"Perhaps." She reached her burned fingers up to touch
her empty eye socket. "These wounds trouble me, Marcus.
The one who gave them to me assaults me through them.
The pain is hard to think through." There was less surprise
in him than she expected. *Talk, then.*

She had not kept herself to herself as well as she had
intended.

There was a detached interest on the priest's face as he
stepped nearer her, then stopped. "An echo of the power
that wounded you."

"Yes."

Again he strode closer, peering at her eye while she
scowled at him. "That is why the eye bleeds when it
chooses?" He reached up and touched the tender flesh
beneath the empty socket.

Dealla flinched, scowling. "When *he* chooses, Priest. Bran
Fionnan. Tell me, can your god protect me from him?"

The priest's probing continued, until he elicited real pain
and she slapped his hand away. He made no apology but

he did step back. "It is a wound that has already been made. An inroad that already exists. I am troubled to hear of this, in truth. Is it possible he knows of our plans? If he is in your mind…"

She sensed a shrug in his voice, and more than that, uncertainty. "I had already considered that. It doesn't seem to be the case. He wants to hurt me, torment me — he drags painful memories and nightmares to the forefront but seems capable of little more." She grimaced, then smoothed the agitation from her features. "But it is not pleasant, which is why I seek your aid."

He bowed, but shortly. "I must apologize for having nothing helpful."

Wincing still, Dealla turned from him and walked to the window, staring through it as she smoothed her fingers along the edge of the sill. A splinter prodded her, and she picked at it. "No. I will go tonight to your church. I will sleep there, and we will see if the boundaries of your hallowed ground are enough to keep out Summer fire."

The challenge seemed to spark something in the man. "A room will be prepared for you at once, my queen. My own, if you desire it." His voice gained a certain edge, and she wondered if he truly had that much faith, or if there was another truth that motivated him.

As lightly as she was able, Dealla chuckled and relaxed a little when there was no mocking echo in her mind. "Somehow I do not think the rooms of a priest would be fitting for a queen. Merely make sure those you ready for me are clean."

"Of course. Shall I await your arrival?"

"Yes. Go, now. I will follow shortly." He bowed, but she didn't watch him leave. The pressure was starting again behind her eye, just when she had thought she was safe. "Damn you, Bran Fionnan!"

His response was an image dragged up out of her nightmares or his own memories. The Red King, smiling in pleasure.

It was a smile that gave fangs to the crescent moon.

Chapter Three

Myrddin had left Kas while his body was still aching and red-marked, and he hummed to himself as he went along now, calmed by the memory. The taste of his lover's skin still on his lips was the best of distractions and, at the very least, he had given as good as he'd got.

Yes. And he liked the way the dark marks had showed up on Kas' pallor. He thought they must look at least as good on him, the ones Kas had given, and found himself reluctant to shift his shape.

He could keep the marks even if he did so, but he knew without trying that it wouldn't be the same. It was time, anyway, to let Uther see something more of him than a boy. Something closer to the truth. Thinking that, and on his own displeasure at what Uther had interrupted, Myrddin appeared in front of the High King without warning, allowed no hint of his approach.

He splashed himself into reality with a flash of green and spring scents, casting the shadow of a boy even though he still wore older flesh. He glared right into Uther's face, so close he could see the reflection of his own mismatched eyes.

"Why did you summon me? You, who says he has no need of magic or omens or their believers, those types of fool? Why, Pendragon? I see no trouble here." He watched the man grow pale as his power rose in flux, snapping around them like the whipping of angry vines. He was irritated at being called, here and now, when he had been enjoying his time with Kas.

When he had plans to make, so that he could try to build a

lasting peace. And this red-faced, red dragon king, he was a necessary element? But Myrddin had seen. He remembered, though the fragments had not yet come together to make a complete picture. Pendragon, yes. A sword he had never seen with his waking eyes…and a boy, as yet unborn.

Peering at Uther, he shook off the memory of things that were yet to come. "Well? Will you speak or do I go? I expected an emergency, Pendragon."

"There is—" Speech snapped out of Uther's mouth, but he sucked in an uncertain heaving of breath and turned his face away before he continued. "A woman." The words were abrupt, short with heat and something that was not quite shame.

"A woman." Myrddin's tone was flat, unimpressed, even as he reeled internally, but Uther didn't seem to notice.

"More than just a woman. The one I want for my queen, but she is wed to Gorlois and not to me. To one of my own men! Or at least, he should be." He stopped again, and Myrddin stared at him harder than before. They were, he thought, approaching a familiar moment.

"Gorlois."

"The lord of Cornwall. He retreated to Dimilioc, just there." Uther jerked his thumb over his shoulder, toward the dim mound of a fort in the distance. "He sent Ygraine to Tintagel, at the coast. She was not averse to me, to my attentions, but he is not a stupid man. Now that he has hidden her away I can do nothing with her, be nothing to her, unless he is…dealt with."

Cold fire burned in the blue of Uther's eyes, pale and fierce in a new way. "He keeps her in the tower there. At Tintagel, without even need for an army around her. Whether he chooses war or only to cower and conceal her, I don't yet know."

His smile was as cold as his gaze was burning when he turned again. "Treason, certainly, if he chooses the first. Reason enough to kill a man, and a widow may remarry. It isn't worth a war, not for a woman. But Ygraine…I want her. Boy…"

He paused, as if only then taking in the details of Myrddin's change in appearance. "I want her, whatever you are. I want her for my own."

A piece, then another, clicked into place in Myrddin's mind. He knew what Uther would ask him for. He held himself still, waiting at the edge of the moment. He was afraid that if he breathed, moved, spoke, he would change something that wasn't meant to be changed.

"I do not want a war, but I will have her. Will you help me, boy?"

The smile that wanted to show on Myrddin's face was sharp enough to cut, but he kept it to himself.

"Do you hear me?"

"Help you." It was harder now to keep the smile back. Myrddin had to hold his breath, and in response the wind darted overhead, agitated, stirring the leaves with restless remonstrance. He ignored it — this was what he had been waiting for.

"Bring her to me! Take her from Tintagel, or bring me to her — is it in your power? It is in no one else's."

There was a darker shift in the breeze. A change in the air, which no longer stayed still between shifts of wind, but waited, breathing. Myrddin peered up into Uther's face and saw that he was serious. *So. For a woman.*

There was within him a mingled sense of rage and completion.

This was the right question. Wrong, but what he had been waiting for. Still. For *this* he'd left Kas behind? For this, when he could have waited until it was Kas who had to leave? Maybe his lover had been right after all.

Something must have showed on his face, in his eyes. He saw the awareness of wild power on Uther's face as it started to writhe between them. "For that? When I told you something important." Myrddin almost laughed. '*Important*'. It was, more than all other things, but to give that away would be to ruin the game. "What does your woman matter to me, Pendragon?"

"I need her. Is it magic?" Uther growled his answer, and a new desperation inflicted itself on his voice, but it was only new to the moment, not to the man. "Tell me, boy! Is that what it is? Has she ensnared me? I think only of her. The sound of her voice, the shape of her face, the scent of her hair. And yet she is not *mine*!"

He turned again, whipping his cloak behind him as he paced, furious, and still, despite his fearful suspicion, almost ashamed.

Myrddin examined the backs of his hands then Uther's face. "There's no enchantment on you, Pendragon. Nothing more than the spell any woman may cast over a man. But she belongs to another, and it would be better for you to find some other lady to be your queen."

"That is the help you offer me? When I had need, you said, and so I called you. I *must* have her. I would have taken her, given the chance, and that even for one night — and Gorlois knew it, or why do you think he hid her away?"

"This is not what we agreed, Pendragon."

A furious energy crackled through the king's movements as he whirled around again, gesturing sharply. "Isn't it? You promised me your aid and that's what I'm asking for!"

"The rape of another man's bride is not a thing for which my *aid* is available." His voice was cold, and Uther's growl in response like the grumbling of an angry bear, but Myrddin stood tall and unafraid before him.

He could see clearly in Uther's mind that it had not yet occurred to the High King to be watchful of himself around Myrddin. He wasn't thinking about what it meant that Myrddin had first been brought to him as the son of no man.

The High King's thoughts were fixed only on the woman and how he might gain her for his own. "You think that's how it would be? She was not the one averse to me or my intentions. Though she *is* another man's bride, she does not want to be."

Myrddin glanced at him, contemplating, but all he could

determine was that Uther thought he was speaking the truth. The surface of his mind was as easy to see reflections on as still water.

Even so, he wouldn't be the first man to have overestimated a woman's interest in him. There was no guarantee, and yet something was meant to come from this moment. From this request...from Uther's need. A woman. The spark of memory lit Myrddin's whole mind for a single instant. *The Sword.*

A boy. Laughter and his own hands, with the lines of an old man engraved deep in them. A boy. The son of a king.

A king without a queen.

"Wait here. I will go find your woman, see for myself what she wants and who she is. Perhaps there is a way... perhaps you will have what you want. Wait here." He repeated himself just to shut Uther's mouth, keep him still, then took a step and vanished from the grass.

As a breath of Spring air, barely flesh, almost mist, he flew to the shore and the tower Uther had named to him. A few men, guards in rust-streaked armor, were scattered among the rocks at the edge of a stony coast, more cliff than beach. Only one among them stood out to him, and Myrddin knew at once that this was Gorlois, Uther's rival.

So. Uther thought he was in hiding, but this man had his secret ways.

The coastline was mimicked in the hard countenance of its lord. Craggy planes had resisted being weathered smooth by time, and the man had a hard jaw, hard eyes, a falcon nose and a dark beard that was sparse as it drew up toward his ears.

Iron-gray hair lay in long locks against a dark cloak of rich burgundy wool, though it was salt-stained by the flying spray. There was a sword at his belt, the hilt well worn. Lord of Cornwall, lord of Tintagel...lord of the lady who was waiting within that tower.

Silently, a green shadow, Myrddin slipped past him and climbed up the rime-crusted stones in leaps and bounds.

The woman's thoughts called out to him as he came closer. Ygraine was a still and silent woman, an image of beauty with a mind like a palace chiseled from ice. Power, she sought. Power, so difficult for a woman to obtain.

She had found a portion of what she wanted in her husband, all but a king in his own land. But she remained unfulfilled, still seeking her own way.

"Be the mother of kings."

The thought had been in her for years. Now the rough penance of her adulterous ambition pursued her with the intensity of Uther's stare. All she wished was there before her, yet so far out of reach. A married woman, she could not be queen. A married woman, she could not give Uther what he craved.

What she, too, desired, if for her own reasons and not the mercurial pettiness of flesh and its pleasures.

Not being able to have her had made Uther want her more. She knew this, had known it from the beginning. Why else had she told her husband, set him afire with jealousy? What had she to lose? The death of a husband, the gain of a king — or perhaps a husband who might supplant his king, properly motivated. As he might have been at the death of Aurelianus!

But what would be would be.

She would wait, Brythonic Helen locked in her tower, staring out at the sea and anticipating the waiting wages of war. She heard prayers rising on the wind, cold men cold-hearted in the chill of the evening, but they were Christian prayers, dim to her and meaningless.

Daughter of the old gods, she was. Proud princess, wild hearted, ambitious...

Myrddin had seen enough. He retreated from her mind. This Ygraine — he would give her what she wanted, though he doubted she would ever know it had been him.

Mother of kings.

He turned away, leaped off the tower and returned to Uther. It had been barely an hour since he'd departed, and the expression on the king's face was purely startled when he arrived.

"You—"

"I have been to the coast. To the tower where she's kept. Ygraine sits alone there, while Gorlois prepares for the possibility of war. He thinks you will come for him first, but that is not what you intend. I wonder what will happen because that is so?"

Golden child. The Sword. It was an internal flash and it passed quickly, but Myrddin could not deny the truth of the vision as it coalesced. "She does want you, in her own way. Your woman." He paused again, but perhaps a moment too long.

Uther clenched his fists. "Boy, if you do what I ask of you, I'll reward you as you please. Wealth, women, a kingdom—"

For a moment Myrddin appeared to consider, allowed a greedy flicker to cross his face, but he knew as Uther spoke that this was what he had come for. This was the moment to which his meeting had led him.

The shine of gold stood out to his inner eye, the blond softness of a mortal child more precious than treasure. "Whatever reward I please?"

"Anything but my crown or the woman."

He stared up at Uther for a long moment then nodded. "The bargain is made, and may you not regret it. I will bring you to your woman at Samhain, Pendragon. You can wait that long. All things in their time. Until then I will see what this kingdom of yours is like. I will see how you fight your battles, who is trusted in your court."

"These things matter to you?"

"No." Myrddin laughed as Uther blinked at him.

It was a lie, of course.

* * * *

Bran left Dealla with the knowledge of what he could do,

if he wanted. How easily he could take control of her, and why he wouldn't do it.

"You would defile me, woman."

More than he'd expected, that enraged her. His last awareness of her as he pulled out of her mind was of wrath crashing around in her brain like a tidal wave.

Opening his eyes, Bran gazed across his forge without seeing it, and wondered. *Play.* Though nothing he had learned from his father told him so, he wondered if this game he was tormenting Dealla with would end up costing him. He was reminded of the adage about eavesdroppers never learning anything they wanted to know.

Maybe he was better off with work instead.

It was true, what he'd told Dealla, threatened her with just for fun. Macsen had been asking him about a Midsummer gift. A Summer tradition, that. From one lover to another. Something precious, something worthy of the feeling and the recipient.

He wondered what the Winter custom was, if this was Summer's. There were powers other than Macsen's in the Red Kingdom. There had to be more than just the Samhain sacrifice. Something for all the beings who fit no definition but their own.

But he was getting distracted again. Something to give Macsen in return...what was fitting? He could ask, but Macsen would offer a teasing answer, or no answer, or demand nothing at all, and that wasn't right.

Fire flared in the background of Bran's thoughts. He had been playing with fangs and bones and chains for ages now, but they had come to nothing because he had never been able to decide what to do with the pieces.

A torc, like Macsen had given him? Rings, bracelets? Bands for his arms, a circlet—he could make any of those things but he didn't see the point. The only jewelry he had worn in Bran's sight was a crown of fangs and bones. "The night we met, he wore it. And when he leaves..." But the images stuck with him. *Fire. Fangs and bones.*

He had a flash of a thought then. Many of the chains he'd made were so fine they might be mistaken for fabric. He'd made them while thinking of Macsen, and he could see them in his mind's eye, the length of them stretched gold and soft and glittering against his lover's skin.

Could he make a tunic, neither jewelry nor armor? Rose gold, not just yellow, and white gold and silver for accents. Could he? *Yes.* But…

"Would he wear it?" Bran rested his head on his hand. He pictured Macsen dressed in Summer power. His lover would be gorgeous in gold… He stopped and licked his lips, closed his eyes to intensify the image and gave himself a little shudder.

Bran cast a practiced gaze over the metals that lay waiting around the forge, chunks of ore and gleaming ingots. Easily, he hefted a stone heavy with glittering electrum and brought it to the fire with him, pushed his hair out of his eyes and set to work.

There was no way for him to know how Macsen would respond, unless he asked, or made it, and asking would ruin the surprise. Link upon link, he began forging chains, individual loops almost too small for his fingers to fasten together.

Bran went slowly at first, careful to match the first few that he had made, but he gained proficiency quickly. He knew instinctively where bones and fangs fit together among the shining loops, shimmering skeletons that became almost invisible as he worked. Then the light would catch the metal just so, and a snarling, skeletal shape would stand out amidst the rest of the gold.

One link at a time, then in parts as the soft chains grew toward completion, Bran filled the metal with steaming Summer until the gold couldn't take anymore. Power spilled out of it and stained the table with sun-bright scars.

The moonlight within him had its place, too. The white gold liked it more than Summer sun, and the silver wouldn't take the sunlight at all. Both metals took his father's power and added a subtle sheen of night to the Summer glow.

Hours passed in silence. The shining gold and the radiant power together took shape beneath his hands, until what was spilling off his table and into his lap wasn't a raw bolt of cloth but a sun-scented tunic, a mesh of chain finer than the finest linen.

It was nearly done when he lifted it in his hands and turned it in the light, pleased with himself. "Heavy, but that won't matter to him." Grinning, he started in on the last few bones.

While he worked, Bran muttered to himself, cursing the links of chain that slipped away from him. Mostly it was Macsen's name that slipped past his lips, the occasional wonder about what he would do, what he would say, presented with this gift.

What *would* he do? Macsen's idea of punishment... Macsen's idea of reward. Bran had been told he would learn both in time, but he was growing impatient. Whenever he'd mentioned it, Macsen had always laughed at him. *"Still thinking in mortal time, on mortal terms? You'll have your chance to earn one or the other, I'm sure."*

Bran sighed. A certain restlessness was blossoming within him. "Miss your hands on me, lover. The way you fill me up and drink me down." How long had it been? Too long, anyway.

Wolf fangs opened and shut in the glittering tunic he held, or the spattered reflection of the forge's fire made it seem so. Bran slid his thumb over the fangs of one of the skeletons he'd already finished, wondering.

The prick of the bite he felt then was certainly real.

Like some unexpected, final tempering, the wolf-skeleton drank his blood and gained the faintest garnet sheen, glistening amidst the gold. For Bran, the sensation was like an echo of what he'd felt the day he'd put on Macsen's torc. He reached up and touched the cold band around his throat. Was his blood fulfilling the spell he'd woven?

Perhaps the gold knew who it was going to.

The second time, Bran did it on purpose. He held his fingers near the open mouth of another fanged skull and waited for the sting, the sweetness of the theft. The more he fed the metal, the more it softened, rustling, the more it gained Summer fragrance, until the aroma had grown to a sticky scent that even he could taste.

One at a time he fed each fang, each skeleton, until there was as much of his blood worked into the gold as there was raw power, sun and moonlight combined. When he finally put the tunic down, Bran was tired. Drained but heated. Aroused in a way only Macsen would be able to satisfy.

He turned and peered out of the window, toward the clear black sky. Every star in existence was a diamond-bright point, piercing the dark, and the moon was nearly full.

Macsen would be home soon. *Soon.*

Bran held the tunic up in both hands, shook it out, and the heavy chains settled into loose folds that appeared to be light as fabric. It was just what he'd intended, but he wondered again if Macsen would really wear it.

"No point worrying about it. I'll find the right moment as soon as it's Midsummer, and then I'll see. It won't be long by Winter time..." He was grinning despite himself. Macsen wasn't expecting anything from him, he knew that, and the Red King had been in a mood lately, whenever he was home. Irritated by the constant summons out of his court and into the wild of Winter.

No amount of blood seemed to help his hunger, and Bran knew why that was, who his lover was thirsty for. It really was time to be done with waiting. For both of them. He sighed and tucked Macsen's gift out of sight beneath other, less important things just in time.

A familiar step sounded at the entrance to his forge. It was a single footfall, but that was enough to alert him when he'd been waiting for just such a sound. "Macsen. *Finally.*"

Cool, strong arms wrapped around him from behind, and Bran relaxed into his lover's embrace.

"Noticed me this time, did you?"

"*Ha.* Like I haven't been waiting for you. Has it been days or weeks or months since you've been home? Have you really got so much you need to do that—?"

"That I have to stay away so long? Yes. Or I wouldn't, you know that. There's been trouble."

"Someone finally challenging you?"

Bran felt Macsen laughing silently against his back, then the weight of his body draped over his shoulders.

Macsen bent closer, nuzzled his cheek, his throat, and answered by his ear. "Brat. How would that be trouble?"

There were layers of irony in the statement, but Bran only sighed and turned his head enough to press his mouth to Macsen's lips. "You say things like that, and *I'm* the brat? Tell me what's wrong, then." Hesitation entered his lover's body, a certain stiffness that was a guaranteed tell. "Macsen?"

"It's nothing. Some of the water peoples are leaving. The selkies have set out across the endless sea."

"The...?" Bran reached up to touch Macsen's cheek. "That freezing ocean? Why? Is it—really endless?"

"Because they're afraid. And I...don't know. Perhaps. Endless in the way the gray of *between* is endless, or magic itself. But it doesn't matter. They were afraid." He scowled and it was a darker expression than Bran remembered. "Better that they left, before I killed them myself."

"Macsen..."

Bran caught himself on the edge of the table as Macsen shifted suddenly behind him, stood straight and took a step back. "Kas was right, the bastard. He was."

"*Love.*"

The Red King paced, restless, near the door. "It's all coming undone. The first few threads are already unraveling. I don't know how or why, but I can feel it as I know my people can feel it, and Kas before us all. Can't you? Or is it still one of those things you no longer know how to recognize?"

"I—"

"Never mind. I only mentioned it because... I don't even

know why I mentioned it. I shouldn't let Kas get to me. I told him it wouldn't matter, and it won't. For you, I..." For the second time, Macsen stopped, and Bran turned himself around where he was sitting. The expression on Macsen's face showed something of his love, and something of the Hunter he was at heart.

"I don't want you to worry about any of that. It's just my concern as king. That's all. My people are the Hunter's people, the chill and shadow of winter's darkest hour. There's no place for fear in that. In them. In me." But he was laughing, and the sound of it was bitter. "It's a lie, of course. I know what fear is. Because of you, and I don't even want to change that."

"Love..." Bran wanted something else to say but couldn't think of anything.

Bitterness spilled out of his lover's every movement.

"Yes. To love is to fear." And Macsen's face. His *face* — but Bran knew what to do then.

"Macsen. I love you." He tugged the Red King down until he could reach his mouth, then kissed him, licking at his tongue until his lover growled at him and slid a hand into his hair. He let Macsen kiss him harder, bite his lip and mouth his way down to his throat. "I love you. I've been waiting for you. Now, take me to bed."

"*Anwylyd.*" Beloved. Macsen's word warmed Bran as it always warmed him, and more because of the surprise in it, the eager truth of the meaning wrapped up in the sound. "You know me so well, so well."

Macsen kissed him again, but this time Bran gave him a look. "Bed, Macsen. Now. I'm not letting you make a mess in here again."

"As you command." There was humor in the words, and the Red King's own kind of submission, but desire, too. Gratitude, and love.

Bran slung his other leg over his workbench, stood and stretched out the kinks in his back, then slipped the fingers of one hand through his lover's and pulled him toward the door. By the time they were outside, Macsen was kissing him again, tugging him through the green of Morgan's orchard and into the palace.

Chapter Four

Bran was already moaning into Macsen's mouth by the time they got up the stairs, and Macsen didn't let him go even to get at the handle of their bedroom door. Pressing Bran against it, he cradled his lover's head in one hand to keep him from knocking it on the wood, and kissed him harder. He marked a trail of red love bites from Bran's jaw to his throat, then to his shoulder.

Pinpricks of blood stood out on the surface of his skin where Macsen had been careless, and he licked them up one at a time, little curls of tongue as he pressed his thigh between Bran's parted legs. Rocking, rubbing on him, already panting for it, Bran lifted his hips away from the door and tried for friction, sensation, anything.

Already his eyes were glassed over with desire, his mouth red and wet where he'd bitten his lip. He clung to Macsen's shoulders with both hands, slipped them down his arms, then around his waist.

He smirked as Bran yanked at his clothes, tried to bring him closer and still went on grinding his cock into Macsen's thigh.

"Macs—*gods*. Want you inside me, want you to touch me…" He growled and Macsen stared at him, then leaned down to kiss him again. Bran shuddered, writhed, the heat of his cock a rigid thickness. Gasping, Bran moaned into his mouth, overcome by his own lust.

If Macsen hadn't had his hand between Bran's head and the door he would've knocked himself hard, the way he was bucking, coming in his trousers. A hot flush rushed over Macsen, that he could do that.

Bran was so eager to have him he couldn't hold back.

Macsen kissed him even more deeply and wanton moans vibrated into his mouth until he stood straight and jerked his lover away from the door. He fumbled it open, pushed Bran into their room and onto the bed.

"I'm sorry I've spent so much time away. Look how much you needed me." He ran a hand up Bran's thigh, over his cock, still hard despite the wet mess making Lumi's silk cling to him. "But when I am called for, the summons stays, pulling at me, until I go."

Blue eyes glowed up at him from under a mussed fall of blond curls. Bran slipped his arms around Macsen and tugged him down onto his chest. "It's what I get for picking a king to fall in love with, isn't it? My own fault. But it *has* been too long. See what you did to me? What would the White Queen think?"

Macsen laughed low in this throat. "She'd be jealous of you, beautiful. Just to see how I touch you, how I want you. How I live to take you, live for the taste of you now." He ran his tongue up Bran's throat then down again, sucked at the darkest mark he'd made and hummed with contentment when Bran lifted himself off the bed and moaned.

"*Love.*"

Bran's hair curled warm and golden around his fingers. Macsen pushed them through it, bent to his mouth and licked at his lips, teasing. "I've missed holding you, touching you. I dreamed of kissing you. You go to Dealla in her dreams, torture her. Why not to me instead? Even in a dream I would make you scream for me."

Flushing, an extra layer of heat across his cheekbones, Bran rolled his eyes. "Scream for you. Ha. I don't—"

"You do. You will." Macsen kissed him to silence the protest forming on his lips. Bran wrapped both arms around him, ran his fingers through Macsen's hair, then tugged, impatient. "More, Bran? Ready for more?"

"Been ready. Maybe next time you leave I should go with you."

Macsen licked the fullness of his lips again, then past them. The red flush beneath the golden skin intensified as lust replaced that hint of embarrassment. Enough to remind Macsen of just how Bran had looked, surprise on his face as he was overwhelmed by pleasure.

"You're even more beautiful when you're blushing." He was pleased with himself when Bran's cheeks reddened again. "But as to going with me...I already said that you could. That you *should*."

Macsen tugged on a handful of Bran's hair and watched him shiver, his breath catch, his tongue dart out to wet his lips. "I am king and you are mine, and it's been too long. So long I almost forgot what you taste like."

"Oh?" The sound was choked, tight with desire.

"Sweet, I think. Like your kiss. But perhaps I remember wrong." He slipped his fingers under Bran's tunic, pulling the fabric up as he went.

"Remember wrong?" Bran was already gasping again, an extra pause between his words. "We can't have — *that*." He pressed his cock against Macsen's hip, and it was harder than before.

Macsen pinched Bran's nipples, teased them with the tips of his fingers, and his lover's eyes flashed, smoky and glittering both. "Can't we?" He pinched Bran's nipple again, tugged lightly, nuzzled his throat and mouthed at the marks he'd left there.

"*Oh*, no. *No*." Bran slid his fingers into Macsen's hair and dragged him down to his throat.

So eager, always so eager. It made the waiting better, knowing that Bran wanted it so much. Macsen licked at the scar marking his shoulder until he knew Bran anticipated his bite, then purposefully chose a different spot and sank his teeth in.

His lover groaned and sighed at the same time. Macsen hadn't forgotten the taste of him, not really, but it *had* been too long. No feast in Winter's wild woods could match this. Drinking from Bran, he had grown used to filling himself with light, but there were new depths to be tasted now, more of the moon than there had been before. Something added to the Summer, more richness than just sun.

Macsen allowed himself one more mouthful before he withdrew his teeth, licking his lips. Bran moaned and pulled his hair, tried to keep him against his throat, but Macsen laughed at him and brushed a thumb over his mouth.

Full lips parted at the touch and Bran flicked the tip of his tongue at Macsen's fingers. He dropped his hands from Macsen's hair to his buttocks, then slipped one down even farther and gripped his thigh. "What are you waiting for? I want more than just your teeth in me."

He was beautiful, wanton like this. Vermilion flame licked at the lines of his body, sneaking up to brush at Macsen's skin. "Impatient, *anwylyd*. Always."

The blue eyes burned brighter. "I'm not waiting. Not this time."

"No?"

"*No.*" A shimmer of flame sprang up between them, consumed the silk Macsen was wearing and left Bran in nothing but his trousers. Lumi's frost had resisted the heat. He jerked his hips up, frustrated, and shoved the trousers down and off, then rolled Macsen over and held him to the bed.

His cock was still wet, slick against Macsen's own erection, then over the taut muscles in his torso as Bran moved up his body. The Red King had no reason not to submit to the kisses his lover pressed on him. Bran's mouth was hot on his lips, his throat, his chest, hot at the tip of his cock when he closed his lips around it and sucked.

Bran lapped at it as he held it in his mouth, then pulled off, crawled up over Macsen's body and kissed him again. "I missed kissing you. The taste of you, the feel of you. Do I have to take you for myself? I will. I want you that much, and didn't I prove I have the strength to take what I want? *Didn't I?*"

Oh yes, he had. The memory was there waiting. Hot,

straining muscles holding him, the fire in Bran's eyes when he had trapped Macsen with his back to the wall of the Summer palace and taken him there. Stretched him open and taken him for himself...

But not now, not today. Not that. Macsen bit the soft fullness of Bran's lower lip, sucked on it gently and his Summer son relaxed just a little. *Submit. Submit to me.*

"Maybe I was wrong, maybe I should let you stay here and take my time coming home more often. Begging me like this...I think I like it." He reached up with one hand, grabbed a fistful of soft, blond hair and smirked when Bran moaned louder as he pulled harder. "Yes, I like it. The more you beg the more it makes me want to play with you."

Bran stole additional kisses, each one more scorching than the last, until real fire caressed Macsen's skin with sensual threads. They glided up and down his sides like eager fingers, with just enough pressure that it wasn't tickling but arousing. "You know I like it when you tease me, but later. I want you to take me, so take me." Macsen said nothing. "If you don't I'll take *you*."

That stirred him. He had no intention of letting Bran play that game, not now, not after all the days he'd spent alone, denying his own urge to return here and — Macsen was up in an instant. He had Bran pinned to the bed beneath him and his mouth at the soft curve of his throat again before he could get out another word.

"Not today, *anwylyd*. Oh no. Today you're mine for as long as I want you, no matter how impatient you are." Bran was his prey and would *submit*. "I will tie you up, if I have to. Or is that what you want?"

"*Ha*." It was a breathless breath of sound, and Macsen barely resisted the urge to lick it off his lips. "Not now I don't. Bastard, what do I have to say to—oh. *Oh, yes*. Jus' like... Macsen—nn—*nnnnggg*."

Bran's words slipped from speech to nonsense, groans and begging as Macsen worked a finger into him. He was so tight. Had it been so long? Hadn't he even touched himself?

Two fingers. Deeper. He curled them, stroked inside, and Bran bucked in his grasp, had to *try* to restrain himself, even after...

"*Bran*. You—" He swallowed and heard his own voice shift register, drop a narrow octave to the wolf tones he had spent a long time trying to avoid. "Missed me so much, Bran?"

Macsen added a third finger to the two already keeping him open and this time Bran had no words for him, just cried out and spread his thighs wider. Macsen stretched him gently, anticipating how it would feel to bury himself in that silken heat again.

"Beautiful. I could never resist you." Pulling his fingers free, he ignored Bran's disappointed groan to lean over him and lick scarlet splashes from his chest. He did it slowly, made sure Bran felt every stroke of his tongue, then lingered with his mouth over Bran's nipples. "Love the taste of you, all fire for me. Now. Up on your knees. Up."

His lover twisted under him, breathing hard and still flushed. He feathered his fingers open across golden skin, over the hard curve of ribs and up Bran's spine as his lover got on his hands and knees.

The sight of him like that was enough to make Macsen impatient himself, but he still took time to slick his cock, tested Bran with his fingers again and watched him open for the penetration.

Good. He lined up and worked the length of himself in slowly, then stayed there, eyes closed, bent forward over Bran's back. Bran clenched tight, shivering, *whimpering*. Sensitive now, but then he'd already made such a mess of himself.

Macsen reached under him, wrapped his fist around Bran's wet cock and stroked until he started begging under his breath. He let go then and sat back, taking his lover with long, full strokes that tormented them both.

It wasn't enough to bring himself over the edge, but it was almost too much for Bran. He arched with every thrust, the muscles of his thighs tight, his toes twitching against Macsen's calves.

Fire had settled in the curves of his body, along the angles of his muscles and into his hair. The soft down on his buttocks tingled with heat. He held him open, watched his cock sinking deep. The way that little pink hole stretched around him —

Harder, then harder again, Macsen thrust and watched Bran undulate, clench his fists in the sheets. He lowered his chest to the bed and braced himself on one forearm, but Macsen caught his wrist as he reached for his cock. He pulled Bran back by it with steady strength, then caught his other arm, too. "I'll give you all the more you want. No. Touching."

"*Close.* Bastard you… Oh. *Oh,* don't stop. Right there, *right there —*"

Macsen held his wrists, thrust faster and ate up the sight of his lover's wanton body. His golden skin gleamed, the corded muscles beneath taut with arousal. Summer fire lashed in all directions. Bran dropped his head forward and cursed, cried out when Macsen slammed into him again, then seemed to relax, even though his muscles were still tense.

Submit. Yes, submit. You are all. Mine.

The breaking of Bran's defiance tasted nearly as good as his blood. The Red King sat back on his legs and pulled his lover with him, then let go of his wrists. Bran dropped into Macsen's lap, drove himself down onto his cock and stayed, shuddering, with his thighs sprawled open and his shoulders pressed against Macsen's chest.

Macsen held his hips and thrust sharply, not relenting even for a moment. Bran dropped his head onto Macsen's shoulder, tempting him with the half-healed wound at his throat.

"Mac — Macsen…*deep.* S'deep, I — I —"

The broken sound of Bran's voice sent a spike of pleasure all through him. "Too much for you?"

"*No*. Bastard, if you stop I'll—*ohhhh* don't stop."

Macsen licked Bran's throat, one long, cool stroke of tongue.

His lover shivered, then sighed. "*Yessss.*" It was barely a word, just a long, sweet hiss of affirmation. He sank his teeth in without waiting, let Bran writhe on his cock and try to push himself over the edge.

When he lifted his mouth, Bran groaned his disappointment. Macsen stroked the twitching muscles in his abdomen with one thumb then tightened his grip on Bran's hips and thrust into him again. "So close, Bran."

"Yes—close—ohhh, please."

"Are you going to let me see, are you going to come for me? So much tighter when you... *Yes*. Just like that."

"Ahhh...ahhh—*ah!*" Bran was shaking, his hands tight on Macsen's thighs. He bit his own lip until Macsen did it for him, sucked on the tears in his soft skin and drank up the cry he let out as he gave in to his release.

Macsen groaned into his mouth and lasted for one more stroke. The eager squeezing of Bran's body around him drew out his pleasure, soft pulses milking him even when he tried to pull out. "No, don't." Bran turned his head and blinked at him, pupils dilated and blue irises blazing. "Stay inside me, just like that."

"*Anwylyd.*"

"You've never taken me like this before. I *like* it this way. Do it again, just like this. You're so deep—"

"*Hmmm*. I could do it again." He held Bran still, pulled out a little, then filled him up again slowly. "If you wanted. Since you like it so much."

"Plea—*ohh yes.*"

Soft, wet noises accompanied every thrust, and Macsen watched Bran's face as he slid deeper. The way his eyes fluttered closed. The way he bit his lip until he was moaning, panting and moving on his own. Macsen teased his nipples, then reached around to stroke him.

"Oh—*oh gods*. If you do that I—"

"Again?" Macsen held his hips and tried to slow him, then kept Bran still with his cock buried deep when he wouldn't obey. "Didn't touch yourself at all while I was gone, did you?"

"No, I-I wasn't thinking about it until you — *gods* Macsen, move, please."

"Until I returned?" He stopped with the tip of his cock hovering at the entrance to Bran's body and held him when he tried to sink down onto it.

Bran gasped in a breath, then another, and squirmed in his hands. "Please don't tease me anymore. I want you so much it burns — it *burns* and I *need* you."

A low chuckle slipped out of his mouth, spilled across Bran's shoulders. He leaned in to murmur against them, kiss his scalding skin. "You didn't know that's how it would be? My Summer son. How little do you guess of your own nature? Have I been too good to you, keeping you sated?"

"Macsen!"

He struggled, squirmed, panted, but he had no leverage and here, in dark Winter, his own kingdom, Macsen would always have the mastery. "I have, haven't I? Spoiled you... And is it fire inside you now, just like on your skin?"

"Ohhh yes, *yes*."

"*Good.*" Slowly, controlling every movement, Macsen allowed Bran to slide down a little at a time. He let him settle, rocking and moaning, muttering to himself 'yes' and 'yes more' and 'gods' and 'Macsen' and 'please'.

Most of all and most enticing, 'please'. Macsen kept one hand at his lover's hip but slid the other over his thigh to touch him again.

It only took a few strokes before Bran let go, cried out hoarse with pleasure and laid his head on Macsen's shoulder. He seemed caught between trying to catch his breath and taking more pleasure for himself and squirmed as Macsen teased his cock with wet fingers.

So wanton, beautiful and begging, not letting him out of his body even now — but that was all right. After so many days apart, Macsen wasn't nearly through with him yet. "I love you. So much, I love you…"

Bran turned his head and pressed his lips just under Macsen's jaw. "Love me more."

'*More*'. "I can never make up my mind…" He caught Bran up under his thighs, lifted him off his cock and shifted him forward onto his knees. "Which I like better. When you say 'more', or 'please'?"

Bran slumped forward, turned his head to the side and pressed his cheek to the bed between the crooks of his elbows. "I c'n…just say'm both." His eyes glinted at Macsen from beneath the fall of his hair. "*Please*. More." He spread his thighs and lifted himself into Macsen's hands.

Macsen held his buttocks apart and pressed one thumb into him. He was so wet…

Bran only groaned and lifted his hips. "Feels — oh, please."

"*Shh*. I'm going to take you nice and slow, and you are going to stay still for me, just like this, aren't you?"

Bran sucked in breath and a ripple of fire fled over his skin as he did so. "Yes, *yes*, I'll stay."

"Good. Don't. Move." He rubbed his cock between Bran's buttocks, pressed only the tip inside, then eased back. "Maybe I'll spend as many days inside you as I spent away from you. What do you think about that?"

"Just don't stop. *Don't*."

Macsen sank all the way in, one smooth, long stroke, gripped Bran's hips with both hands and squeezed. Fire around him. Fire beneath him. Why had he stayed away so long? *Never again*. To tease was one thing, but he had missed his Summer son too much.

* * * *

The attackers came out of the dark. Neither Winter hunters nor wandering Summer *sidhe*, but human women. Even in the blackness, Lughaid immediately recognized the armor of Dealla's huntresses, and with them, the thrice damned priests she had sworn to her service.

In many years of rites, he had never met a god as jealous as the one those men claimed to serve. And the men themselves... There was something of the old Roman arrogance about them, as if despite their claims to worship the god of the Jews, they had still been infected by some spirit of that city.

It was on their faces now, that arrogance, and a certain greed — for lives, if not for gold, but they would win nothing but death this way. Refugees fled before them as the swift flicker of iron fell where it chose.

Priests and women cut down many where they stood, too shocked to move, or too afraid. But these raiders prowled with purpose and peered into the shadowed faces of their victims with cold intent.

They were seeking, not something, but *someone*.

The blood drained from Lughaid's face. He turned and ran as fast as his old legs could carry him, toward the center of the grove and the tent in which Aisling stayed. They must have discovered that she lived, and that she was here.

Certainty gripped him with icy talons. If they found her, they would kill her. There would be no way out then. No hiding place, no safety for anyone in Ireland, not for a thousand years. But he froze in horror as the center of the encampment came into view.

Aisling's tent was already burning.

The canvas roared under the weight of fire. The princess was nowhere in sight, only three huntresses, smirking. Expecting accolades, were they? Praise, for the murder they had committed?

Lughaid sank to his knees, drained of all hope. Once again, just as with his son, he had failed. *Too late*.

The women started toward him as he fell, recognizing his robe and, perhaps, his face. Two retreated, but the third did not deviate from her approach. The black pass of her blade through his gut was almost painless, a single stroke of fire.

Just a reflection of his burning hopes.

Then she twisted it as she pulled it out. Gasping, Lughaid put his hands to his belly. Wetness but no warmth. Shock had drained half the feeling from his fingers already. It was not very far to finish falling from his knees to the ground, but the impact still shocked the breath from him, and it was very hard to take another.

Lughaid watched the canvas of Aisling's tent as the fire intensified and the fragile structure collapsed in a rush of flame. But he hitched himself forward and tried to focus his wandering eyes.

Was she... *No*. It couldn't be and yet...

Aisling lay unburned at the center of the inferno. The Summer mark at her breast was brighter than the blaze, and when she stirred it was as if she were just coming awake. *Then* there was a scream. The princess scrambled out of the embers, scattering ashes, with terror reflected in her eyes, the clothes burning off her body but her skin untouched.

As she did so Lughaid heaved in the most painful breath of his life. "Ais..." Too quiet. She'd never hear him over the fire. "Aisling!"

The cry brought blood to his lips but it drew her attention, made her eyes grow wide. In a moment, she was on her knees beside him, her naked skin too white where the ash hadn't stained it.

"Lughaid, they—you're bleeding!" She paused and her face changed as she pulled his robe away from the gash, but he did not look down. "This wound is—"

"*Too late*. Listen to me. Flee this place while...*ahh*. While you can. They think you dead, they won't follow. Go to Britain. Ask the High King for the way...into Spring. Make *peace*. You understand? And then..." But his breath failed him. His hands were cold, his lips numb.

"Into Spring. But Dealla—"

"It won't...matter. Unless."

"We can have the green again. I understand, but... Lughaid, I can't do this alone!"

He smiled at her, or tried to. He was so tired now, cold

and so tired. "Take…your hunter. Into…" He sighed. "Very green, the Spring…" Lughaid heard her calling his name, over and over. But why? He was so tired. And he had nothing left to say.

Lughaid's message lingered in Aisling's ears as he closed his eyes for the last time. Go with her hunter? But where was he? Perhaps even he…?

The thought terrified her. "Cathán?" she shouted blindly into the night. "Cathán!"

The princess tried to stand, but before she could stumble to her feet a pair of hands pulled her back. She rolled over as a male body tumbled her into the grass and pinned her down. Aisling only realized it was the man she'd been calling for when Cathán leaned in close to her face.

He was over her like a lover, but for the fear-wild beating of his heart and the quick, black darting of his eyes. He bared his teeth as he glared at the world in motion around them.

For the first time Aisling saw more than just a hint of the *other* in him.

She was almost afraid, but *sidhe* or not he was still Cathán. Aisling stayed still as he peered into the night but she whispered quick and sharply the task she had been given. Lughaid's words. "*I must go to Spring!*"

Straddling her hips, he pressed his face near her throat, breathed in. Out. In. What was wrong with him? But he was speaking then. "It's no good. You will never get away, unless I take you with me, and to do that I… Stay. *Still.*"

He reared up over her and sank bright teeth into the heel of his hand. Blood flowed, too red, and he began to paint her skin with it. Her face, her throat, her heaving breasts. The bare skin of her arms and the goose-fleshed trembling of her legs.

The scent of it surrounded them, not like the scent of blood at all. Not iron, this odor, but salt and copper. Something of the sea. His mother, she remembered. His mother, he'd said, was a selkie.

Then he was over her again, wrapping her in damp cloth that she belatedly realized was Lughaid's torn and bloodied cloak. He held her to the muddy brush, and the hum of his voice came close by her ear.

"Don't move. Say nothing. Breathe as light as you can while I run with you." His face was wild, transformed.

"Cathán?"

"Something is changed, is happening. The air is whispering." As he spoke Aisling glared at him, demanding an explanation with her eyes. "The Summer King, my lady. *Dark Summer's King*. Only a potential, yet to be acknowledged...*ahh*. But soon." The words were a ghost of fire on his breath, haunting the shell of her ear.

"Can't you feel it? Perhaps it is your fault, my lady." The Summer mark on her breast tingled as he gazed at it, and his stare wandered upward on a drunken path toward the horizon. "A thousand years we've been waiting. All that was dark has been kept in the light for so long."

The curve of Cathán's smile grew to match the crescent moon. He closed his eyes and the lines of his face no longer seemed human at all.

This time, though he didn't say it, Aisling heard the echo herself. *Summer King*.

The land beneath her had begun to remember to whom it truly belonged. The presence in the ground swelled, clamoring against invisible senses she never used. She opened her eyes with a startled gasp, expecting to see fire all around her.

The night stayed dark.

Cathán pushed himself to his feet then, grabbed her hand and pulled her along with him until they were racing across the hillside, sprinting toward the coast. The ground fled beneath her feet at impossible speed, and he didn't stop at the water but pulled her along its surface.

The gray of the sea flowed by swiftly. The whole of the night was an equal blur. The air burned her face, her lips, and dried the moisture out of her mouth as she gasped for breath.

When they finally stopped, Cathán dragged her off the beach and up into the darker shadow of the dunes.

His fingers trembled as he touched her. The man's whole body trembled and she wondered if it had cost him something she didn't understand to paint her with blood and rush her across the water.

His eyes were strange by the light of the moon crossing the zenith of the sky. His irises were as black as his pupils, the whole of his stare too wide, too quick.

"Cathán…"

"You should be safe on this side of the sea. Your sister and her women have no presence here, no influence. And will to evil or not, she has not much longer to live."

Aisling remembered without need for reminder that feeling of danger and longing rising in the wind. *Summer King*. She shuddered and Cathán touched her shoulder.

"You will be queen soon. In all the ways that matter, you already are. You could have sent another in your place, chosen someone else. Are you sure you want to do this?"

She couldn't prevent the hiccup of laughter that escaped her mouth. "Want? No. But I must. I knew Lughaid was right about that the moment he said it. And now that we're here — but you need to rest before anything else. You don't…"

Aisling hesitated, then settled on the vaguest description as being the most accurate. "You don't look well."

But he shook his head and paced restlessly around her, as if to mock her suggestion. "No. *You* need rest and I need to find a town with a market. You can't go anywhere like *that*." His gesture took in the whole of her condition, her blood-stained skin and the torn cloak that was her only garment, before he grabbed her hand and pulled her farther along the shore.

The sand was cool and damp when he stopped and pressed her down onto it. The tidal scents of shore and seaweed were intense but oddly comforting. They reminded her of Cathán's own scent, the heavy salt of it.

"You'll be safe here. I'll return as quick as I can." He squeezed her hands, and it was only then that she realized she had reached out for him, was holding his fingers tightly in her own cold grip. "I *will* return for you. There's nothing to fear now."

She did not ask why, if there was nothing to fear, she was curled in the black shadow of a dune, out of sight of anyone but him.

* * * *

When Cathán reappeared just before dawn, some of the wildness had faded from his expression but not from his eyes. "Here. Change into these." He pressed worn, clean leather into her hands, clothes like those she'd worn when she had been hunting with him, then turned from her.

Aisling used Lughaid's cloak and the cold seawater to scrub herself clean of ash and Cathán's blood, then dressed in the clothes he'd brought. When she touched his shoulder, he turned around and examined her.

"It will have to do. Come here, I'll comb your hair. This High King, do you know where he is?"

Aisling frowned then relaxed despite herself as the warmth of his fingers separated her hair and he combed it smooth. "I know where he *should* be."

He didn't answer, only gathered the locks away from her ears and forehead and braided them, then settled something heavy onto her head. She reached up and touched smooth, cold gold. A circlet? *How had he...?* "Cathán—"

"Did I not say you are *queen*, my lady? Now, which direction?"

"North, and east—ah!" She cried out as her feet left the sand, and she fell against his chest. Aisling pressed a hand to his sternum and scowled when he didn't put her down. "Cathán!"

"But I move faster than you over land, my lady. Not just over water."

She thought he was smiling, but it was a long road, and time was short. She let him carry her.

Chapter Five

It had been a long while since Myrddin had lived at a human pace.

This stint with Uther's royal household was the first time he had done so since his mortal roots had passed away, since his mother had died. He found it less than relaxing. The world of real things advanced at a frantic pace even bright Spring couldn't match. Everything mortal was in a fervor to do what it felt it must do, before the end came.

Still, by the close of his first day, Myrddin knew what he had to do to get what he wanted. It was all too easy for him to inspire awe in mortals. The simplest flutter of illusory silk could turn a serving girl into an empress for an hour. A twist of the living core of a man, and a priest became a braying ass for all to see.

When the king asked him why he refused a seat at his table, Myrddin gave Uther a taste of clear Spring wine and laughed at the way it went to the man's head.

The second evening, in the dim quiet of the crackling fire and the mutter of low voices ranged around Uther's great chair, Myrddin brought out his harp.

"What are you doing, boy?"

"Amusing myself. What kind of court is this?" But when he started playing there was a disrespectful mutter from the cordon of priests that always lingered near the throne.

"A mere bard."

Myrddin only smiled. He called a wavering haze out of the twilight and fog curled across the floor, lapped up the open door and recoiled from the fort's old walls. Kings and ladies, beasts and gods strode out of the music and onto the mist. Uther and his company gasped first in fear, then in wonder.

After that night, the priests stopped their ears, but their daily exhortations couldn't keep the rest of the court from listening.

Myrddin sang the stories of his mother's people, the great heroes and their loves. Lingered on romance – couldn't help it. His heart was longing for his lover, even though he couldn't go. Not yet.

Not until he had made a place for himself here, until he was sure that even the Christian priests, who would remember him resentfully, would at least remember him. And so instead of going to Kas, he sang of beauty and its easy vanishing beneath the twin weights of time and pain.

At night, he made himself scarce. Alone, Myrddin went into the wild, thinking that he might meet Kas in the cooling summer woods. There was never anyone waiting for him, and he wondered how long he would have to stay away to make Kas fulfill the possessive promise he'd made.

Each morning, he returned to Uther's camp and noticed the accumulation of more trouble. Despite a general appreciation for his magic, his music, there was still more focus on the promise of the future that lingered around his presence. On the interpretation of omens and their influence over future events.

Again and again, until even Uther looked at him askance, he was asked what the omen of the red dragon meant. The High King had admitted that he was the same boy who had revealed that mystery, the 'son of no man', to reassure his court of Myrddin's presence.

The questions continued, but Myrddin remained reluctant to answer. If he had wanted to interpret what he had said more thoroughly, he would have.

Meddling with mortals in this way had its risks. He knew that. *Knew* that. It created disorder in the fabric of things, as much as that which he was trying to fix. Could he use chaos to correct chaos? He wondered, but the decision was taken from him soon enough.

Time was no longer his friend.

Uther's priests scoffed and gave their own meaning to Myrddin's words. In their explanations Myrddin heard a whisper of death that had nothing to do with his own desires. If he did not offer the correct interpretation, or at least the one he wanted, those priests would turn his own omen against him.

Finally, on a morning of red sun, he decided to give Uther what he had been asking for. "You've bothered me for more than you wanted at first, Pendragon."

"Have I?" There was no humor in the High King's features, and Myrddin sighed. Had he already waited too long? "Samhain is still months away. It causes me trouble even to acknowledge you and your pagan festival, yet here you sit, doing nothing for me."

Myrddin bridled, despite his intentions. "Nothing for *you*. Do you think that's why I have come? No. *No*, not for you, not for any mortal."

Something ferocious moved for an instant Uther's face. "And yet you had no trouble letting dragons into the wild of my kingdom, opening up the mountain, creating doubts in the minds of my men!"

"Do you want an explanation?" Uther was silent. "No, that is not enough for you, is it? Your priests have offered you prophecies, and now you want one from me. That *is* what you want, isn't it?" Myrddin almost laughed, but the taste of it was too bitter. "A lie that might come true. A metaphor that will be easy to forget when it becomes inconvenient." He whipped around and faced the court that hung on their every word. "Do you want it, all of you?" And again, evergreen, like pulled thorns, "*Do you want a prophecy?*"

There was silence, and that was his answer, and it was yes.

He drew himself up. "I gave you the omen of your kingship, Pendragon. Victory for the future, against the

Saxon foe that has defied you. But now I tell you that every victory is temporary, except the one that is swallowed whole.

"I see a Red Dragon returning out of the west. Before his children can come to him, he will revert to his old habits and tear himself to pieces. Dragons are cannibals, King, but their failing is not the failing of beasts. Before flesh, they go seeking what avarice breeds in them. One treasure…or another."

Uther frowned at him, but Myrddin could see on the king's face that he didn't understand. Well. That was the way of prophecies, wasn't it? One never knew how they would play out until they had already come to pass.

"Children, you say."

"Yes." Myrddin glanced from Uther to his daughter, a quiet slip of a girl. "I see your son, earning his crown, taking it with his sword."

Uther's stare fixed on him. "A son. A *son*." His eyes glittered, relieved, proud. "And what of my daughter?"

Myrddin turned to consider her again. Uther's bastard daughter was a green-eyed girl child with her father's red hair. He had seen her in the Spring madness, the girlish features turned womanly with the passage of time.

There was something about this bastard princess, this Morgause, that terrified. So much so that Myrddin could say only one thing. "She will become a beautiful weapon. A terrible blade. Both your children will be crowned, but which will wear more blood, I wonder?"

The eldest priest interrupted, stepped out of the crowd but not quite far enough to put himself between Myrddin and Uther. "The king has only *one* child."

Myrddin shrugged. "The son will come."

A spiteful, derisive expression twisted the priest's face further. "Oh? And when will that happy event be?"

But that Myrddin knew better than anything else he could have been asked, and this time he did laugh. "When? This is the time of the summer born. At Samhain, he'll be conceived with the Winter, then born and given to me with the dying of the light."

'Given to me', he had said, but no one seemed to notice. Not even Uther. Had he not yet guessed what the price of his woman would be?

"What else can you tell me, boy? Are you prophet or sorcerer? Druid? Bard?" the priest asked.

"Everything and nothing. As I am all those things and none of them. I have told you what I wished to tell you. I have told you many things you need not know, but still you ask for more." Myrddin closed his eyes and let out a breath that infused the air with spring. "We are close to the time when stones will speak to you."

"When stones...?"

"You will drink ash, and the day you go to the battlefield wounded, you will not come from it again. The hand of God will strike you down."

Uther's stare did not shift. "I do not mind a death in battle."

"You will not die in battle. Did I not say? The hand of God will strike you down."

The High King shrugged, but when he turned, he seemed satisfied. "The hands of God hold the fates of all men."

Myrddin watched him walk away. The man had obviously not heard the warning, but perhaps that was not his fault. *He* had not meant for Uther to comprehend.

* * * *

The warmth of the afternoon brought a clamor of voices at the fortress gate. Interested, Myrddin wandered over to see the source of the fuss, but most of the noise came from inside. Outside, he saw only a single pair, man and woman.

The man he didn't know, though he had an aura of... something. But the woman. Aisling? Yes, that was her name. She had changed from the first time he'd seen her, innocent in unconsciousness, but he recognized her still.

Sleepless decisions and new horror were written in the lines that marked the corners of her eyes. Yet she stood tall when she was let through to stand before Uther and introduced herself as Queen of Ireland. "I've come, Lord, to ask for the way into the Wyrdwood, or permission to go seek it myself." Her eyes were bright but hopeless as she bowed before the High King. "In the service of peace, I beg of you. Allow this."

"Beg of me. *You* are the new Queen of Ireland?" Uther laughed richly, but Myrddin compared them in silence.

Uther had had too much of wine and women since he had become king, but Aisling was gaunt and beautiful in her huntress' leathers, her hair bound by a crown of plaited tresses and a fillet of gold. Yes. She was a queen, and Uther a king, and the difference between them was as obvious as life and death.

Peace, she wanted. Passage through Britain to the sacred gate of Spring. Peace. *Well, what would Macsen think of that?*

Myrddin wondered. This woman was seeking in the wrong direction, with the best intentions, but here and now was not the place to correct her, nor to reveal himself as he was. Not as the Spring King, not as the Lord of the Wood or the son of its god.

Uneasy, he eyed the priests as they approached, thinking of his father's radiance as he had seen it last. Diminished. Asleep in the Spring. No. There would be no sharing in the here and now, but perhaps he should open the way for her.

He wanted to see what she would do, this twice-marked woman, on his side of the Avalon gate. The boon she wanted was not in his power to grant, regardless, but he could send her to Winter.

Addressing Uther, he leaned forward. "Pendragon, you should give her the guide she asks for. Or permission, at least." Myrddin ignored the way Aisling's companion suddenly focused on him. "It does no harm to you, and this woman is much better than the other."

Irritation darkened the expression on Uther's face, stalled

his affirmation as he tried to find issue with the suggestion or the request. "I don't want trouble. Vortigern was a fool to hire these women, to go after the Red King. *Milesians*. Pirates and fools, the lot of them. As if Pict and Saxon raids weren't enough trouble."

Myrddin laughed silently as the woman shrugged. "I only try to build something out of this that might become a lasting peace." For the first time, there was a hint of emotion in her voice. Anger or desperation? "Will you at least let us pass?"

Uther examined his fingernails, then flicked a careless hand in her direction. "Go, and good riddance to you. Let the *sidhe* take their own revenge. I'll not waste my people on you. Northwest, across the bogs, I'm told the hills will be a city of glass that does not belong to this world. If the way is open."

There was hesitation in the woman's voice. "A city?"

"Sometimes it is a city. Sometimes it is an isle, or a forest. I have never gone there. It is not a place for mortals."

Myrddin blinked at Uther's description, but he could see how it might seem that way, on days when the veil was thin and the immortal gleam passing through.

"Now go, I said! Do not make me repeat myself again."

Myrddin watched the woman leave. She would have no trouble crossing the country, he was sure. With a breath of power, he reached out and opened the Avalon Gate.

* * * *

Summer was falling apart. In bits and pieces, the edges of the golden kingdom were scattering, no better than puffs of dandelion seed lost to the wind. Tighe watched the whole season walking a line along which murmurs and confusion met the silence of death.

Those of Summer's people who had dared venture back to the hollows of Ireland had been slain, and many of those who had gone after them seeking revenge. The Milesian huntresses and their priests were dangerous, but equally dangerous was the lack of response from Summer's Queen.

Tighe's mother had vanished into some secret recess and was nowhere to be found, not even through the will of Summer. He had wandered for days, searching for her, following paths that wound in circles and ended where they began. It had grown tiresome quickly, and today, instead of trying again, he had decided to seek out Faelan.

He wanted to clear the air, fix whatever it was that had gone sour the day his mother had ordered Faelan off with Bran and the Red King. There was distance between them now. He and Faelan had shared an easy, comfortable closeness since the moment they'd met. So much so that at the very beginning it had confused and disturbed him.

Now it was missing, and that distressed him instead.

"Faelan? Faelan, are you home?" The Summer wood had opened into the clearing where Tighe's own house was, but he'd just *left* home.

"I'm here, Tighe." The call came from inside.

He slipped through the door, then into the bedroom.

Faelan stood naked, contemplating a pair of tunics that were laid on the bed in contrasting splashes of blue and sunny orange. "I thought you'd gone somewhere."

His lover had spoken without so much as glancing at him, and Tighe stopped in the doorway. "Is that why you came back?"

"What? No, but you weren't here when I did. Something you need, prince? *My prince*." There was a hint of Faelan's usual playfulness in the words.

That was enough to pull Tighe over the threshold and into the room. "Just you. I wanted to see you." Tighe stepped closer and wrapped his arms around Faelan's shoulders. "You keep disappearing, and I've been searching for my mother, but that hasn't worked out so well."

Tighe tried for humor, but Faelan twisted in his arms, and his eyes were dark as he answered. "I have not been disappearing. And your mother is the problem, the reason why I…" He shook his head. "Everywhere is trouble, Tighe. The corners and the edges of things…"

"They're coming apart. I know. But what would you have me do about it? I wanted to find my mother so I could question her, not confront her. Not like that."

"That's what you say every time—" Faelan dropped his gaze.

Tighe thought he knew what his lover was going to say. "Even the last time?" He tightened his embrace, bent his head and brushed Faelan's lips with his own. "I've been regretting letting you go ever since. Wondering if I could have done something else, said something else. I don't know what, even now, but I—"

Faelan's scowl intensified, and he avoided a deeper kiss. "Tighe! Have you been paying attention? Before I even left with your brother and—before I even left, six of my brothers were dead. Dead! And our queen is vanished now, without doing a thing about it. Out of sight as if that means out of mind."

He let out a huff of breath, pulled out of Tighe's embrace and returned to their bed. "Who are we to go to with our troubles, all of us? Some come to me because I'm close to you, and you are Summer's Prince. Even if you're half mortal. Even if you—" But he cut himself off with an angry exhalation, turned and picked up the blue tunic, slipped it over his head.

Tighe caught hold of his arm again and pulled him close. "Stay. Please?"

For an instant, there was a sliver of heat in Faelan's glance. It vanished as if snuffed out, and Faelan shook his head. "I can't. I have—plans."

'Plans'. "Faelan…"

"Someone must do *something!*"

Tighe let go of him and closed his eyes. The same argument. They'd had it before, more than once. *Maybe this is why we… Maybe it wasn't because he left with Bran. Maybe this is…?*

He opened his eyes again. "How do you expect to find her, if even I can't? How do you expect to start a rebellion with no queen here to rebel against?"

Faelan paled then scowled at him. "How do you know what—?"

"I didn't know anything. I do now." He fixed his gaze on the palms of his hands, not trusting himself to meet his lover's eyes. "Did you think I'd tell her, is that why you didn't say anything?"

"Tighe." Faelan slid warm fingers into his hair, along his cheek, and made him look up. "It's not me who doesn't trust you, it's not even a matter of trust. You *see* too much. Everyone knows that. And I'm sure the public good isn't the only reason so many are so willing to go on a rampage."

Tighe had no answer for any of that. It was all too true, and he'd always known it.

"My prince, you're Summer's son, true enough, but..." Faelan shrugged, and Tighe furrowed his brow in aggravation.

"But. Always. If there was just—" But Tighe's thoughts overturned, because there was, in fact, *someone.*

I saw it in Bran. The Summer sun eclipsed. Twice now, my brother has defied the Summer, shadowed the sky.

Faelan wore an unfamiliar expression. "You're thinking what I've been thinking, aren't you?" His eyes had gone both soft and hard. "Many saw your brother in the throne room, holding off your mother's fire for the sake of that girl."

Tighe let out a heavy breath. "Yes. And you were there, when he confronted the Black King. Others who were near, who saw the sky go dark, they suspect, too, don't they?"

The words stayed unspoken between them, heating the air. *Summer King.*

"Bran needs to acknowledge his power himself if he's to challenge Mother, try to make her act or give him permission to do so. Give *us* permission." But Tighe's face twisted into something grim, and he couldn't prevent it.

Give you *permission*. Faelan and everyone else, but never him. It was too dangerous.

Even as he thought that, the swelling possibilities were within him, things that history and myth and his own good sense had always warned him against.

He *could* ride a horse into the mortal world, never let his feet touch mortal ground, touch nothing that did with his own hands or anything in them. It was dangerous, so dangerous. It was tempting fate.

He thought it would equally be tempting fate to let his *gancanagh* lover go alone among mortals. And more than that, Bran was... "It's not fair to him, you know. To my brother. He wants nothing to do with ruling. The moment I called him Summer King, I saw that." But he fell silent. That bordered on telling too much, even to Faelan.

His lover only shrugged. "Maybe it's not fair. I don't know him like you do, just that he's desperate for his beloved."

Tighe gave him a glare that might have shattered some other being, but the mirror at Faelan's heart held as it always had. *Gancanagh* power showed Tighe only his own fear. His future, emptied of this single being he had come to love.

But Faelan didn't seem to sense the intensity of his stare, was still caught in the threads of their conversation. "It has to be your brother. There's no other choice, prince. I'm of dark Summer, and I'd follow him. He has the night in him, not just the Summer sun. All he needs to do is take what's always been meant for him."

"I—" Tighe took a breath and tried to shrug. Only one shoulder cooperated. "I'll send Bran a message. See if he'll come here. I expect he has no desire to hear from me at all." He winced and lifted one hand to his jaw, remembering. "That's all I can do. He wasn't very happy with me last time we met, if you recall."

"Tighe..." Faelan reached for him, but this time Tighe was the one who turned away, as if he hadn't noticed.

The fear, irrational as it might be, was too much now.

Thinking of his brother restored the anxious-angry feeling of anticipation. Worry that sooner or later, probably sooner, Faelan would just go. Do as his nature demanded, and…

Stop.

Thinking about it.

"If he says yes, I'll talk to him. Don't worry." Tighe stared at the wall over Faelan's shoulder. "Anyway, didn't you say you had plans?"

"I did. I *had*. It doesn't matter now."

Tighe settled himself on the bed, rolled onto his side and turned his gaze to the window. "You should go find out what they're saying, so I have something to tell my brother. It's not like I can go, you said it yourself."

The blue tunic Faelan had put on drifted onto the bed beside him, and Faelan stepped naked between Tighe and his view. "There's more than one meeting, more than enough muttering to overhear later. I'm not going anywhere while you're like this."

"Like what, exactly?"

"My prince. I don't need eyes like yours to see there's something wrong. Something more than just what's wrong with Summer." He pushed Tighe over and climbed on top of him. "You won't tell me what's wrong. I know you won't, or you would have done it already. But I'm not going anywhere."

"Faelan…"

"I feel like time's running out. Like it's not just Summer that's failing. I don't want that."

A flush of heat and fear rushed through Tighe. He reached up and brought Faelan down into bed, wrapped both arms around his lover and held him against his chest. "I don't either. I don't—*I don't*."

They lay together, a tangle of limbs and breath, until Faelan dozed. Tighe watched him for a while, contemplating the softness of his sleeping face, then slipped out of bed and out of the house.

Jeweled wings beat overhead, a thousand glints of avian

promise, and he called toward them. "I need to send a message to my brother. Which of you wants to go?"

A golden flutter came near him, a green-eyed bird he recognized as the first he'd ever made.

"Are you my volunteer?" It alighted on his finger, and Tighe composed his worries and Faelan's, all the Summer trouble, into as concise a message as he could manage. "Bran, I'm sorry. *I'm sorry*. We need your help. Summer is falling apart and Mother is… I don't like asking. I'm *sorry*. But you're the only one who might be able to do anything. Please come."

Before he had finished, Faelan came up behind him, yawned and draped his arms around Tighe's shoulders. He stood listening, and Tighe watched him watching the glittering dart of his messenger as it disappeared into the distance.

"Will he come, do you think?"

Tighe rubbed the heels of his hands against his eyes. "Probably. Even if he doesn't really want to. He apologized once, for relying on me. Bothering me, he said. So he will probably come now that I need him."

"But not for a while, so come back to bed, Tighe."

He turned and gazed into Faelan's eyes. Warm fingers squeezed his shoulders then slid up into his hair and tightened there.

"Please? Come back to bed."

"All right. Just for a little while." He tried not to say it as if he thought that was all they had, but the way Faelan kissed him told him he had failed entirely.

Chapter Six

Aisling traveled north, following the pulse of power at her breast as much as the directions of Uther Pendragon. It led her all the way to a glass hill, visible beyond green water.

The Avalon Gate.

A circle of stones marked the transition between one world and the next. Each had been engraved with spirals that were almost invisible beneath a coat of growing things. The air at the center wavered like a summer mirage, but the breeze that came to her from the other side was cool.

It smelled not of the bogs but of a growing wood and… apples?

The sweetness of the fragrance was enough to make her mouth water. The more deeply she breathed, the more the air stung her lungs, her lips, until she couldn't help but lick them, hoping for a taste that wasn't there. When she finally shook herself and took a step forward, Cathán took her elbow. "This place is dangerous. Don't forget you're only mortal."

Aisling looked at her hands, the lines in them, the tightness of the tendons at her wrist. "As if I could."

She took a deep breath and plunged into the Spring.

As she stepped through the circle, a glittering wood surrounded her, without transition. Green leaves hung over the haze, each one a jewel suspended. She turned, and the circle of stones was still behind her. The ancient triskelions were black where the sunlight touched them but glowed in the mist, and they seemed older, far older, than those on the other side had led her to suspect.

"My lady."

She was turning before Cathán spoke, feeling more than just his eyes on her. Watchfulness seemed to come even from the curl of the ferns and the moss on the standing stones.

Aisling took a step forward, and a growl came from the forest. She saw them as soon as she heard them — wolves moving in sharp outline, the froth of their saliva a threat on shining teeth.

A stag scattered the pack. The young buck scrutinized Aisling with mismatched eyes, one green and blue, a stare that brewed silence. Dark Spring was all around her, and she tasted the question that had driven her here before she spoke it. "Green King, where are you?"

"Where are you? Where are you?"

Aisling stared. She had not blinked, but the stag had vanished, and now before her were the tiniest, most perfect beings she had ever seen. Human in shape but green as the leaves, winged with fractures of beating light. "I — Can you help me? I've come from Ireland, to find the Green King."

One of the tiny mouths became a round 'O', and the *sidhe* let out a scream of flute noise. Pure notes in rising tone startled her backward until she felt Cathán's chest against her shoulders and glanced at him. "Cathán…"

"Careful, my lady."

"Careful?" *Sidhe* flitted in front of her. Tiny fae called out music to each other, beckoned her forward. She ran her fingers through a cluster of white flowers and they tumbled away from her touch with the sound of bells.

Music without melody. Calling her? *Yes.* And she wanted to listen to that call.

This Spring kingdom held something as fleeting and lovely, as nearly human, as anything immortal could be. There were spirals of knotwork in the smallest shadow of bark, minuscule patterns in the green-glass luminescence of beating *sidhe* wings and blinking *sidhe* eyes.

A little at a time she was pulled forward, laughing.

"My lady, wait!" But though she heard him calling, the green pulse of the wood was louder. She went from one shadow to the next, with him just behind her. "Aisling, they'll kill you. They'll dance you to death. Aisling!"

She danced down an endless hill and dragged him with her, across water that flowed but still carried the unbroken reflection of the sky. It wasn't his hands on her, finally, that stopped her, but the wet pressure of his mouth on her lips.

The shock of it, the heat of Summer pressed to her mouth here in the Spring, was enough to make her blink and wake up — to make her hear the echo of his words and the truth in them, before she gave in to his kiss.

In the moment after, she felt the pounding of her heart even in her fingertips. There wasn't anything to say. Everything she needed to know was in his eyes, on his face. Surely it had to be the same for him.

But the moment was interrupted by a voice from behind her. Aisling whipped around at the sound of it, too *normal* in this place.

"Hello, princess. Or is it queen, now? We meet a third time."

She blinked, even more confused by the sight of him than the sound of his voice. A boy. A *boy*? What was he doing here?

But Cathán was before her in an instant, sharp teeth showing openly as he held her with one hand. "This one, he's dangerous. Too dangerous, Aisling. Stay away. Stay just there."

The boy stepped forward or — something. He was no longer where he had been, but only an inch away, glaring into Cathán's face with mismatched eyes. One blue, one green. *Like the stag*.

"Yes. I am." The boy's words echoed. Cathán shoved her back, and Aisling had only the vague impression of green in motion around them, the boy knocking Cathán about as if he were a plaything. "Don't. Get in. My way."

Eyes peered at her from the shadow of every leaf. Laughter

rocked the trees like storm winds. Wolf song came from nowhere, and the boy was… Where? Where had he gone, and where was Cathán?

The boy was beside her then, holding her hand, bowing over it—then, once again, he was several feet away. "Welcome, Queen, beyond the Avalon gate."

She eyed him, then the green of the wood. "Where's Cathán? What did you—?"

"Oh, nothing terrible. Nor do I have something terrible in mind for you. Come. Walk with me. Talk to me."

She stared at him from under her lashes, wondering if she dared ask her unanswered question again. Then she pressed her hands tightly to her elbows and wrapped her arms around herself. "I am Aisling. I came to— Lughaid said I should come here. Apologize to the Green King, or offer recompense. Whatever was necessary."

He peered at her, his eyes growing wider and brighter. "And the old druid?"

"He's dead. My sister's women raided the grove. Nowhere is safe now, and without the spring, we'll never have anything but death."

"I understand. But I can't help you."

A cold prickle flushed through her chest, followed by a painful pressure. "You are the Green King."

"Yes."

"But…" She muted her immediate protest. Only a boy? Obviously not. And his denial was more important than his appearance. "No—*no*, please! I'll do anything, give anything up, but don't…"

He had already turned away from her. "You misunderstand. I am no longer preventing the spring. Only Ireland is trapped in Winter's storms, and I am not the one you must appeal to. Go ask the Red King's favor, if you dare. *I* cannot help you."

She lunged forward. "Wait! Please. Do you at least know the way?"

The Green King turned very slowly to inspect her again,

wearing a strange expression. "Into the Red Kingdom? Yes. But your companion is more than capable of leading you there." He paused, amusement on his face. "Assuming you can convince him. It's a dangerous place for someone mortal."

Aisling shrugged. "That doesn't matter. I won't run away, not now. Thank you."

His amusement intensified. "For what?"

"Seeing me."

The Green King laughed at her. "But I had already seen you before, young queen." In a blink, he was—taller. A man, not a boy. Then he vanished into the green, even as she remembered. She had seen him in the High King's court. He was the one who had spoken to Uther in her favor.

There had been no sense then of the power he had revealed to her here, and she couldn't even guess at the game he was playing. It didn't matter. He was gone, and though he had said 'companion', Cathán was nowhere in sight.

The music rose again, enough to disorient her breathing with its rhythm. She did her best to ignore it, remembering what Cathán had said. But where was he? "Cathán? Where did you go?" The trees threw her voice at her, wild echoes that beat across the narrow clearing.

"I'm here. But we should go. Now, while we can, before the danger in this place becomes unfriendly." Cathán's voice came from behind her, but when she turned, Aisling flushed hot. His clothes! Where had his clothes gone?

She couldn't get away from the sight of him, couldn't bring herself to turn away or close her eyes. Her fingers wanted to touch every inch of naked skin she could see.

"Cathán, your clothes…"

"Taken from me. And my knife, and the tie for my hair, and my boots and bowstring. Punishment, perhaps. I should be so lucky, if that's all."

The trees laughed, agreeing. 'Lucky'. 'Lucky'. Like the echo of her voice had done, the word bounced around them.

Aisling licked her lips, having her own thoughts. *Lucky.*

But she was forgetting something. Something…about Cathán? His beautiful body.

No. A cold wind passed over her, and that was reminder enough. "We have to go. Into Winter, into the Red Kingdom."

He stared at her. "Are you *mad*? I could go there, and perhaps I'd be safe. But you? No, Aisling. You're *mortal*. A morsel."

A curious feeling came over her. "You've called me by name ever since we entered the Spring." She tilted her head, but the change in perspective altered nothing, except to make it more difficult to keep her eyes on his face. "Do you call me by name only now that you won't obey any longer?"

He took a startled step back from her. "Ais — my lady. I…"

"Don't stop. I didn't say to stop. I've been trying for so long to get you to…but it's also true that you made yourself my guide. Now I must go into dark Winter, and I need to know if you will help me." She took two swift steps toward him, closing the distance between them, and peered into his eyes. "I am queen, or I am not. Make up your mind."

The defiance left his face a little at a time, until he shoved his hands past his forehead and into his hair. "Yes. I'll lead you. I said I would, but you don't know what you're doing. It's a long journey, and I can't protect you from Winter's hunters. They won't see you as mine to protect."

She took another step. Music, again. It reminded her that she wanted to reach out and — "*Oh.* I didn't think you'd be so hot." Cathán's skin was smooth under her palms, then rough with short curls, the hair on his chest like that of any man.

She slid her fingers up to his shoulders, and he trembled as she touched him.

"*Aisling.* You shouldn't —"

"Be doing this? But, Cathán…then neither should you."

He froze, his hands on her hips. "I didn't — I'm sorry. I didn't m —"

"Don't say you don't mean it! I do, *I* do."

"Woman." There was a groan in his voice, and she pressed herself toward him eagerly. "It's only the Spring. It's only…"

"No. Take me to Winter and I'll beg you there instead. Or home, or anywhere. Haven't you noticed that I…?" But she stopped, flushed and couldn't say anything more.

"You'll be my woman. I won't share you, queen or not. *Ever*." His eyes held all the fire of his Summer self.

Aisling smiled at him. "I know."

* * * *

Through the wide, open window in the wall opposite his bed, the Red King watched a strange procession of beings leaving dark Winter and making their way toward the mortal world.

Not only the selkies had asked to leave the borders of his kingdom behind them. Others were just as eager, though their reasons were different. For the first time, large numbers were returning to their first home. Not the wild golden borders of the Summer kingdom, but the cold-blighted forests of Ireland.

The Green King may have restored the Spring, may have forgiven, but Macsen did not. Winter would slay the buds, sink its teeth into every leaf and sap the warmth from the sunlight. The storm would stay until he had what he wanted.

He could not torment Dealla directly but…

"You're thinking about that woman again."

The door clicked shut after the words.

Macsen turned away from the window and found himself staring at his lover instead. "What makes you say that, hmm?"

"You have that murderous look." Bran started across the room, wreathed in the scent of his own blood, and Macsen took an involuntary step toward him. "Your eyes are tight and your teeth are showing, but she's not here for you to strangle, lover."

"*No.* How unfortunate." Bran grinned at him, and it was then that Macsen noticed his hands behind his back, the tension in his posture. "What are you hiding? What are you keeping from me?"

"I'm still not sure I should show you, but it's the right day."

"The right day?

"Midsummer." Bran's smile widened. "I was just in time. Did you forget? You were the one who told me—"

A grin spread across Macsen's face. "*Ahh.* So you have a gift for me. Is it what you've been making all this time? The something beautiful? Even before we went to visit your father, you said...but you wouldn't give me a hint!"

"You can judge for yourself if it's beautiful. I— Well, *here.*" Bran held out what he'd been hiding.

Was it a bolt of cloth? It was dark gold with a reddish glint, but it was metal. Macsen had never seen chains so fine, so soft. He picked the thing up and the folds opened in his hands, fell into...sleeves? A tunic. And *what* a tunic.

It was heavy, but that didn't mean anything to him. Beautiful? No, it was gorgeous. There was Summer and blood in every link, ripe and overwhelming. This was why the scent of Bran was everywhere, and he was to *wear* this? "Do you know what a torment this will be? The scent of you on me? Come here. *Come here.*"

He dragged his lover near with one hand, trailed his kisses down Bran's throat and bit him. The temptation was too much and he had no reason to resist.

But he only allowed himself a mouthful of sweetness, the bright blood burning on his tongue, before he lifted his lips and caught Bran's chin in his hand. Macsen dissected his flush, the dilation of his pupils and the soft, swift humming of his heart. "Why do you let me? Why do you like it so much when I steal your blood from you?"

Hoarse and hot, Bran snickered, then pressed his body

against him. "'Steal'. But you don't. It's mine to give and I like to. Haven't I told you before? It feels good when you get your teeth in my throat, you don't hurt me. Can't hurt me."

A pulse of need flushed through Macsen and he caught his breath, licked his lips. "No. I can't, can I?"

Bran's eyes went bright and sharp at the same time. "Do you regret it?"

Macsen nudged his head to the side, bent over the oozing wounds and lapped at them. "I would never *hurt* you, but there are some pains that can be pleasure. I'd like to do those things to you…sometimes."

There was a pause. "Things."

"*Yes*. I want to tie you up, Bran. Torment you, make you beg, make you burn for me. Except that you already do. Except that I can't hurt you."

The heat in Bran's eyes surprised him when he glanced down and met them. "You could ask. If I gave you permission, the oath between us wouldn't…then you could do whatever you wanted, couldn't you?"

Macsen held his breath and managed a single word. "'Permission'."

There was more heat in Bran's gaze than he had ever seen. The blue of his eyes was alight with lusty fire, intense and golden. "Because if that's not the problem… I like that pain, the kind that isn't really pain. When you take me and I'm not ready, that burn when you stretch me open. The way you denied me when you tied me up."

"If you keep talking like that…"

"Then what?" It was a breathless dare, but Macsen only lifted his eyebrows.

"Brat. Be good, for a little while. I want to see if this is as beautiful on me as it is on its own." Bran's flush amused him, the way he seemed startled by the tunic in Macsen's hands, as if he'd forgotten about it. Macsen handed it off just long enough to strip out of the one he was wearing.

Something between the glow of the Summer sun and the

heat of Bran's embrace clung to Macsen the moment he put on his gift. It was heavy, as he'd expected, but softer than silk despite the fact that it was made from links of gold.

It made him hungry, breathing Bran's scent with every inhalation, holding the taste of him on his tongue just because he was dressed like this. It was so distracting it took him more than a minute to calm the riot of his senses and study what he was wearing.

The fine chains held together a wilderness of predator shapes, all the world's hunters prowling, heads lifted, fangs bared, eyes gleaming. They had flakes of gemstones for irises, drops of jet for pupils, and they *stared* at him. They stalked through the chain as through forests or fields of grass, warm on his skin. Wolf-skeletons opened their jaws to howl in unison. Macsen admired the workmanship as much as the scent.

"A kingly gift." He leaned a little closer, caressing Bran's cheek as he flushed, then bent to hide his smirk in the curve of Bran's throat. "Thank you. But what should I give you in return? You never told me what you wanted. Now look at me, caught empty-handed."

Bran arched as Macsen licked at his throat, sucked at his skin without biting to break it. His eyes were hooded with desire, dark, dusky blue, as they had been since Macsen had said…he wanted to hurt him.

Hurt you with pleasure, anwylyd. The only thing I will ever, ever hurt you with. "Won't you tell me what it is you want? I will give you the perfect gift, if only you tell me what it is." Macsen kissed him again and when he lifted his mouth, Bran was staring at him with — what? What was that in his eyes? *Passion, yes.* But something more.

"Give me Dealla, lover. Be the Red King for me. Give me her life, after you take it away from her."

A slow, cold shiver worked its way down Macsen's spine. "Is that what you want?" The expression on Bran's face didn't change. Summer murder, stunning enough to make him ache with longing. "Really what you want, *Valravn*?

That's as much a gift for me as for you. Even if I've wanted it, I—"

"More than wanted." There was a hint of a grin behind the darkness, but only a hint. "You're obsessed, but I understand, and there's no point postponing it any longer. Her dreams are dangerous, and you'll kill the country, not the woman, if you don't restrain the Winter."

"Can't have that…" But it was only a murmur. The request had added need to Macsen's desire. That bloodthirsty brightness on Bran's face always brought him undone. "We will go, and I will hunt her for you. But first I want to teach you what I meant. I want to break you, just a little. Make it hurt and see if you like it."

"Yes."

"And then…"

"And then?"

Macsen traced Bran's mouth with his thumb. "You like to watch me kill. I remember."

Bran looked up at him, licked his own lips and hesitated. "Yes. I do. You're never more *you* than when you're killing and I love you." He paused, as if he wanted to say something else, then shrugged. "I love you."

Unable to resist, Macsen closed the space between them and kissed him. "And I love you. Come with me now."

"Bed?" Bran's voice had gone husky with desire, and he chewed his lip as Macsen stood straight and smirked down at him.

"Not yet. Some things, Saoirse is not ready to bring to me. *To us.* Certainly not the toys I'll use on you tonight."

"Toys." Bran's throat moved as he swallowed.

"Yes. Come with me." Hungry now, needing, Macsen took Bran's hand and warm, callused fingers closed around his palm as the Red King led his lover deeper into the palace than he had gone before.

Bran peered at the red-glowing roots around them as they went down the long spiral of the stairs they usually took up to their bedroom. Down, past one level, then another, to a door that let them into the third.

There was only the one door, and the stairs continuing into the dark, but Macsen tugged at Bran's hand and brought him over the threshold when he lingered, peering down.

"You can wander later, if you want. For now…" He stood Bran before a long wall hung with gleaming coils of rope and lengths of chain. Knives, with dangerous edges and more dangerous points.

Shackles for wrists and ankles, collars of black metal and silver and ice. Clamps. Cages. Rings that weren't blood and Winter magic like the ones Macsen had used on Bran before, but polished wood and gleaming iron. Toys the exact shape of Macsen's own cock, and some that were smaller — and some that were thicker. Blindfolds and wraps and ties and —

Macsen watched the track Bran's eyes made from one thing to another, saw his breathing quicken, heard his heart beat faster. "The ropes, Bran. Not the rest, not yet. Unless…" He left the word hanging there and waited for Bran to say something, if he really wanted more.

"Unless?"

"Unless there's something else you want." He left unspoken that he still wanted Bran tied up for him.

"I… Half these things are…" Bran paused and gulped, but Macsen noted with amusement that his lover's cock was rigid, a hard and obvious bulge even through his clothes. "How?"

Macsen came up behind him, cradled the back of Bran's head in his hands, then slid cool fingers across his shoulders and down his spine. "But you know how, beautiful. First I tie you up, leave you nice and open for me. *Vulnerable.* Then…"

Dilation in his pupils. Quickening of his breath, and his voice hoarse when the pause had been drawn out too long for him. "Then?"

"I want to stretch you, tease you, put one of those rings on your cock and leave you for a while, ice just the shape of me inside you. Leave you, let you feel it. Burn with it. Until you finally can't beg me for more. Until you beg me to let you… *ah, but I won't*. Not even then."

"And—" Bran's voice broke on the word, cracked and died, but he licked his lips and continued. "And the knives?"

This time, Macsen's own heartbeat increased, pounding in his chest. "I had pets before you. Mortals. Those were to tease myself as much as them." He tightened his hands at Bran's hips despite his intention to leave *that* in the past.

His lover's gaze was suddenly steady on him, despite the way Bran bit his lip. "Were? So you wouldn't use them on me?"

With difficulty, Macsen ignored the way Bran's pupils had dilated. "Bran. Not that. Not now. That is…different, and I already make you bleed for me."

A momentary scowl flickered across Bran's face. "But you just said it's different. I *want* different. Everything you like, I want." He turned his gaze to the wall, took a step away from Macsen's hands and pulled down a thick coil of thin, black rope with a red sheen. "Here. This one. And if you won't…"

"I won't."

Disappointment woke on Bran's face.

But you do not yet know what you are asking of me, lover.

"Then do what you said." There was frustration in Bran's voice, and passion, too. "Put a ring on me and stretch me open for one of these—*toys*. Tease me and—and…"

"*Say it, Bran.*"

His eyes glittered, hard and bright as sapphires. "Make me beg. Hurt me like you want to. Make me beg and cry for you."

Macsen wrapped both arms around his waist and licked at his throat. "I could do it here. *Right here.* But there are others who come this way. There have been more mortals among us lately, others taking pets and keeping them, though I do not. They might see you, so I'll be good."

A hard edge came over the softness of Bran's features,

neither foreplay nor teasing. "And do you *want* pets? Or did you just stop because—?"

"I stopped because of you. Because I needed no one else, nothing else, once I had you." He reached out and brushed his fingers over Bran's lips. "So I thought, but I've learned better. I cannot take your life from you. Don't want to. What would I do then, without you? But I must have lives, even if that need isn't the same as how I need you. You know that. You have to know that."

A guilty flush colored Bran's cheeks. "Yes. I just—I'm sorry."

Macsen flicked a grin in his direction and gave it sharp edges, filled it with lust and promises. "*Sorry*. And so you should be. Now I will *punish* you."

White-hot, Bran's excitement flared across his skin, then subsided.

Macsen eyed him intently. "I think…a blindfold."

"Blind…fold?"

"You won't know when I'm going to touch you, or where. Everything will feel stronger. *Sharper*." He took one down from the wall and picked up the toys Bran wanted, too, a metal ring for his lover's cock and Winter ice exactly the length and shape of his own erection.

Bran squeezed the rope he was holding as his gaze fastened on the things in Macsen's hands, and Macsen nudged him toward the stairs.

Chapter Seven

Macsen shouldered open the door to their bedroom, nudged Bran inside and sent him stumbling toward the center of the room with a little shove. The heat of his skin had given way to ice that crawled up almost to his shoulder.

It melted as Macsen let go of him, but he shivered with nervous anticipation regardless. Macsen had only tied him up once before, but he'd liked it, wanted more since that first time. It was just that asking for things like that was difficult. The Red King hadn't been Bran's first lover, but he'd been his first *sidhe* lover.

There had never been a human Bran had trusted enough to tie him up, even if the thought had occurred to him while he'd been a captive—which it hadn't. With his human lovers, he had only ever played at submitting, just enough to confuse them when he'd finally taken control. Men, women, it hadn't mattered. They'd come to him because he was beautiful, Summer-bright and taboo.

Macsen was... Macsen had *always* been different, even if perhaps his attraction had been from the same source at first.

"Give me the rope, Bran."

Bran held out the coils and Macsen snatched them from him, squeezed them in both fists and stalked in a tight circle around him.

"Now you strip for me."

He pulled his tunic over his head and tossed it aside, pushed his trousers down and nearly tipped over when he bent to grab them off the floor and Macsen closed in behind him. His touch was *freezing*, and his hands molded themselves to the curve of Bran's buttocks.

He slid one up to Bran's neck and held him where he was when he tried to stand straight. "*No. Just like this, I think. To start.* Spread your legs a little more—yes. Now, arms behind your back."

Bran snorted and glanced over his shoulder. "What are you doing? I can't stay like this!"

He didn't miss the feral curl of Macsen's lips, but he lost sight of it as Macsen stepped completely behind him.

Then he felt the ropes.

Cold, that was the first sensation. Colder than Macsen's grip on him and tighter than his fingers as he wrapped loops around Bran's wrists and up to something that he couldn't see. It took his weight off his legs and balanced him a little, but he was distracted by Macsen's hands working again, knotting the rope up around his shoulders, then down. Smooth lengths of blood-scented silk bound his chest, his hips, his thighs, even his ankles.

Then Macsen came around in front of him, the ends of the rope in his hand, and *pulled.*

Bran's feet left the floor. He tried to catch himself out of reflex, but his hands were bound and all he did was twist as Macsen pulled him up, until he was suspended in mid-air, bent at the waist with his legs held apart and his arms behind him.

He tried to scowl, but Macsen only snickered, hung the rope on raw mist and stepped toward him. He took Bran's face in one hand and tipped his mouth up to kiss him. *So cold.* His mouth, his tongue—he nipped Bran's lips, and it was like cutting them on ice.

A single drop of blood fell from his lip toward the floor when Macsen let him go, but he caught it on a fingertip and licked it away. "Won't waste even so much as that. And the sight of you, all tied up… But this isn't enough, is it?"

"Not enough?"

"You were to be punished." An instant of darkness fled through Macsen's voice, then returned, entwined with eager humor. "Remember? I think you do."

"You—" He twisted, tried to get some leverage, but had no success.

"Be still now."

Bran obeyed, and black came toward his eyes, accompanied by Macsen's fingers. Then he saw nothing at all. The blindfold cut off the light completely, sealing itself over his cheekbones.

"And this too." Macsen slipped a familiar restraint over the tip of Bran's cock.

Smooth, cold metal, the ring squeezed around him as it slid over the head, down the shaft— *Gods. So. Tight.* It settled at the base and tightened more, or maybe it was just that he was more aroused. Bran gasped out a moan and tried to buck his hips toward Macsen's touch. The ropes held him still. He barely budged—and where was Macsen? What was he doing?

Bran could hear him chuckling, but nothing else. The sudden chill of his lover's fingers on his nipples forced another gasp past his lips, then a moan. "*Macsen*. That's—"

"Intense?"

"Ye...*essss*." Macsen replaced his fingers with his mouth, but only for a moment before he vanished again.

Minutes passed, or maybe longer, and Bran jerked when slick, cold fingers slipped between his buttocks. They made little circles around his entrance, exposed for easy access by the way he'd been bent and tied. The tip of one finger barely pressed inside him and he moaned, rolling his hips.

With one hand, Macsen held him open, and with the fingers of the other he stretched Bran a little at a time.

"Macsen *more*, more, *please*."

"More?" One slender finger worked all the way into him.

Bran sucked in a breath, squeezed tightly around it and groaned when Macsen twisted it inside him. "*Yes*. Want you inside me, want you to take me."

"It doesn't matter what you want."

"Mac-Macsen! *Oh*. That's not—fair."

Two fingers, both curled inside him, rubbed back and forth. It was just enough to make him shudder. He wanted cock, wanted to come, wanted… But Macsen was chuckling, wolf laughter lower than his usual tones and rich with bloody desires.

Doesn't matter what you want. The words were written across the front of his mind in blinding white. The sound of Macsen's voice, rough with lust and sharp with authority, had scraped over his nerves and left them raw.

Of that, too, he wanted more.

The chill of Macsen's hand slid from his buttocks up to his shoulders, then raked down Bran's spine, the Red King's nails four lines of cold fire that made him arch and moan. There was a wet sting, and he knew Macsen had spilled blood. Tensing, he anticipated the touch of his lover's mouth — and there. Just above his buttocks. Soft lips whose curve of smile he could feel on his skin.

His lover followed one of the lines of blood he'd drawn with gentle touches of tongue, all the way up to Bran's shoulder. Then he licked up the next…and the next. Two of Macsen's fingers were still curled inside, stroking while he thrust them in then out.

Bran was so hard it hurt. How could it hurt and feel so good at the same time?

"Oh. *Oh.*"

Three fingers. Macsen pushed them in more roughly than before, rotated and spread them.

"You're dripping all over the floor now. What a mess."

"Ah — *uhhhhng.*" Bran surprised himself with the guttural sound of his own groan, with how little he cared that Macsen was laughing at him.

Then the fingers were gone and something thicker, harder, *colder*, was inside him. He knew this feeling, the rigid shape filling him up. "Yes, yes, yes. Take me, love, *please.*"

But Macsen stopped moving as Bran begged for more, and he was still laughing.

"Please!"

"Did you forget, Bran?"

Slowly, very slowly, Macsen's cock pulled out of him, then slammed in. Cold. So cold it was fire. Bran realized then and let out a broken cry.

"Yes, that's right. It's not me inside you. Do you like your toy? The feel of my cock stretching you open, even if it's not? Does it hurt yet? But sweetly. I want it to hurt *sweetly*."

Bran didn't expect Macsen's fist around his cock, the quick, rough tugs. He cried out once then dropped his head forward and cried out again and again. "*Please*! Love, I— Please! Ah—ah—ah—*ah*!"

Every time Macsen's hand slipped over the head of his erection, teasing the sensitive tip, he cried out and tried to roll his hips into the touch. His pulse was focused in his cock, the ring painful pressure that only made him want more. Pain. *Pleasure*.

"So wet for me. Even with the ring on."

But Bran couldn't answer him. *The feeling*. Holy *hells*, the feeling. His whole body vibrated with want and he clenched around the toy inside him as Macsen teased it in and out. Bran still burned where his lover's nails had cut him, still tingled where his tongue had left his skin wet and cool.

Then the bastard pushed the toy all the way inside again, let go of his cock and left him there. A soft whine escaped Bran's control, then a whimper of need, but there was nothing else. No more sensation. Just his body tightening and relaxing, wanting and wanting.

"Macsen." There was a heavy moment of silence, and Bran sucked in a breath. "Macsen!"

"*I'm here*." But the humor in his voice told Bran he'd let that quiet fall between them on purpose. "Did you think I'd leave you? Like *this*? How could I do that, hmm?"

Bran was growing used to the blindfold, and he turned his head instinctively to track the sound of Macsen's voice.

"How could I? You're so beautiful, so vulnerable...and all mine."

Little touches tormented him then, brushes of Macsen's

fingertips and tongue that left Bran anticipating a feeling that might come from anywhere.

Instead, the ropes around his thighs and calves tightened unexpectedly, pulled his legs up farther until they were bent at the knee and spread even wider. The change in position shifted the toy inside him, rubbed the freezing length of it over nerves already throbbing for release.

"*Gods…oh, gods.*"

"Too much?" Macsen's voice came from just in front of him.

Bran jerked forward, as if he could reach out for him, but he couldn't. Damn it. *Damn it.*

"Did I spread your legs too much, Bran?"

"No, n-no."

"*Good.* How do you feel?"

"Like I'm going to die if you don't—"

"Does it hurt?"

Bran nodded, almost frantic. A cry escaped him as Macsen's palm connected with one of his buttocks, a sharp smack that left a sweet sting on top of the other sensations.

"So good, hurts so good, *Macsen, I*—"

There was a sound he couldn't identify, and something soft, almost tickling, brushed his stomach. He sucked in a breath, almost laughed, then cried out again as Macsen closed his mouth over the tip of Bran's cock.

That tickling—his hair. And the noise—Macsen was on his knees under him, on his knees with that terrible mouth on him, sucking him while he twisted the—

Oh, gods. He *was* going to die.

In and out. Wet, rough tongue. Soft lips and occasionally the graze of dangerous teeth.

"Need to *come.* Macsen…"

His mouth retreated from around Bran's cock, and he almost cried. More, he needed *more.*

"I am not stopping you."

The cool flutter of Macsen's breath on his straining erection made him whimper. "Can't, I—? How can I? *Please.*"

Take the damn ring off and —"

"*No*. You'll have your pleasure with it on."

Struggling now, Bran jerked against the ropes. "But I *can't!*"

"Yes, you can." And though he couldn't see it, he could hear Macsen's smirk in his voice. "Eventually."

A little at a time, Bran relaxed despite himself — or rather, settled into his torment. The toy was torture, and the cool sensation of Macsen's mouth running up and down the length of his cock the most terrible tease.

A tingling, burning feeling crept upward from Bran's toes, along the bottoms of his feet, up the backs of his legs. It settled in his cock, swollen and pulsing, then spread up to his nipples and even his lips, still torn where Macsen had bitten them at the very beginning.

There was a dull ache in his muscles, behind the cold of the ropes tingling on his skin. He shifted to soothe it, moaned as the toy rolled around inside him, then licked Macsen's fingers as he touched Bran's lips.

Kissing them, he moaned when Macsen pushed two into his mouth and let him suck, but he wanted *cock*.

This time he got what he wanted. Macsen pulled his fingers away and Bran panted his disappointment only until he felt Macsen's erection against his lips, leaned forward as much as he could and sucked the tip into his mouth.

Macsen groaned, a deep, thick noise that gave Bran a jolt of heat. Fire, he was on *fire*, and he wanted his lover to keep making those sounds. A little at a time, Macsen eased his cock deeper into Bran's throat, gave him more until he was thrusting almost all of it in and out.

"So hot in your mouth. Tongue just like that, *just — yesssss*." It came out of him in a long exhalation, barely more than a hiss. Bran tasted the cold, salt pulses of his release, tried to swallow them all and still felt wetness dripping out of his mouth, sliding down his chin.

More. He darted his tongue out, wanting. Macsen chuckled, a breathless, lusty sound. The roughness of his tongue rasped over Bran's cheek then slid into his mouth, sharing the taste of Macsen's pleasure as he kissed him.

Only when he pulled away did Bran become aware again of his own denied arousal, the painful throbbing of his cock, the ring so tight now, *so tight*.

He bucked his hips, couldn't help himself, felt the air cool on the wet tip, but nothing like relief. And that damned toy! Every time he moved it shifted inside him, but never enough that he could make himself—*gods*. He'd never needed anything in his life as much as he needed release right now.

"Please. I— It hurts, it— It's so good but I can't, I can't, oh—bastard, you—please!" He only stopped begging, cursing, when he was out of breath, but Macsen let go of him, took the toy out and left him empty.

Bran *howled*, bucked in his bonds and cried out for anything, anything if Macsen would just make him come. The absence of sensation was more painful than being overstimulated. One of Macsen's hands was on his face then, undoing the blindfold, and Bran sucked in a breath and squinted against the dim light of their bedroom.

He was too high strung to notice the slow descent of his body, but he unbent his knees as the rope loosened, and the floor was cool under his feet. Macsen was cold and solid supporting him, and he leaned into his lover when his legs refused to hold him.

Blinking, he finally opened his eyes all the way. Whatever Macsen saw in them must have compelled him somehow. He dragged Bran up to his mouth and into a deep kiss. This way, Bran could at least do *something*, and he rubbed his swollen erection against his lover and shuddered all over when he slid his mouth from Bran's lips to his throat.

"Can you stand now?" Bran took a shaky breath as Macsen's question filtered into his awareness. *Stand?* Slowly, testing, he settled his weight onto his own legs and Macsen let go of him. "Good. Stay still while I finish untying you."

The rope came undone easily and fell to the floor in glistening coils. When his hands were free Bran stretched his arms, turned his wrists, then reached out and grabbed his tormentor, held Macsen tightly and kissed his laughing mouth. "Been good, haven't I? Been patient, I—*please*."

"Need something, lover?"

"Macsen!"

"On the bed. On your back for me." Bran almost threw himself onto the bed then reached up for Macsen and saw him standing there, staring at him.

"Look at you. So hard." He got to his knees between Bran's thighs, wrapping cool fingers around his erection. He stroked up once and Bran dropped his head to his pillow, pushed his hips up toward Macsen's fist.

"Next time I do this to you I'm going to have you inside me, Bran. But not now." He pushed Bran's legs farther apart, settled himself between them and thrust deep with one smooth stroke.

Bran gasped then stuttered out a cry as Macsen drove into him harder, slammed his cock deep with one relentless thrust after another. He was instantly at the edge of the climax he'd been denied. Even with the ring on he was so. Damned. *Close*.

Macsen closed his teeth around Bran's throat, and an instant of pain was followed by the dark, familiar pleasure. Pinpricks of agony bolted through him, then the blinding, ecstatic pressure of his release. Hot pulses of bliss ran into each other, and the tightness of the ring let him feel every one.

"Again."

It was a hoarse demand, thick with all his lover's own needs, but Bran tossed his head on the fur beneath him, tried to breathe and wasn't sure if he succeeded. "Macs—*ahh...*"

"I said. *Again*."

Dimly, through a static haze, Bran heard himself sobbing, his own cries and moans as Macsen kept pounding into him, stroking his cock. He was going to come again, he was *going* to, even if it hurt, even if he was too sensitive, even if —

Bliss. A static, pins-and-needles tingling of pain, then rapture, flushed through him in a hot, white rush. Macsen thrust into him one last time and stayed buried there, groaning his own release against Bran's throat, but Bran rocked under him, clutched at his shoulders and keened until his voice gave out.

The surge of that second climax left him tired and tingling when it finally faded. He thought he wanted a bath, and maybe to sleep, but he moaned as Macsen pulled out of him and almost reached out to drag him onto his body once more.

Soft words spilled into his ears. "Can you sit up, *anwylyd*? Are you hurting still?"

Warm fingers slipped up his legs, rubbed where the ropes had been tied, then tugged the ring off his spent cock.

Even that gentle touch made him moan again. "Doesn' hur'. Wan' you t...'gain." Bran's tongue felt thick in his mouth. His words were slurred, but he didn't care how he sounded, how Macsen must be smirking at him.

"Again? Yes. But for now you need a little spoiling. Can you stand?"

Bran lifted his head and glanced toward the end of the bed, pushed himself up on one arm, then dropped back with a muffled groan. "Maybe. Don' really wanna."

"*Brat.*" But Macsen's voice was soft with affection, and he drew Bran close and tugged him to his feet. "I'll carry you if you don't walk."

Yawning, Bran leaned precariously to one side, then straightened up. He ran a hand through his hair and held onto Macsen with the other as he yawned again. "Don't think I care. Is the —?"

The door to the bath opened and closed on a shadow. Bran blinked at it, confused. Saoirse?

It was the girl in shape but not in substance. She slid out

of the steam that had escaped the bath and into his sight but ignored him, as if aware of how uncomfortable he was to have her near now.

"Red King." She hooked one hand around the other elbow and swayed in place, not quite a bow. "The bath's hot and ready for you. Unless you're going to sleep, I'll bring fresh clothes up, too."

Macsen didn't shift his gaze from Bran's face, ran his fingers through the hair that had tangled over his eyes. "Yes. And food and wine for Bran."

"*Hmm.*" She hummed her agreement and flashed a smile in their direction, then slipped through the door, thinning as she went until she was just a shadow again.

Bran watched as she retreated, confused. It had been a while now since the lessons they'd shared with Ffion. When had she learned to do that? When had she stopped being human enough that she could?

Moonlight lay on the steam, broke on the surface of the water and beckoned Bran into the bath. He wasn't surprised when Macsen came with him, closing the door behind them, but he was when his lover settled himself first, then pulled Bran down to sit between his thighs.

"Hmm..."

"What?"

"This is new. I like it." He tilted his head and caught Macsen's mouth, kissed him before he could reply.

"Good. *Now.* I told you I'd spoil you. What do you want?" Macsen's answer was soft against Bran's cheek, his throat, as the Red King wrapped him up in both arms and embraced him.

Bran squinted at him, a sly expression. "This is nice, but you are cold, even if the water's hot. Can't you fix it?" He turned his head just a little, more than enough to give Macsen a hint of what he was really saying.

"Cold? You can fix that, you mean. But who is spoiling who now?" He licked the drops of water from the top of

Bran's shoulder, the curve of his neck, and sank his teeth in so gently that it was a moment before he could tell that Macsen *had* bitten him.

The shadow that embraced him made the difference, the way Macsen flushed with heat behind him. His chest first, and the length of his legs pressed along the outside of Bran's. Then his fingers as Macsen slipped them around Bran's waist and down over his stomach — and finally, his mouth, as he slid his lips up along Bran's throat again to kiss him.

He was breathing hard by the time Macsen pulled away from his lips. "Better?"

Mischief in his lover's violet eyes. Mischief in his hands, as they passed over his body.

"*Ha*. Worse."

"But I'm not cold anymore."

He leaned his head onto Macsen's shoulder, and gazed at him through half-closed eyes. "No. Now *I* am *hot*."

Macsen slid his fingers down, took hold of Bran's straining erection and stroked slowly. "Even after all that? I thought I had tired you out."

Despite himself, Bran flushed. "I can't help it!"

"I don't want you to." Hot now, the brush of his thumb across Bran's nipple. "I like the way you burn for me." But Macsen chuckled as he said it, the low, dark laughter that only stoked Bran's lust. The rest of him had been overstimulated, but his cock was almost neglected, and the smooth strokes of Macsen's fist were bringing him swiftly to the edge.

"I love to watch you like this." The Red King brought his fingers over the tip of Bran's cock, then down under the head. "Watch you give in to me so thoroughly..."

Bran laid his head against Macsen's shoulder again and reached down with one of his own hands to encourage him. "Please? Do that — do that — *yes*." Sweet and quick this time, his climax washed over him then receded.

Macsen kept up the same easy rhythm until every last

pulse of pleasure had been drained out of him. He eased his fingers over the trembling muscles in Bran's stomach, up his chest and down the length of his arms as he relaxed.

"More?"

Bran shook his head, keeping his eyes closed. He stayed that way for long minutes, until Macsen finally nudged him up and slipped out from behind him.

Stretching his arms along the rim of the bath, he only glanced up when Macsen massaged his feet, then slid both hands up Bran's legs. He thought his lover was just touching him at first, but there were suds then, Macsen's fingers slick with soap, caressing Bran's thighs.

But it didn't matter where Macsen was touching him. The sight of him on his knees in the water already had Bran half-hard again.

His lover was smirking. "Do you need more after all?"

Bran put his arm across his face and laughed while Macsen slid his fingers up Bran's torso and sprawled them open across his chest. "Yes, damn it. I can't *help* it, you just—I *want* you."

Macsen pulled him down into the flow of hot water and rinsed away the suds. "Nothing makes me happier. Don't you know that? But you should eat. Drink. Before *I* have dinner. Before I give you more of what you want...and I want."

Bran lifted an eyebrow, but Macsen reached one arm behind him, then pressed a perfectly ripe blueberry past his lips and into his mouth.

"Mm—where did this come from?"

Macsen nodded over his shoulder. "Saoirse said she was bringing your supper, you heard her."

Bran glanced back. On a table that had been empty when they'd come in, there was a full plate now, a carafe and a pair of cups. "When did she...?"

"While I was washing your feet, lazy."

Bran reached across and took a handful of berries, tossed one at Macsen's head and rolled his eyes when sharp teeth

112

snatched it out of the air. Then he snickered as Macsen made a face and swallowed. "Too sweet."

"Oh? I thought you liked sweet."

Midway to his cup, Macsen's hand paused in reaching. "In my blood and my wine."

"Picky."

"*Yes.*"

Bran flushed at the intensity of Macsen's expression. He dried his hands to give himself something to do, then applied himself to meat and bread while his lover lounged beside him. His fingers were always touching Bran somewhere, but he only sipped at his own glass of wine even while he watched every bite make its way from Bran's plate to his mouth.

"If you're hungry, love..."

"Yes."

Frowning, Bran turned to study him more fully. "Then—?"

The Red King shook his head. "It's not the same, you should know that. Nothing else is for me what blood is. I just like to watch you." His pupils dilated as he spoke, darkening his eyes from amethyst to indigo. "The enjoyment you get from it. The way you lick your lips."

"So...where does all this come from, then? I've wondered." He waved half a loaf in Macsen's direction, took a bite. "Somehow I don't see you as a baker."

"Where do you think?" Macsen knit his brow in amused consternation. "We steal it. It's some of our only fun, since the Summer war is over and our new fight all but resolved."

Bran sat forward sharply and splashed water everywhere. "*What?* Steal?"

Tongue touching his teeth, Macsen saved Bran's plate, lifted his eyebrows at a soggy half loaf and plucked a washed-away blueberry from the water. "Oh, yes. Sometimes I go with them. The raiders, the hunters. It's only fun."

"But—"

"It's Winter's way, Bran, and older than I am. I've been king for a thousand years and even before me this is how things were done."

Bran sighed, shook his head and took another bite of the half of his bread that had survived. "You are...and I suppose you think it's more fun now that—?"

"It's for you? Yes. But it doesn't change the facts, and really. Who in the Red Kingdom would I get to bake bread for you otherwise? Hard enough to make the meat last long enough to cook it."

Bran lifted an eyebrow while he chewed. "Mmm... Saoirse?"

Macsen laughed, reached across Bran's body and stole a strawberry from the edge of his plate as he was returning it to the table. "No, I don't think so. But she'd hunt for us if I asked. Should I send her on the next trip?"

Bran snorted. "Ass. Not what I meant." He bit the other half of Macsen's strawberry, leaned back, then stretched and slid completely under the water. When he surfaced, his lover was standing behind him, reaching down for him.

"Come here. Let me finish what I started." Bran sloshed to his feet and stood still while Macsen lathered his arms and chest. The soap smelled like pine, sharp in his nostrils, and the scent woke him up a little after so much drowsy pleasure.

Bran rinsed quickly, shook water out of his hair and snickered at his lover's scowl when he splashed him. He stayed close to Macsen's side as they got out of the bath, dried off but didn't dress. He fully intended to bring Macsen to bed and sleep until he was awake enough to deal with the Red King's enthusiasm for the hunt. Already there was a certain glint in his eye.

Bran sighed and yawned almost simultaneously. "I know, I know. You want to go kill her. *I* want a nap."

Macsen prowled the edges of the room. "*Nap*. You can sleep after I drink her up. You ate already, but I am hungry, and through spoiling you. Come with me."

"I'm tired..."

Violence flashed across Macsen's face, all his desires

restrained and refocused now that he had soothed himself as much as he could with lust. "*Tired*. You aren't tired, you're lazy, dark Summer drowsy, and I—"

"And you're *hungry*. All right, all right. We'll go." He grinned, reached out and brushed his knuckles across Macsen's cheek. "We'll go, and I'll watch you make a mess of her. Then you can make a mess of me again, because you'll want to, and I'll want you—and *then* I can keep you in bed and you won't be able to complain."

"Won't? I'm sure I'll be able to think of something."

Bran threw him a grin over his shoulder, reached for his tunic and tugged it over his head while Macsen dressed in Summer gold. Bran didn't bother with trousers or boots, ran his fingers through his wet hair and willed the fire to dry it.

It was only when he dropped his hands that he caught sight of a glint past Macsen's shoulder through the open window. Something small and bright was speeding toward them. "What's…?"

"Bran?"

He slipped around Macsen's side and peered out. "That's one of Tighe's birds."

"Your brother's?" Macsen came up beside him and his eyes turned to follow the direction of Bran's gaze. "I thought those were your mother's messengers. It was one of them she sent to me when you…left." He stopped, reached out and touched Bran's lips with gentle fingers. "I've never been so pleased by a message in my life."

Bran smiled at him, but the expression faded to a frown as the glint of gold descended from the Winter sky and alighted on their windowsill. "Have you come for me?"

"*Bran, I'm sorry. I'm sorry. We need your help. Summer is falling apart and Mother is… I don't like asking — I'm sorry. But you're the only one who might be able to do…anything. Please come.*"

The words made him go still. There was a quiet desperation even in Tighe's apology, which told Bran that he had to respond. "Macsen…"

His hands went tight and cold on Bran's hips. "Don't say it."

The sigh that escaped him had Macsen's hands clutching tighter before he even managed the words. "I'll be as quick as I can, but I have to go."

Hungry kisses climbed his throat, sharp with teeth and promise. "*Not now*. We were already going. I have a gift to give you."

He turned as Macsen came up behind him, rubbed his cheek against Macsen's, then kissed him. "I know. *I know*. A gift I want."

But he gazed intently at the little bird, the glittering of the hard, bright eyes. What would the difference be, in Summer and Winter time, if he were to wait? There was no more urgency in Dealla's death than there had been five minutes ago, but his brother…

Tighe had been mistaken, to let their mother send Faelan after Macsen. To say nothing, even at their mother's command. There had to have been something he could have done. Even just to stand in front of him and let him see his face.

Bran would have known then that there was something wrong. Would have questioned, would have— But that mistake wasn't enough that he could ignore this. The message promised a mess. "Like I need another one of those."

It was a very quiet mutter, but Macsen questioned it anyway. "*Anwylyd?*"

Bran shook his head without elaborating. "I'm sorry. I know it's an interruption, but I have to go. After everything that happened last time we met, I don't think Tighe would be calling for me now unless it was something important." Scowling, he peered out at the snow. "At least, it had better be." His frown deepened, and he reached up to smooth his hands through his hair. "I don't like what that sounded like. I don't like that at all."

"I could come with you. That might—"

Bran nudged his lover with one shoulder, turned in his arms. "That *would* cause even more trouble. I'll be there and home again before you notice I'm gone, just…just get ready for our hunt, yes?" He leaned up and Macsen's lips parted for his tongue, enticing him into a deeper kiss. "I'll find out what's bothering Tighe and come right back to you. I can keep an eye on you, you know. While I'm gone. If I miss you."

"But I can't, and I miss you already. There hasn't even been time for me to have my fill of you since I returned." The soft touch of Macsen's tongue against his throat sent a shiver through Bran's body. "Not nearly."

Bran grinned despite himself. "As if you could."

"Brat. But it's true—so help me, it's true." Macsen held Bran tightly, kissed him hard and deeply, then nudged him back. "Go, if you're leaving. Go, or I'll keep you until it no longer matters. Keep you right here—"

Bran slipped out of his arms and squeezed his fingers before he let go. "Now, we can't have that. Then we'd get nothing done. Nothing at all."

He was out of the door and down the stairs before Macsen could hold him.

Chapter Eight

Bran was far more irritated with his brother than he'd let on, and it showed the farther he got from Winter. If this wasn't something important, if that desperation in Tighe's voice was for some fool's errand, or because he was feeling guilty…

Scowling, Bran quickened his steps. As it was, he could barely bring himself to care if his mother was well or not. She certainly hadn't shown much care for *his* well-being, his feelings, his choices… She had taken her vendetta with the Red King to a breaking point, *Bran's* breaking point, and she should have seen it coming.

"I warned her enough times." Since the moment he'd realized what she had set in motion, tried to do to him, to Macsen, all his thoughts of her had been angry. He was almost as angry with himself for not recognizing sooner what would come of her loathing for his lover.

My mother. My enemy.

At the same time, the damage her selfishness had done to him was enough to make Bran wonder what it had done to his brother. What it might still be doing. Six hundred years Tighe had spent suffering with no apparent escape under the yoke of her very existence.

But much as Tighe's message had conveyed need and trouble, it had told Bran nothing about the real problem. Maybe he was worrying too much. '*Summer is falling apart, and Mother is…*' What? What was she now?

The border of gold blossoms was before him then, and Bran sped past it. He opened himself to the rush of heat that accompanied the season. If nothing else, he would have fire to enrich his blood, make Macsen drunk on Summer again.

Perhaps he'd share the Red King's idea of a feast with Dealla, before Macsen took *her* blood. Smirking to himself, Bran passed deeper into Summer, but he was distracted quickly from pleasant thoughts. The farther he advanced into the wood, the more disturbed he was by what he saw, what he felt.

The secret laughter of the trees was a raucous cackle, the greeting of the birds a vicious buzz. Tiny beings danced in and out of his awareness, some of them translucent, some of them only ashes, drifting flakes of leaden gray instead of living flame. The beasts of the wood fled from him, ears flat and eyes dark. As if they were mortal.

Bran hurried forward, concerned now despite himself. Was it this strangeness that Tighe had called him about? The wood opened a way for him, led swiftly to his brother's house and to his brother, sitting outside it in the clearing with his head in Faelan's lap.

His eyes were closed, and Faelan scrutinized Bran in silence for a moment. The *gancanagh* nodded once, something not quite a greeting, before he brushed his knuckles across Tighe's cheek. "Your brother is here, prince."

"*Bran.*" Surprise sharpened the lines on Tighe's face as he sat up. "I wasn't sure you would come."

"No? Why is that, I wonder?"

Sardonic words, but his brother only flushed a little, apparently ashamed. "I *am* sorry. I told you that. I still don't know what I could have done, but that's not why I called you here."

Bran shrugged, stopped a few steps away from them and crossed his arms over his chest. "Good. So, what, then? Things have gone strange since I was here last."

Something of a shrug shivered across his brother's shoulders. "Yes. That's why I called you. The thing no message could say. Summer is…disintegrating." Tighe paused as he stood, brushing grass from his tunic and apparently gathering his thoughts. "There've been too many lives lost and Mother's done nothing. Less than nothing, she's gone. Wherever she went, I can't find her."

Bran lifted an eyebrow. "What does that have to do with me?"

As if it were the most obvious thing in the world, Tighe gaped at him. "You can defy her! You stole the Summer from her already, more than once, even if just for a moment at a time."

"I don't—"

But Tighe went on as if he hadn't heard Bran's interruption. "And the girl. Your human, you saved her. Protected her. I can't stand against Mother like that. There isn't enough Summer in me, and nothing else to make up the difference. But your father gave you what I lack."

His brother's gaze was steady, but Bran was already shaking his head. "I didn't come here to lead a rebellion, to go to war! You said you needed my *help*, but this is…" Then he scowled, anger flaring into fire on his skin.

Faelan was suddenly grinning, and his brother was *chuckling* at him even as he spoke to clarify his amusement. "No, Bran, you misunderstood. We want you to take away what doesn't belong to her. We want you to be dark Summer's King, not lead a… No."

It was Bran's turn to let out a choked mouthful of laughter. "*What*? I don't know how to be king!"

"And you think your Macsen does?"

Bran glared at his brother. "*Yes*. He has responsibilities and he fulfills them, even when he'd rather not. Those take enough time away from us. It's been weeks since he was home, weeks of Winter time. Do you know how long that is? Do you know how long it *feels* like? He calls me impatient, but I— And then he was barely home, and *you* interrupted the minute I had him to myself again!"

He turned and paced away, fire licking over him, flaring at his brother and seeking to comfort Bran himself. "We were going hunting. We were… And I— *no*. I won't be your king. Everything in Summer always wants something from me and gives nothing back!"

His brother stared at him, kept staring.

Faelan only shrugged as he finally stood and turned away. "I thought as much. We'll have to do it ourselves."

But Tighe shook his head, reached out and stopped his lover with a hand on his elbow. "No. Bran, you don't understand. You already *are*. You were born to be dark Summer's King. Like the brother we had before. The one Mother…lost."

"The one Macsen killed, you mean. *Ha*." But he stayed where he was, said nothing else. His father had spoken similar words. That he belonged to his mother, that he had been born for her.

"Before. After the…when I returned from meeting my father." He turned, looked Tighe straight in the eye and frowned. "You said it then. That what the Summer King… but I've never been given a throne, never been crowned. I'm not a king!"

Snorting, Tighe shook his head. "This is Summer, not some mortal country. You have made your power known over even the queen. She was only ever meant to rule bright Summer, Bran." His voice turned bitter. "I would take it from you if I could. Just to keep myself from begging. But I will if I have to."

There was something—fear?—glittering in Tighe's eyes, usually so unreadable. "Please, brother. Take what is already yours."

Bran glanced between his brother and Faelan, hesitating, but still shook his head. "I can't. I *can't*, don't you understand?"

Tighe was still staring at him as he backed away, but Bran made it only a few steps before he grew aware of something *pulling* at him. What was it? Where was it coming from? In Summer it was bright midday, but the vision suspended in front of his mind's eye was vibrant dark.

He experienced a duality of awareness, a doubling of vision. Summer was before him, but there was also the moon, a narrow crescent blinking like a sleepy eye. Was it his father calling to him? Bran peered through the open door of his own power, into the mortal world, and he saw —

No. "No!"

* * * *

Silent, invisible, a shadow among shadows, Macsen snuck out of the Red Kingdom, across the water and onto the Irish beaches, following Dealla's trail. It was a trail of witch-power, her fury and her stench entwined.

He had waited impatiently, pacing in his bedroom, mouth full of hunger, before it had occurred to him that waiting was unnecessary. Bran had said he could get ready, hadn't he? She was only a woman. Like any other prey, he could stalk her, track her.

Her odor and that of many other mortals started at the coast, a months'-old trail of scent that led him inland. He would wait for Bran before he killed her — she was his gift, after all — but he could find her before his lover joined him. He was too keyed up, too ready to postpone the hunt.

Macsen wanted her life too much.

The last thing he had expected was for Bran to run off to Summer. As if his brother mattered when — but no. That was his way of thinking, not Bran's. It was one of the things he loved about his Summer son.

Macsen ran his hands up the sleeves of his tunic then licked his lips and started along the track again.

Just like he'd thought, the scent of Bran and his blood clung to the soft, silken mail. His throat was tight with thirst just breathing that smell. If he focused on it, it washed away everything else, even the taste of the woman he was following, but Bran wasn't there. What to do about his hunger? Dealla was for his *Valravn*...

Perhaps the women and priests who followed her could serve as appetizers.

He closed his eyes and for a moment the tangle of scents

around him was almost too much to bear. Macsen let a howl escape him then bit back the night song and ran in silence through the Irish wood.

He took the first woman he encountered with the speed of an arrow in flight, caught her by the throat and bled her without taking time to savor her life. It was only a drop, a trickle against the flow of his need. As fast as he had struck, he darted away, along the bulge of the tree line toward his next victim.

After the fourth, Macsen turned inward, seeking other prey. Dealla had arranged her defenders in circles, but he was close to her now. The forest was thick with her odor. Was she watching? Did she see her death approaching?

The trees thinned as he prowled ahead. Now that he was closer he could feel something of Summer, burning behind his prey. Weapons? What a fool she was. Macsen stepped forward into a clearing without pause, straight into the face of her women and the priests standing beside them.

Dealla whipped around to glare at him, shouted something to her women, but he ignored her for now. His hands were already on the throat of the man closest to him, and he sank his teeth in deep, savoring the crunch of the bite.

All that he was convulsed in the next moment.

A blessing slept in the man's blood. Divine power fought him, defied submitting to the Red King's control. For a moment, which became many, unbroken, Macsen was frozen in place. Outside, he had become still and smooth as glass, but inside he was at war.

"This is not for you!" It was a scorching voice, the source of the defiance in the priest's blood.

"Yes..."

"No. This is not – "

"It will be –"

"For you."

"Mine!"

Fire without fuel, sharpness without an edge, a sourceless light expanded within him then expanded again, seeking to escape.

But it had come to the Red King in blood.

He had hunted it, slain its bearer and drunk it down. It was his now. The voice wanted to argue but the truth remained. Already, the blood was becoming part of him, the lightning weight of it.

On the heels of that anger and disappointment, the wrath of a god dispelled, another rage began to lap at him. Familiar this time. Old power, Summer power. The deadly vengeance of the brightest season was all around him.

Macsen tried to blink but he was a moment digesting that priest. The raw flower of some foreign divinity was still blossoming in his own veins. The sudden weight of Summer ensnared him, was too heavy to move in. He turned his eyes enough to get a glimpse of himself and saw chains. Not just the soft fabric mesh of his tunic, but real chains, shackled to his legs, his hips.

Fire pulsed from his body. He was aware of nothing, suddenly, so much as the scent and presence of Bran. His power, his love, torrid desire and the sweetness of his blood.

Valravn. A kingly gift.

The tunic he'd been given wrapped him in a column of flame. The screams of the women near him, consumed by it, were loud in his ears. He felt the blaze as only a brush of warmth, even as it rose up a second time, devouring everything near him. Then the bright sunlight in Bran's gift faded to a low ebb, and frantic, angry fingers stripped the softness of the tunic from his body.

The gold of the chains they wrapped around him, instead, sapped every bit of strength he brought to the surface to contest them. Summer's wrath was bound up in them, Summer's vengeance, and he knew immediately where such power had come from.

It had been weapons she'd stolen, after all. Weapons from the war against *him*.

Dealla's women netted him, bound his shoulders, his chest, pinned his wrists by his hips. The chains dug into his skin and scorched him. So heavy. The old Summer he remembered, not the sweet, new wine that was Bran.

Every movement he managed cost him an excess of power. There was too much fury, too much sunlight in these bonds, even for him. *This* was why that woman had stolen Summer gold?

He lifted his gaze to meet Dealla's eyes and could only think that he was sorry.

Sorry, because Bran would come home now and he would not be there, would not be waiting. Would not be *here*, as he had planned to be, with Dealla's life in his hands ready for the taking.

She had caught him off guard, and this time it was his own fault. The fault of impatience and greed. But despite himself, his frustration and anger at being taken by surprise, he was curious. Dealla glared at him with hatred but also with a smirk of victory. What did she think she'd won? She had captured him but she couldn't keep him. Couldn't kill him. And when the trap wore thin…

It would, one day, wear thin. He smiled, then let out a sharp breath when she whipped her sword up and sliced through his throat. Blood sheeted down his chest, already frosting over as the wound healed.

He surged forward, snapping his teeth, and the chains drew tight. Again, there was a thrust of agony, the fire of Dealla's blade sliding through his ribs, seeking out his heart, but this flesh was mostly a game. Did she really think she could kill him this way? And more than that… "That sword does not belong to you, woman."

"No? But it seems to do its job well enough." She jerked it out of his body and appeared to be satisfied by the red flow from the wound…until it staunched itself.

Macsen was amused. "A sword is for killing."

"A sword is to cut! It is enough to know that it hurts you."

"What do you know?" He shifted just a little, testing, but the women holding the chains exerted themselves together and threw him on his back. More gold was layered over him at once, wrapped around his ankles and wrists and over his chest.

If only it were Bran's power, not the old, dark Summer. This could be trouble, and his lover was going to be angry with him regardless. He grimaced at the sky as the women heaved him into the bed of a cart and started to pull him away. They were taking him somewhere else, then.

Bran was going to be very angry. He could apologize — *would* apologize... Macsen turned his gaze in Dealla's direction. "Oh, but you. *You*, he will make suffer."

The huntress slashed at him as he started laughing again. He ignored the dazzling little flashes of pain until the chain at his throat went taut and a slash of gold swept between his head and his shoulders for a second time.

Agony worked its way upward and downward from the wound simultaneously. Dark blood gushed from the separated flesh, but it was a seam in a moment, then a wash of red where no cut showed. Glaring at her, Macsen licked his own blood from his lips, barely amused. It hurt, certainly, but he thought the wild anger on her face made the experience worthwhile.

She smirked at him with something in her stare that spoke of the madness Bran had promised. There was an echo of beloved fire burning in her glance, too.

Macsen closed his eyes to it and sighed. "So unhappy with me. I should have waited for him after all."

"What is it you're muttering? I have you at my mercy now, be *silent!*"

"Mercy?" Macsen chuckled deep in his throat. "You have nothing but the power to hold me here, and that is not *your* power, but Summer's vengeance. I bought it for myself and thought I had escaped, but no debt goes unpaid."

She was momentarily transfixed as he spoke.

"No debt, woman. If you had been wise, you would have turned away from your father's path. Bran would have spared you. But now..." He would have shrugged, but his bonds prevented even that. "Time is not on your side. You cannot kill me."

"No?" Dealla closed her lips over her teeth and smiled tightly at him. "Beast. Then when we have brought you to the dark place we will keep you in, know that you will never leave it again."

Her mouth shaped a snarl, and it was just too much. The Red King closed his eyes and started to laugh again. He could feel it already, as the moon rose over him. Bran's sudden awareness of what had happened, his fearful denial, and his wrath awakening in response to Macsen's pain.

But the Red King spent that first, long night of his captivity more disturbed than he wanted to admit. He had only wanted to find the woman. And now —

"My lady, should we bring him down into the cell?"

The words, muttered as dawn approached, surprised him just a little. 'Cell'? Macsen's unease, like his anger at himself, increased.

Rage roared through him, but the Summer weight was enough to hold him, even then. It was not to be borne! And yet to struggle was to give Dealla pleasure, and he refused that even more than the chains.

Testing, he shook them once, pushed against them with his whole body, then collapsed onto the cold, smooth wood of the cart bed. The weight and heat made him drowsy, and he almost gave in to the compulsion, sank not into sleep-darkness but the start of some rich and vivid dream.

It was dispersed by the pressure of rough hands dragging him up and out of the cart.

"That's far enough. Stake him out in the open and leave him to enjoy the sunrise."

There was a chorus of agreement and Macsen hissed his displeasure when the links were drawn taut, then passed over him *again* as he was laid out on the dirt.

How many fathoms of chain had the damn woman forged? Just to keep him... But perhaps that was the only sensible decision she'd made. Then the metal was tight across his throat, forcing him to lift his head, and he bared his teeth.

Already the eastern horizon had a vermilion edge.

Slowly, as the light touched it, the gold bound around him kindled into flame. Smokeless tongues of fire lapped out of the chains, grew into a calescent pyre, and shapes danced in the inferno, raced one another across Macsen's skin.

Dealla stayed and watched the fire run down his body, blackening him with burns that healed only to blister again. He made no sound, only stared at her. Chained as he was, blinded by the blaze, he still saw the moment when she grew aware of her own fear and turned away.

* * * *

Moonlight rushed through Bran, as undeniable as the horror of what it was showing him. He couldn't think, couldn't breathe. Something cold twisted his stomach, despite the white scream of an inferno all around him.

In the space between one heartbeat and the next a sound was wrenched out of him, something between a sob and a groan, The inner vision showed him little details. Chains, gold and hot and glittering. Spilled blood on Macsen's naked chest, red then white with frost. The flash of a fang as he bit his lip. Pain in his eyes, and defiance of it.

Whatever torture Dealla intended for him had already begun.

The moonlight caressed the chains that held his lover, but though Bran strained his power, his *sight*, he couldn't touch them. To see was not to be there, and the sun was already rising, dissolving the thread of lunar power. The mortal dawn thinned out his awareness, and the last thing Bran saw was a blaze rising from the individual links of gold.

He found himself on his hands and knees in the bright glow of Summer, and his brother steadied him while he rose jerkily from the ground.

"Bran?"

"That bastard. Bastard! He just couldn't *wait*!" The fire of

Bran's anger, misdirected, pushed Tighe until his brother stumbled. "Damn your timing! If you'd sent that message tomorrow, or yesterday — I should have ignored it. I should have just gone with him like he asked and damn the consequences to this place!"

Macsen's pain was a hot shadow cast across his mind. The oath that bound them pulled at the threads of his thoughts, but he had better reasons for keeping Macsen safe, didn't need *that* to move him. "I have to go to him. I'll kill her myself, I—"

"Bran, *what are you talking about?*"

Infuriated, he whipped around to face his brother. "We were going to kill her. Dealla. He was going to kill her for me, finally make an end of her. My midsummer gift."

My fault. Again. He felt suddenly sick. "But because you sent me that message, because I *cared* and I *listened* and came here instead of—" He choked on a 'ha' of half-hysterical laughter. "He's so greedy. So impatient. He says that *I*—but he went after her alone, and now she's chained him up."

"The Red King…"

"Yes! She melted down the weapons she stole. She made them into chains!"

Tighe's face showed surprise and understanding and horror by turns.

Bran clenched his fists. "I've fought her before. You know what happened. I'm not sure anything different would happen now. But it doesn't…it won't matter when he's free."

"Bran—"

"You can deal with Mother, with Summer. I don't care, I never wanted to. I don't *care*." His voice broke and he bit off the rest of his words, shook his head and turned from Tighe.

"If you become king, you'll have greater power."

His brother's words were a lure. Bran knew it, *knew* it, but stopped anyway.

"If you become king, the season will follow you. Faelan

can tell you, if you don't believe me. He and his brothers are of dark Summer."

Fighting himself, Bran brought his frustration to bear on his brother. "What are you telling me? That I should become king to make Summer go to war for me?"

The expression on his brother's face changed, and he knew that if not for what Bran had just revealed about Macsen, Tighe would have been laughing at him again. "No. Become king and *let* them go to war. The season is screaming for vengeance, but Mother has done nothing. That woman you hate, did you think you were the only one? Her huntresses and the priests of some foreign god kill any *sidhe* who dares enter Ireland, even now." Tighe fixed him with a flat, gray stare. "So your Macsen is in danger? He's not the only one."

Bran held his breath and closed his eyes. In truth he didn't know what to do. He had *seen* his lover, wrapped in chains, his own blood on his skin. Dealla hadn't taken him to her palace, but had set him in the courtyard of some building he'd never seen.

Bran was no hunter. How would he find out where they'd gone?

He would cross Ireland from border to border if he had to, burn every fortress, every forest to the ground. But he remembered, too, the way his power had failed him before.

He was no fighter, either. He had never learned how, had made the weapons but not used them…and he wasn't a killer like Macsen, wasn't possessed of the instincts of fang and claw. "How. How do I become king? Tell me." He looked at his brother and saw his own resolution reflected in the black centers of Tighe's pupils.

"I don't know." Despite his shrug, there was relief in the relaxation of his whole body. "You'll have to take it from Mother, if she won't give it to you."

A deep breath. Another. They did nothing to cool his anger, his guilt. "She will. The only reason I was even born was so that she'd have someone to take the half of Summer she didn't want." The words tasted bitter.

"Bran..."

"Where is she?"

But to his frustration, Tighe shook his head again. "I don't know that either. I told you, I was trying to find her, and you know it shouldn't be difficult. But the Summer wood makes no road to her, and I've checked the palace a dozen times at least." He shrugged a tight, uncomfortable shrug. "Summer is falling apart. Dark and bright both are going to pieces."

Bran narrowed his eyes. "I don't *care*. I saw that, coming here. It matters even less to me now than it did then."

Faelan took a quick step forward. "It should! If Summer falls apart, where do you think your brother — ?"

Tighe restrained Faelan with a hand across his chest. "That's enough. I'm the responsibility of *me*."

"Like hell you are. I — "

"*I* don't have time for lover's quarrels." Bran shouldered his way between them, squinted into the wood then closed his eyes. "The two of you can argue when I've found..." But then he frowned, turned again and peered into the distance.

"She's close. So close she could be *here*." The white fire of his mother's presence was faint but not far. Now that he was actively seeking it, there was no avoiding it, but...it was...dispersed. A fragile web instead of a burning lattice.

"What are you talking about? Bran?"

But he started off in the direction the feeling was strongest without another word. Be dark Summer's King? For Macsen he would suffer far worse consequences than that.

Tighe followed a few paces behind his brother and watched the Summer rise in him. Whatever was leading Bran on, Tighe couldn't feel it himself, couldn't see it, yet it was obviously something real.

The first clearing they came to held their mother, coalescing out of Summer light and fire.

"*My sons...*" she greeted them, but she was fading in and

out of solid being, from flesh to flame and back again. She wisped toward them and Tighe had to turn his eyes away.

Her brightness was blinding.

"So you'll come to Bran and not to me, is that it? Or is it that you know what he's come for, and didn't care before?"

She flared at him, and seemed to solidify in her fury. "It is all I can do to contain the Summer! Soon there will be no difference between summer and Summer, do you understand? My power alone is no longer enough to divide them."

She took a shuddering breath and fire spawned in threads and gouts across her gown, in her hair. The flames turned to buds that opened to drop petals of ash. "What would you have me do? Go myself into the mortal world and slay this woman? I would fall apart, and after me, Summer."

Laughter seemed to dissolve her, push at the boundaries of her flesh once more. "Everything is out of balance. Even the warning that the Black King brought me did not prepare me for this! And the only one I could ask to help me…"

Bran stepped forward then, his eyebrows drawn together and his expression dark. "You mean me."

"It *must* be you. I would turn to your brother if I could, but the weight of it would crush him. But you, why would you help me now?"

Her plaintive tone seemed to arouse no sympathy. Impatient, Bran tried to hurry her along. "The weight of *what*, Mother?"

The words escaped her on a gust of hot wind. "Dark Summer. It's been a thousand years without its king. It was never meant to be mine and now it is too much! But there is no one other than you, and I cannot even ask it of you."

The wood rustled in anticipation as Bran took another step. "Why would that be? Because you tried to separate me from my lover? Because you are selfish enough to take everything from me?"

Bran was fire and moonlight, bright enough now that it was impossible for Tighe to see either of them, his brother or his mother.

"*My treasure.*"

"I'm not your treasure! I'm not to be owned, not so precious, not so *shining* as that. I'll be king, do you understand? I'll be your equal, just to stand better at Macsen's side. And I *will* stand at his side."

Cautious now, as if sensing trouble, she finally questioned Bran's fury. "Something…what's wrong?"

His aura grew murderous, but he said nothing, and Tighe answered her quietly. "The Red King was taken. The Milesians have him captive. Bran came because I asked him to, but now he has vengeance of his own to seek."

She brought her gaze to his brother's face. "I would apologize, but you're in no mood to hear it. All I can do is offer my help—"

"You need *my* help." Bran glared at her, defiance in every line of his face, in the subtlest hints of his posture. "How do I take it?"

"Take—?"

"*Dark Summer*. The throne I don't want, that I need, that I was born for!"

Fire expanded between them, sudden and hot enough that Tighe retreated a full step.

"Follow me." Their mother spoke with assurance, but Tighe was waiting for the moment when she would realize what he had seen months before.

Summer King. In almost every way that mattered, Bran already was. What was left for her to share with him? He followed the path of ash and blossoms their mother left behind as she led his brother out of the clearing and deeper into the Summer wood.

Tighe stopped, startled, at the sound of Bran's confused 'ha', and came out of the trees to see surprise on his face and hear recognition in Bran's voice.

"This place… I know this place. I've been here before."

Dark woods around them. The ruins of the Summer King's palace before them, the gate broken and overgrown, the old hall covered over by golden hay. The chittering of birds and insects was an irrational hum, no longer a coherent melody. "You have been here…before? By accident while you were walking the wood, then. No one comes here, treasure," she said.

Tighe winced. She should *not* have said that.

Bran turned a blistering stare in their mother's direction. "No? This was the *first* place I came to. One of the *dullahan* loaned me a horse, and my beauty brought me here. Right here." He had been walking forward, but he stopped and cast his gaze over the remains of the old king's palace.

"This is why, isn't it? Because it was meant to be mine. Because everyone knew but me." Bran swung his stare in Tighe's direction, and it had neither softened nor cooled. "You called me Summer King."

"Yes. Sorry, Bran. I see what I see." But he could say nothing more. Their mother stepped between them, and in that instant became a being of light, summer vines and blossoms straining, no flesh evident in any shifting shape of her.

"*I don't want to wait any more.*" Her voice echoed, no longer merely sound. "*Step into the fire, my son. Take away the night.*"

Bran glanced at Tighe, but he only shrugged. This was nothing he had seen before, no ritual, no magic. The heart of the Summer was moving over their mother in a way that blocked all other things, even from his sight.

"*My son. Bran Fionnan.*" Her words, too, were becoming fire. "*Bring your heart into the heart of Summer with me.*"

Bran appeared to hesitate. Then he stepped forward, took their mother's hands, and there was a shift. The season snapped into flux as the magic *howled*, racing outward like a wild beast set free.

Chapter Nine

Bran felt the sun inside him, outside him, a rapid and stunning blaze. It melted the bright Winter frost of his clothes from his skin, and he had a moment to regret the loss of Macsen's gift. Then it went out, and the quiet spaces of his mind grew abrupt with noise. From where?

Everywhere.

Why?

Because you are King.

The noise was a celebration. The sun darkened into eclipse overhead, and all around him were the thousand voices of dark Summer. The words joined out of jumbled cacophony into something like real music.

Summer King. So long, we've waited.

'So long'. Yes, that was the feeling most familiar to him out of everything that touched him in the blaze. Not his mother's love, the shrinking vanity of it. Not his brother's presence, revealed as a blaze of doubt. Not even the angry ache of fearful loss, empty spaces eager to be filled again, as was the empty space beside him.

None of that, but the feeling of waiting was what he knew best. Impatience and its price.

He'd spent so many years biding his time that there was nothing in the world more familiar, more painful. A wave of sympathy radiated from him into the land, the too-green, too-bright half of Summer that should be dark. He, too, had no more desire for daylight's intrusive glare. Better the quiet of twilight's peering eyes, the firefly and the muted hum of dusk.

Sunset flared through him as he reached for it, and red

incandescence blinded Bran from himself before it darkened further. Dimness came with the moonlight, midnight rippling outward from where he stood.

His awareness raced through the green of the land. The new Summer King touched its every shadow, encountered every leaf, slid into the petals of fragile blossoms and refracted into shallow drops of dew. Lives buzzed in his ears, an awakening of many beings.

Bran remembered dark Summer as it had been when he'd crossed through it with Macsen and Faelan, seeking his father. The only relief from the light had been at the edge of the mountains, where the moon rose and paled the Summer sun to something less straining. All those watching eyes, all those whispers that had clung to his footsteps then... Now they were naked before his awareness, just waiting to be acknowledged.

Some of them grew fuller in his mind as he focused on them, murmuring in sharper voices. Bran could have summoned them if he chose, but each one he turned to, even the wild equine shadow of his beauty, was already racing toward him.

When he opened his eyes again, the season was in motion around him, already changed. The sun was making a slow descent to the horizon and the moon was rising.

He tasted wind, or the hush of grass in the wind, or the whisper of a thousand feet-not-feet, running-gliding-flying closer to him. He was very still and very silent, listening and feeling all of it. It was almost enough to drive him mad, but there was an open door in his consciousness that he recognized now for what it was.

Summer's heart. Midsummer's midnight. A shadow and the hiss of steam that came from a distant fall of rain on eager embers. He could mute it all if he closed that inner door. The feeling of a shouting multitude was dimmed as he did so, washed out by his own power, his own thoughts, to a mere whisper.

It would never be truly silent again, but that whisper was

so near silence he could ignore it. The quiet left him with nothing but the layers of his own feelings, each one peeling away to reveal a deeper pain. *Macsen*. Fury filled him. There was sadness, too, but — *rage*.

He'd never before felt anything like this, *anything*. It fed on the new tie that bound him to the Summer, and the Summer fed on his feeling, came ever more awake, more alive. The whisper at the back of his mind was close now, echoing the scream of his own desire at him.

Find Dealla.

Yes, find her.

Go into her country, find her, and burn them both together.

Burn it all.

Fire flickered into life at his feet, and he took a step toward the rush of dark Summer's people as they approached him. "Bran…"

He ignored Tighe and glowered at his mother. She was only bright Summer's Queen now and her face was… changed. "It's done. It's mine. You have no claim to dark Summer any longer, so go. Go to your own palace, your own bright Kingdom. You'll find it less strain on you, I'm sure. Do what you will there."

"And you? What about you, my son?" A dazed, wan sadness, sadness spread too thin, was in her voice.

"I'm going to Ireland. I'll do what must be done, what you refused to do. But first…I will see if Winter wants to go to war." The blaze coalesced around him, until he was dressed in shifting, lucid flames, to replace the bright Winter frost that dark Summer had melted away.

He regretted the loss of the tunic, the trousers, but even the heat at the heart of Summer hadn't touched the torc around his throat. That mattered more. Gently, he stroked the cold band with his fingertips.

A smoldering wave of shadows came up from the wood, from the water, and fixed their gazes on him, silent as they had assembled. Bran stared back. He had nothing to say to them, unless…

As one, they bent the knee. As one, they bowed to him. "Summer King. Command us." It was the voice of the *dullahan*, gravel out of rusted bone.

Bran took a step forward, and a way opened through the ranks of many moonlit and blazing beings. "Come. Bring your weapons, your power, your anger and your allies." The volume of his own voice surprised him but he wasn't bothered by it. "It's time. Past time. We go to wake the Winter and then…"

He only smiled. He did not need to say more. Laughter was spreading among them, angry howls and the suckling murmur of hungry ghosts.

Tighe stood to one side, aware of a conflict of conscience that was purely his own, on top of the wild pressure that was his brother's will to violence.

Whether it was his long association with Faelan or some subconscious choice he had made, he felt within himself a shift in allegiance. His brother was now his king, as his mother had once been his queen. He could not deny the urge for vengeance that was part of that change.

The intensity of the fire had branded the horizon, burned out the sun and left even bright Summer near darkness. The dark Summer powers, long kept in lands of exile, were all in motion. Those who had already professed their own violence were only an accent when once they had been the crest of the wave.

Summer's people would win the land that belonged to them by right. The last, tenuous threads of the old oath had been shattered forever. There was fire in the dark, laughter in every shadow, a racing silence moving among the Summer branches with a blood-thirst to rival the Red Kingdom's hunters.

Tighe felt their urge, their need, as he had felt Faelan's, intensifying every day since his *gancanagh* brothers had first begun to die. It was Faelan who was the source of his own conflict. Faelan, who had already girt his sword about his waist and raced off with sharpness in his expression to join the horde gathering at his brother's feet.

Faelan, who had kissed him goodbye, surely expecting that Tighe would obey good sense and stay here, where he was safe. But his lover was so eager to hunt down those mortals. How did he plan to do it? What power did a *gancanagh* possess, except…his body? His lust.

How could he think that Tighe would just let him go? Not try to stop him? "It was always stupid to hope, but I do love you, Faelan, I do."

Tighe laughed quietly at himself. Was it even a decision? He could stay and go on waiting. Wondering. Hating every minute of it and hating himself. Or he could go and risk the danger he had avoided for six hundred years. With hesitant steps, he slipped away from the teeming masses, through the wood against the tide and into the dimmest corner of his own smithy.

Flowers had grown up around the sheath of the weapon he pulled out of the shadow, and one or another of the little birds he'd made had built a nest in the angles of the hilt. Glittering feathers and fragments of shell delicate as stained glass had been left among the woven Summer grasses.

He brushed them aside, then drew the sword and eyed the edge critically. Only once, since the Winter war had ended, had he had reason to touch it. That had been to put it here.

It wasn't as if he could use it to fight mortals, even if it was just as sharp now as it had been when he'd put it away. It would be as deadly to him as to them. Even so he belted it on then turned. Through the little clearing around his house he saw gold firefly light still fleeing through the wood.

The gathering was all but finished. Already he could see the blazing focus that was his brother moving away. Tighe glared in consternation at the streaming train of Summer's people then whistled for a horse and stood waiting.

A solitary shadow detached itself from the flood and came to stand before him, sparks fleeing the constraints of its mane and tail.

"You'll bear me into the mortal world, follow after my brother?"

The beast's neigh of assent was almost a screech, and Tighe mounted with a feeling of dread. It only grew stronger when the direction of the long Summer ride became clear to him.

Bran led the whole of them into the gray between, then into Winter, shaking the borders of the sleeping season with the passage of his host. He had meant it, then. "Wake the Red Kingdom", he had said.

Winter. What was there for them now? Tighe picked out those he knew in the distance. Bran, riding at the head of them all, and Faelan some distance behind him, his teeth showing as he smiled and sang a death song with the rest of his brothers. The *gancanagh* were all too beautiful, hard to look at standing together like that, but only one of them made his heart ache.

The ache intensified as Tighe joined the crowd and was rushed across the bitter border of the Red Kingdom. He was surprised to find that the cold bit at him, but that was all. Everything else in dark Winter was sleeping, as if pretending to be dead.

The air in the Red Kingdom was still and more than cold. No breeze stirred to welcome Summer's King. Neither Winter hunters nor Winter prey were in motion, and Bran rode slowly through the wood, seeking signs of life.

Everywhere, there was the same unbroken sense of stillness. As he came near the palace, it was even more pronounced. No music in the court. No dancers. But on the dais, curled up like a sleeping wolf in the space between his seat and Macsen's, there was Saoirse.

Bran slipped off his horse and ran to her, shook her shoulder.

It took too long for her to blink her eyes open, to wake up, to see anything but sleep. "Bran? Bran..."

"I'm here. Saoirse. Saoirse!"

She lolled in his arms, boneless, breathless. "The Red King. Where? There's only sleep, and I don't…understand."

Cradling her reminded him of her youth, of all that had been stolen from her. "Your sister took him, Saoirse. Dealla has him captive in Summer chains. It's why she stole those weapons, but I'm going to set him free. Must the Red Kingdom stay sleeping, or will it help its king?"

A slow, cold light kindled in the girl's eyes, stronger as the moments passed. "The Red King is captive?" She stood, swaying, and shouted at thin air. "Ffion! Wake up! The Red King needs you!" And again, when only silence answered, "Ffion!"

"Ssso…Illoud. Ssso…*hhhhmmm*." Snow blossomed upward, coiled into shapeless attempts at shape, then returned to a drift. "Ssshhhh. Sssleep nnnow."

Saoirse descended the steps in one movement and *kicked* at her. The drift hissed upward, then flew down as an angry rush of wind. Saoirse hissed back at it, and when talons shaped from the frost clawed at her face, she struck them away with her staff.

It was the one Bran had made for her years ago, but he had no idea how it had come into her hands. One moment they were empty, and the next it was there. She dealt a heavy blow to the snow as it fell, and in a moment it was Ffion again.

She took on shape more strongly while the wind intensified. "Stupid girl. You woke me, and for what? *Hmm*? Ungrateful, you are."

Bran watched, amused despite himself, and Saoirse bared tiny pointed teeth. "Ungrateful? The Red King is captive, and Bran's brought Summer to us, all of dark Summer together at last. They're going to war, and we should go with them."

"The Red King…?"

"That *stupid* woman's chained him up in Summer gold. Weren't you listening, didn't you hear at all? What's *wrong* with you?"

Ffion's eyes darkened in Bran's direction. "Summer…"

Saoirse interrupted her with a scowl. "Dealla stole it, with her huntresses. Just like Bran was stolen once."

Additional sharpness formed itself around Ffion's voice. "Stole. And our king? And Summer goes to war."

Bran stepped forward and looked Ffion in the eye. "Will you tell the rest of Winter? Rouse them out of their sleep?" He stared in the direction of his forge for one black moment. "I have work to do in the meantime."

"Rouse them?" Her voice was a yawn, but she peered at him intently. "And tell them what, I wonder?"

He glanced up sharply. "Tell them that they can stay here, sleeping, or they can help us find their king. There are no hunters like those in the Red Kingdom, are there?"

Ffion huffed at him. "No. Of course not." She swirled off in a rush of snow and, almost at once, there was a change.

Bloody intentions rose around them. In the wake of the Winter wind's renewal, Winter's hunters were coming awake, and angry. Bran felt Summer's impatience, tangled with his own, but this was how he would find Macsen fastest.

Saoirse came up beside him and tugged at his sleeve. "Bran, there's someone in Winter who doesn't belong. A mortal, a woman. She's coming this way. I think she's been coming this way for some time, only I've been sleeping since the Red King left. Someone is bringing her, someone…who is human-not-human. Someone like me?"

Suspicion curled Bran's mouth into a frown. "Go find her. Them. Bring them to me. I can't think of a single good reason for a human woman to be here."

Saoirse nodded and sped away from him, into the wood. He watched her go until the red smear of her hair vanished in the snow, then went up the steps to the dais. He almost took his seat, but his eyes strayed to the empty throne where his lover should have been.

The searing new power he'd gained was restless, as

impatient as he was to do something, and for Macsen he would do *anything*.

Even break the oath he had made to himself.

The fire in the forge was dim, but as he approached it roared up in welcome, licked at the ceiling then retreated to a white-hot glow. A hundred flickering firelight reflections shone at him, and he spared only a moment in contemplation. Star-steel? Gold? Electrum, silver, onyx, obsidian...? *Yes.*

Bran shaped the metal with his bare hands, with the pressure of the flame and all the agony of his rage. Star-steel for the blade. Gold for the hilt. A pair of ebon eyes, wolfish, staring, embedded in the glint of the metal. He thinned the edges, deepened the blood channel, then did it again.

He wanted it sharper. Sharp enough to cut the moon out of the sky.

White gold flowed along one side of the blade, and Bran filled it with sunlight, then with Summer. Atomi fluttered just out of the way, drifted interested among the sparks and tested the new edge with their light and dance. The smallest among them cut her toes on the point, but none approached the other side of the blade.

That edge was black and whetted with pain, all dark Summer's rage and Bran's own agony. It drank the light as Bran focused on it, ran his fingers across it, and sliced, not his skin, but the shadow of his soul.

Macsen. Blood but I'm coming, spilled but I'm coming, for you, just... Macsen. Oh, my love. Wait for me. Just. Wait. I...

He jerked his hand away, breathing hard. So, it would cut more than flesh, this sword. It would cut where wrath and desire told it, cut into darkness and draw it out.

There were howls on the wind as he laid the finished blade on his worktable, and only then realized that a good deal of time must have passed. Bran watched the moon passing through the swift shadow of its phases, then sucked in a breath, caught up the sword and slid it into his belt.

The moon.

If he walked that road, followed that power...Macsen's dreams. Could he find them? Touch them. Touch *him*. Tell him. Bran stepped out of the forge and onto the snow, reaching for the moonlight with his own power. A brilliant silver lattice built between them and turned the face of the moon into a peering eye.

A dream. Where was the Red King's dream?

A ripple of awareness thrummed through him as he passed along a fragile trail of moon-dust and into the dark. Macsen? Oh, no. Blood and broken shadow. *Macsen*. Oh, no...but yes.

"Macsen. I'm coming for you, we're all coming for you. All of Summer. All of Winter. I'll burn everything until I find you."

There was no response and Bran wondered if the dark of the dream he had found was a mirror for some murky place in which his lover was being kept. *"Macsen. Love!"*

"B...ran...?" The answer was sluggish. The dream, too, was sluggish, the link to it draining to maintain.

Bran could give himself no flesh, maintain no image, but he couldn't tell if it was because Macsen's sleep wasn't deep enough, or because of the distance and the dark, his own lack of practice.

"I'm coming. For you, love. Do you hear me – do you understand?" He sensed a smile. A flicker of the old glory that was Macsen's amusement. Then there was a jerk as his lover was woken by something stronger and more immediate than the spell of Bran's presence.

Shaking now, he closed his fist around the hilt of the sword he'd forged. Macsen was suffering, and from his own experience, he could guess how badly. Why was Winter so slow in waking around him?

Then he paused, his thoughts on hold and his whole body flush with a single truth.

Macsen was not the only one he could reach through dreams. No torment Bran could inflict on Dealla from this distance would be enough, but maybe he did not need to hurt her to help his lover.

A cold, sick shudder twitched over his skin at the thought of what he was going to try. The first time it had occurred to him as a possibility, he hadn't been able to think of anything that would make him do it, but now…

Now, he knew what was enough.

He closed his eyes to Winter and peered through mortal moonlight again. Bran sought his own power, the thread of fire connecting him to Dealla, and it was there. He didn't recognize the place where it drew him but he trusted the sight the moonlight had granted.

The sunlight was all but stripped away when he passed his presence over the fences and into the grounds of an unfamiliar church. The air stung as he slipped through it, foreign power displeased with his presence. Something stronger urged him forward.

The Summer fire was already latched into Dealla's flesh.

She had tried to hide behind a barrier that he wouldn't be able to pass, but the cold power of the moon reached her through every space big enough to let in even a single mote of light.

Hesitant still, he reached along the dim thread of fire that connected them, slid along the length of it and into the slick, coiled darkness of her mind. What he saw on the surface of her thoughts was enough to enrage him more than he had already been.

Blood on the walls. Blood on her hands. *Macsen's blood.*

There was something wrong with the image of him printed in Dealla's mind, and Bran's concern gave him away to the woman whose thoughts he had invaded. His pangs were an alien emotion manifesting in the midst of her own celebratory feelings.

Bran singed them all away with his own wrath. "*Woman, I know. What you've done, what you're trying to do. I will* undo *it.*" He felt her fury, her helplessness, and intensified his hold.

Deeper. He would go *deeper*. Beneath her surface thoughts, beneath all conscious purpose to where her brain was coruscant with firefly thoughts. He found lightning-lights in motion and tried to burn them out. But fast as he disturbed and disrupted them, there were always new sparks in the deeper darkness.

He reached out instead and took hold of the long, bright filaments controlling her movements. He grew aware of the feel of the mortal world and an echo of agony as he caused Della's hand to lift, the fingers to open and close.

So. Just as he'd thought, he could do this. There was a flicker of heat over what he could see through her eyes, but it would be enough. The woman stumbled when he made her walk, but that was the full extent of her resistance. He made her peer down and saw that her clothes were still wet with blood.

Macsen was close, then. Very close.

Bran forced Dealla out into the night, where the moonlight intensified his hold on her. Impatient, he walked her from one end of the priests' compound to the other. The men were everywhere, and women in leather armor, but no one said anything to Dealla, for which he was grateful.

Walking her body against her will was like moving a stiff puppet on threads of fire. He suspected that speech would be beyond him, and did *not* intend to linger in her flesh, to learn more than was needed for his single purpose. He wanted her hands to open the doors, her fingers to undo the locks.

If once Macsen was free of those chains, nothing she could do would be enough to protect herself from him.

Between the church and the collection of wooden buildings the priests lived in, a pair of women stood guard over a low, dark entrance. It seemed to lead to some kind of cellar. *There?*

The confirmation was in Dealla's thoughts, no matter that she tried to hide it.

The guards nodded as he compelled the woman past in silence. The farther he went into the passage, each step he pushed her through, the more Dealla's resistance increased.

Bran tightened his will and focused through the haze of heat that divided his awareness of her sight from his own closed eyes in Winter.

Blackness. Tunnel vision, and the vanishing point of a gleam of gold at the end of the way. There was a slight curve to the left, and Dealla staggered. Still Bran forced her forward, until he could finally see Macsen, spread across the wall of a cell.

He was draped in length after length of chain, locked one to the other, like an ugly mockery of the gift that Bran had given him.

But his body was... *Oh, love.* Blood and shadow.

No flesh.

Macsen turned his attention toward the door of his cell at the sound of Dealla's footsteps. There was something off in the way she approached. The muscles in her legs twitched, and her fingers grasped at the empty space in front of her as she stepped forward. The lines of her face were flat and expressionless, and she brought the scent of moonlight with her.

Bran? The thought, even as it occurred to him, was beyond his comprehension. He knew his lover had been able to influence her thoughts, her dreams, but this was something else. Dealla said nothing, no threat, no taunt, as she opened the barred door of the cell.

The Red King glared at her in silence, focused on the thread of fire that divided the pupil of her eye. She reached for the locks of his chains with spasming fingers, and for an instant Macsen tensed his whole body.

But the moment the woman had hold of them, one of the guards darted through the door, laid hands on her and tried to pull her away. "My lady. My lady!"

No words answered her, and the fingers of her queen kept reaching blindly, even when the woman fumbling at her arms called for help and brought Dealla struggling out of the cell. Her face distorted with a terrible expression of loss and desperation before she slumped forward and went limp.

When she stood straight again, there was nothing but raw loathing on her face.

"My lady?"

"You've done well. I am myself again." Dealla drew her sword and the glint of her eyes fixed on the gilt edge of the blade. "Yes. Myself again." She jerked open the cell door, and it clanged against the wall.

Macsen had only a moment to consider the change in her before there was pain. A hot stab in his gut. A sharp rip upward. She was no longer trying to kill him, just cause as much suffering as possible, and at that—

At that, she was certainly succeeding.

She had already drained him enough that keeping his own shape was almost impossible. The skin Dealla's sword was parting was no longer even skin, but merely a film of blood that flowed away from him and took strength and power with it.

But the loss of strength did not dull the sensation or his desire to kill her. Macsen filled his mind with the way she would be at the end. The way her gaze would blank and dim. Then he turned his thoughts to his lover, trying so hard to set him free.

He knew how it must have pained Bran to attach the sick twisting of Dealla's mind to his. Somehow he had made use of that for more than madness, but the witch had anticipated his attempt.

Despite himself Macsen let out a pained huff of breath when the edge of her sword whipped across his eyes. *That* was a new type of agony. The admission of his sound amused her, but her chuckle was dark and lasted only a moment.

"Is there anything in you but blood? Bloated thing. Perhaps it will only take time to kill you, drain you. *I have time.*" Too slowly, the vicious spread of her smile came into focus.

When the women dragged Dealla out of the cell, Bran was consumed by a silent howl of rage. He sped along the line of fire, through the moonlight and into his own consciousness.

Damn it. *Damn* it! Even when he could control her body, he couldn't get what he wanted from her. Bran reached out again for moonlight, seeking Macsen this time, but the sun had risen in the mortal world and the passage to his lover's dreams was denied him.

He would try again in a few minutes. There was that, at least. Time passed swiftly here. *Macsen. Love. Here there is always moonlight. I'll find you. I'll give you easier dreams, if only you sleep.*

A second time, looking through the eye of power, the wide focus of the moon, he stretched out his awareness. *Dark.* No light at all in that cell... He tried to follow the bonds between them instead, the bond of their oath, the bond of their courtship, their love.

There. A thread of his own power, faint as the first star at twilight. It was a shadow, the part of himself that belonged to Macsen now, as did all things whose blood he'd drunk. Again and again Bran tried, until the recoiling power finally found his lover asleep.

The dreams of his Red King were blank, as unformed and shapeless as they had been the last time, but now, furious, Bran drew on his own strength. He gave Macsen their bed, the softness of the furs on it, drew the heavy outlines of their bed from his own memory then laid his dream-self down to wait on it.

It wasn't long. The scent of his power, of him, were enough to bring his lover speeding toward him through the gloom. Here, in Macsen's mind, Bran saw the Red King as he saw himself, a wolf of shadow and blood. It was only when he reached the side of the bed that Macsen became more like his usual self, but the edges of his body were blurry.

"Hello, love. You said you wanted me in your dreams." He reached out and Macsen came to him, totally trusting, nuzzled Bran's throat then nipped him.

"A dream… Is this another dream?"

"Yes. Dealla took you from me, but she can't keep me away, not completely, no matter how dark, how deep she buries you." Bran ran his fingers through Macsen's hair and wished for more than the misty echo of sensation.

"I've come home, but it's not the same, not home without you. *Bastard*. Why couldn't you wait for me?" He pulled at the soft red strands wrapped around his fingers, but gently, until Macsen lifted his gaze. "Why couldn't you just *wait*?"

There was heartbreaking regret in the violet eyes he loved so much. "Because I'm greedy. Because I was stupid. Because I never thought that she— I am sorry, Bran." Macsen leaned forward, crawled up the bed and pressed his mouth to Bran's throat.

Bran was partially mollified, because the reasons were true. Even if he didn't like them, at least Macsen could admit it. "Idiot. *Bastard*. I tried to make her let you out, but see what she's done to you? The next time you say I'm impatient, I don't know what I'll do. *Something*."

"Yes, *anwylyd*. Whatever you say. But I wonder…" He licked his lips, and Bran already knew what he was going to say. "I wonder what you taste like in a dream?"

There was something disturbing about the apparent intensity of his hunger, and Bran tilted his head to the side and offered himself completely. "I don't know. You should find out."

"Yes? *Yes*…"

Chapter Ten

There was mad promise in the thin stream of light Bran's throat gave up to Macsen's teeth. Even in a dream he was sweet, but the taste was a reflection. Memory only, not brand-new bliss. A soft stream of power, the heart of the moonlight that had brought Bran to him in the first place.

When he lifted his mouth, Bran observed him too closely, peering at his face. "Something, Bran?"

"*Something*. She's hurt you, and that cell she's keeping you in is almost beyond my reach. I'm waiting for Ffion to do a little rousing. I forged a sword – you've never seen such a sword, Macsen." His eyes glittered fiercely, the most solid part of him. "No one has. I never wanted to make a weapon again, but this one is for me. Summer's King should have a sword, don't you think?"

"Summer's King? So, you took the throne at last." There was only curiosity in Macsen's question, rather than concern or upset.

"No." It had not occurred to him that he might actually *have* a high seat of his own, until Macsen mentioned it. Tighe had said it was unnecessary, but… "Not the throne, just the kingdom. Mother gave it up and now it's mine. And we're coming for you – as soon as your Winter hunters are awake enough to lead the way."

"Bran?"

The heat of his hands clung to him, as if he wasn't just a dream. "I am coming for you. I'll burn Ireland to the ground if I have to. I understand now, what you meant about love. It *is* fear, but it's more than that, Macsen. The only real bliss, the only kind that matters. The only kind that lasts."

He was glowing now, the light inside him intensified, almost fire even though there was no sun in it, and only a whisper of Summer. "We'll pay her back together for every pain she's caused you." Then he reached out. "Come here. Come to me and take from me, take me – even if it's just a dream. I've missed you."

"'Just'? What's 'just' about it? My eyes are closed, but you are still here with me." The borders of the dream fuzzed outward, until Macsen was left with only their bed and Bran. He had been dressed in white and gold, but now his clothes disappeared, leaving sun-bronzed skin and the pale flicker of lunar flame. "So eager."

"You say it like it's a surprise. I need you, even if I'm still angry with you. If you'd just *waited*. If only you hadn't left – "

Macsen ran his hands up Bran's arms, then down his spine, and kissed an extra apology onto his lips. "I only meant to find her. I never thought…but there's more to those priests than just the name."

"I know. The sword she cut me with was blessed by them."

The shadow of a smile passed across Macsen's face. "You did worse with fire. But I – "

Sharp, short words silenced his attempt at humor. "Arrogant. Impatient. *Selfish*."

Grimacing, Macsen wrapped both arms around him, kissed him again, once, twice. "Yes. All those things. I am sorry. I am. More than you know. They even stripped your gift from me."

The barest hint of a smile turned up the corners of Bran's lips. "As if I care about that. We'll find it, or I will make it for you again." Then he paused, frowning a little. "Actually, I've lost mine too. The clothes you gave me, the White Queen's frost. Dark Summer melted them off me."

Gentle, reassuring, Macsen brushed the backs of his knuckles across Bran's cheek. "Does it matter? She will make them anew, if I ask. But I shouldn't have come, and…"

"And you're a bastard who doesn't deserve to be feeling sorry for himself." But this time Bran kissed *him*, tugged him closer and murmured against his mouth. "We don't have much time, and I want you. I need you, Macsen. Please?"

He spread Bran's thighs with his knees, ran freezing hands up the length of his arms to his wrists and pinned them over his head.

In a flash that had nothing of fire about it, his lover vanished, and the bed beneath them, and the dark of the dream. Macsen groaned, blinking, until his eyes obeyed him and opened. Squinting, he glared at Dealla as she lashed him the rest of the way into consciousness with a length of chain.

He sneered at her as if the sudden renewal of agony was nothing more than an inconvenience. "Did you have to wake me, woman? I was having such a good dream." He was delighted by the way her eyes narrowed, the tiny lines at the corners deeper the more he disturbed her. "Haven't I proved that killing me is far beyond you?"

"*No.*" She spat the word at him, and the new, sudden light in her eyes showed her madness clearly. "Not yet. Perhaps not ever."

Macsen snarled at her, not defiant but mocking. The burning of her sword as she drove it through him was only familiar now. He let no agony, no torment, shake his smile. He would never deny the pain she had caused him, but still, he had no fear of her.

He closed his eyes and remembered the dream. Comforting. Soothing. Bran's mouth hot and precious under his tongue.

The memory faded in the face of reality when he opened his eyes again. Comfort might come for him as soon as he sank into the darkness, but it was comfort of the cruelest kind. *Still.* Perhaps he should share it. "Summer is on your doorstep, woman. Why aren't you running?"

Her wide-eyed stare bored into him.

For the first time in his captivity the woman was shocked silent, but it didn't last.

A flicker of terror sparked to life behind her glance. A stricken expression, that faded almost before he could enjoy it, passed across her face.

"How could you know that? How could he reach you, even here?"

Macsen observed her shock, surprised himself. Did she really think he would answer? He started to laugh and couldn't stop, even when she stabbed him again.

It was only pain, and Bran was coming.

* * * *

The woods of dark Winter were dead quiet, and the silence was more than disturbing. Aisling walked with one hand wrapped tightly around Cathán's fingers and a prickling sensation at the nape of her neck. Days now. Weeks? Months. Time, impenetrable in its passing, had only looked askance at them and continued by.

There had been moments like this before, but this time the feeling grew until Aisling couldn't take another step, froze where she was and heard a voice before she could check behind her.

"Hello, sister. I'm sorry, but I'll have to kill you if there's no good reason for you to be here."

"Saoirse!" Beside her, Cathán studied the girl, unchanged still, in silence, then took a step so that he stood with his body angled across Aisling's.

"Hmm..." Saoirse leaned forward on her toes. "Your lover smells like selkie, Aisling, but if you've come seeking refuge this is the wrong place. *I* will not protect you. Why are you here?"

A hot flush stung Aisling's cheeks and she bit her lip. "My... How could you know that he's my —?" She paused again. "'Smells like?'"

"Give me your reason, not questions!"

Inhuman impatience sparkled at the points of her sister's teeth, and Aisling swallowed. Changed, and unchanged? No. Saoirse was on the verge of terrifying. "I've come to petition the Red King, to save Ireland from the Winter."

Her sister bent over and curled in on herself with sudden, racking spasms of laughter.

She took a startled step back. "Saoirse! It's not funny! We've been to Britain, through the Avalon gate and into dark Spring. I braved the Green King and the gray of *between* to come here, and now this?"

Saoirse leaned up on her toes and pressed as close as she could to Aisling's face. "*This* is the Red Kingdom, waking and going to war to find its king. Oh, you aren't funny, you are far more than that. You should have stayed in Ireland if you wanted to *petition* him." There was a pause, as if the girl was considering whether or not to tell her something, then words that shocked. "Dealla has taken the Red King captive. Only Bran Fionnan is here now, and not for long." A slow shiver worked its way over Aisling's body as Saoirse settled onto her feet again. "Tell me, does he have fond memories of you?"

"I don't know why he would have any memories of me. He was Dealla's captive, not mine."

A low hum, neither approving nor more dangerous than any other noise, slid out of Saoirse's throat. "None is better than bad. Bran is Bran, but he is also dark Summer's King, and angry. But we are all angry, Aisling." She turned and slipped to a further shadow.

Aisling blinked.

"Hurry up, if you really want to talk to him." Saoirse sped away without another word, and Cathán caught Aisling up and helped her along behind her sister.

Cold, vicious, the Winter wind bit at her cheeks as Cathan ran faster, keeping up with Saoirse's shadow but never the girl herself. Finally, Aisling had to close her eyes to the cutting pressure of the air, and only opened them when her lover stopped short and almost dropped her, then set her on her feet.

Bran Fionnan was stepping down from a dais when Saoirse raced into the court and stopped him, but at first Aisling thought he didn't even see her. He walked straight by and only paused when Saoirse caught hold of his arm.

"Bran. Bran! It was my sister, it was Aisling and her lover. Not anyone dangerous."

Aisling was very still as Bran turned to contemplate her.

"Your other sister? I barely remember her. Why is she here?" He turned to Saoirse again.

Aisling stepped forward and gave her own answer. "I came to ask the Red King to spare Ireland the winter. Saoirse said that Dealla has him captive. I don't know why she'd do that, even if she had the power. She wants him dead."

Saoirse glared at her. "Dealla wants everyone, everything dead. Or turned into a monster. Like her." She ran her tongue over the points of her teeth.

Inhuman brightness in her sister's gaze made it easier for Aisling to talk to Bran Fionnan. He had never been mortal, was not supposed to be. "I could be of help, I think."

The cold blue of his eyes darkened from cornflower to cobalt. "Then be so. I have no time to waste on you."

"If the Red King has not been killed —"

Laughter interrupted, wild and inhuman and all the more terrifying because it once had been.

"Dealla, kill the Red King? No, she can't do that." Saoirse's voice was as eager for violence as her laughter and the pacing steps she took around them now, weightless on the snow.

Aisling shuddered. "If he's alive, I know where he's being kept." He said nothing, didn't answer her, so she repeated herself. "I know where he's being kept. There's only one place Dealla could hope to keep the Red King, even in chains."

"*Don't.*" All the humor had gone out of her sister's voice. There was something both warning and protective about the way she leaned forward over Bran's shoulder, despite the fact that she still appeared to be only eight years old.

"No, Saoirse. It's all right." The sharp expression on the girl's face retreated at Bran Fionnan's words, but it did not dissipate completely. "You, woman. If you know where he is, tell me now!"

"There's a cell beneath the church that belongs to Dealla's priest. Marcus Pontius is his name."

His mouth shaped the priest's name silently after she spoke it.

"He came from Rome, years ago. Father gave him permission for his mission, his church. Beneath it, there is a cell. The priests have hallowed that ground, and the presence of their god forbids certain kinds of intrusion. More than that, the cell is lined with gold and iron and silver."

The *sidhe* shook his head. "That wouldn't be enough. Not to hold Macsen."

Aisling shrugged. "I have only heard rumors of his power. Perhaps it would not hold him on its own. But as I meant to say, his chains are made from Summer gold, not just mortal metal. Nothing else would work so well to restrain dark Winter's King."

Bran Fionnan's stare deepened in fury as she continued.

"Dealla and those who serve her have always known the Red King's weakness. Why else do you think they dared steal *you*?" For a moment, she thought she had said too much.

Then he took a step forward. "You know the way to this place."

It was what she had wanted to avoid, above all other things. A direct confrontation with Dealla. She was such a coward. Such a coward! But she didn't want to do it. She remembered what Cathán had said to her then, his question. *'Do you want to?'* No. Not any more now than then.

She felt his silent presence behind her, protective, reassuring, even though she knew suddenly there was

nothing he would be able to do here. And her answer…
Wasn't there, hadn't there always been only one answer?
"Yes. I know the way. I'll lead you."

But the Summer King's denial was immediate. "No. You'll ride in the vanguard with me, and Saoirse will watch you. In case you decide to change your mind."

Vanguard? Change…my mind? "What are you talking about? I—" But she protested in vain.

"Summer is going to war, and I remember you. For many years I watched you, never beside Dealla but sometimes behind. Following silently, doing as much harm in your own way as she has done in hers. I'm not sure of you, woman. It's Saoirse I trust. If it wasn't for her I'd let the Winter have you."

Aisling swallowed and for a moment was unable to find a breath.

He was obviously entertained by her sudden, renewed awareness of danger. "Yes. You know what that means. But I have only the most tenuous control over them as it is, and so you will be with us. Saoirse…"

Her sister stepped forward with an expression as cold as the ice. "A wrong move, a wrong word, and I'll kill her. I don't owe her anything."

"*Saoirse.*" The new Summer King's voice was amused and only a little chiding, but Aisling found herself unsurprised.

Was he not the Red King's lover?

* * * *

Saoirse crossed into Ireland at Bran's side, one eye on her sister and the other on the swell of rising fire that was dark Summer's people enraged. They had come for the Red King, but it was their own vengeance they were taking now, one human, one huntress at a time. Yet it was not the racing flames that held her attention. The mortal lands that she had known were a new world to her, and she didn't understand why.

New starlight. Same old stars.

Forgetful of everything else — the reason she was there, her sister beside her, Bran's grief and wrath — Saoirse bent forward over the mane of her horse and slipped her toes down to the beckoning ground.

Wildness raced up through her feet. She threw herself onto her back, blinked at the sky and felt the ground breathing under her. Was it her lingering mortality that had birthed newness in the world? Was it everything about her which had changed?

Then the moment passed and the next brought only pain.

Saoirse sucked in a gasp, and that, too, was agony. Dissonant chords played in her flesh, one after another. Why, *why*?

But she knew why.

She had been warned but she had not been thinking. The air had intoxicated her with the familiar music of her abandoned mortality, and now she paid the price. The years she had lived in the Red Kingdom washed over her in a moment, while the panting laughter that had brought her down from horseback became panting screams. Hands were on her shoulders, but the touch of them was only another fragment of agony.

As suddenly as it had begun, the wrenching stopped. Her arms and legs still throbbed with uncomfortable echoes, but the feeling was fading as quickly as it had overwhelmed her.

"Saoirse! What was that?" Bran shook her, new lines of worry that he did not need etched in his face.

"Nothing, I...it was my fault. I've grown up a little. *Oh.* Maybe more than a little." She stood, but her legs felt like strangers. She was...taller. How odd. And her limbs seemed as unaccustomed to her weight as she was to the new distance between herself and the ground.

But she smiled at Bran and folded up her worries for later. "I'm sorry. I didn't mean to waste time." She swayed as she crossed the grass to her horse.

"But you aren't hurt?"

Saoirse shook her head at him. "No. I'm only shaking now, and even that is almost gone."

"Then what are we waiting for?" Fire curled into his breath as he turned and called over his shoulder. "Onward! Southward!" He turned his horse and went forward, the blue of his eyes all fire despite the rising moon.

Behind them, the mingled Summer horde passed over the land and everything burned in vengeful reflection of their new king. The stars went out, or seemed to, in a sudden flare. Summer's people stepped into a wood and the trees went up with a roar.

The blaze seared Saoirse's cheeks, scorched the wind-blown length of her hair, dried out her mouth and left her gasping even while she laughed. Dealla had survived a springless year and the worst of Winter's winds. Now, Summer had come, with a firestorm that rained from the sky like chunks of the burning sun.

* * * *

Tighe rode alone among the Summer horde, keeping to himself, but he followed when Faelan moved away with a smaller group.

He didn't want his lover to hear him, see him, didn't want to answer his questions with fear, or his concerns with suspicion. Didn't want to hear him say all the things Tighe already knew, about how dangerous it was for him to have come here...but he followed all the same.

From a distance, he watched as Faelan used lustful power to distract his victims. The Milesian women were spread thinly, not an army but a scattering of foes that seemed to rise out of the ground as the Summer host raced onward.

More of the women appeared the farther south they went, but even in the face of Summer violence, at first they seemed unable to put up any resistance to the *gancanagh* drug.

It gave Tighe a twinge, watching the easy way Faelan

smiled at them, flashed the emerald gleam of his gaze in their direction. He didn't respond to the mortals he seduced into his arms, but the eagerness didn't leave his expression, either. The blood he spilled only seemed to spur him on, up through the spreading center of the fight and past the focus of power that was Bran.

Tighe watched them both, his brother and his lover, the one unfurling to show an ever-brighter rage, the other slipping like a golden shadow from one woman to the next.

Here and there were screams that weren't human but *sidhe*. The huntresses had been trained too well for all of Summer's people or Winter's hunters to escape, and a gray smoke of witch-magic darkened the eastern landscape and blotted out the stars.

Much to his surprise, the prince caught sight of his mother moving toward the smoke, shedding fire as a snake sheds its skin. Had even she come after them?

But he turned west and saw his brother riding alone. The red light of the setting sun clung to him, and to the flickering point of his sword. The weapon shone, but not just with newness. The glittering truth of its golden edge escaped even Tighe's sight, and the other was so black it disappeared into the approaching dark.

The blade flashed and turned in Bran's hand as if it were alive, and he killed without pausing to glance at the huntresses he had slain. His brother had eyes for only one woman, who fought with a fervor that seemed more inhuman than those she faced.

So that was Bran's enemy. *Dealla*. She paced among her women ceaselessly, and where she appeared the Summer tide seemed to slow, though it did not stop, pushed back by exhortations and spells and the woman's own sword.

With her to lead them, three score or more of huntresses formed a skirmishing line. They curled inward to protect their own flanks and fought through *sidhe* wherever they met them but turned ever away from Bran. The women were moving south instead, the direction Faelan had gone.

Tighe spurred his horse after them with a sick sensation of fear that tightened into nausea as he sped along. He had been afraid of seeing Faelan give in to his own nature, fearful of the lustful desire of a *gancanagh* for mortal love. It had never occurred to him to be afraid for Faelan's life.

But Tighe heard the echo of his lover's words, all the angry danger that had been waiting in them, and knew that had been foolish. *Six of his brothers have been killed.* Trembling now, he scanned through the fire, across the field, into a burning wood. Where had the *gancanagh* gone?

For the first time in his life Tighe was grateful for his sight. The familiar mirror of Faelan's essence stood out like a blazing star and he focused on that to the exclusion of everything else.

The sword in his lover's hands was dark with blood, and there was strain on his face as the Milesian women pressed forward. Faelan and his brothers had not been made for this kind of fighting, and the women were no longer taking notice of the *gancanagh* poison that tainted the air. Bloodlust had overcome all other urges.

He galloped forward, and the prince's gaze caught on the point of a single spear, on the intentions in one woman's eyes. She was focused on his lover as a wolf might focus on its prey and Faelan was facing in the wrong direction.

"Faelan! Watch out!" Tighe spurred his horse, overcome by terror. He couldn't lose him now, not now, when he hadn't had a chance to tell him the truth, to say— But his cry had turned Faelan's face toward him, not his danger. Tighe swore and leaned forward over his horse's neck, drew his sword and tightened his fingers around the hilt.

He barely got between them in time.

The blade in the prince's hand struck true and sent up a red spray of blood from the woman's severed throat, but the thrust that saved his lover completed the forbidden connection. A cold tremor sped up his fingers from the hilt of his sword as the link was made between Tighe and mortal ground. The moment fractured into many pieces, each one distilled.

How glad he was to have saved the one he loved. How glad to have breathed mortal air again. To have seen the world again, so unlike the *sidhe* forests he'd grown accustomed to. This world…doomed in the moment of its first blossoming, and still so beautiful.

He had time for only that moment. He saw the spear drop from the dead woman's fingers at the same time that he saw Faelan was truly safe, but his strength was already fading. The feeling that had started at the tips of his fingers lanced his sword hand with pain and raced up his arm.

Tighe tumbled from horseback, the reins like lead weights instead of leather in his grasp. Faelan was there to catch him as he fell, an inch from the ground, but it was too late for that.

The air, so clean just a moment before, was thick as soup now. The prince couldn't feel his hands, his legs, Faelan's fingers touching his face. It wasn't fair, it wasn't fair, it wasn't *fair*. But if it had to be one of them, if it had to be—

This is better.

The green eyes over him were blurred with tears. Tighe couldn't hear what Faelan was saying but it didn't matter. He knew. He tried to reach up, to brush the dampness away, but his fingers were already dust. The Summer power that had sustained him for six hundred years was ripped from him, left as only a shadow, which scurried away from his consciousness and took half of what he was with it.

What is left?

But he was silence then, stretched across the world as thin as light.

* * * *

Bran heard Faelan's scream of grief through the roar of his own heartbeat and the blaze of fire, and only then realized both that his brother had come with them and that he had fallen.

The echo of Faelan's loss came through the subtle threads of dark Summer, and Bran slammed shut the internal door. It was enough to see that pain on the *gancanagh's* face. He didn't need to feel it, too.

Lava coursed through his veins regardless. Beauty raced him across the battlefield, and when he reached Faelan, Bran slipped from his horse and stood very still, watching his brother fall apart.

Dead, he was...dead. Disbelief had no place in the moment, but all the same he still couldn't believe it. Behind him, his mother washed up on a wave of ashes. Turning, Bran could barely take in her presence. When had she come? Why? Why had either of them come here? But she made a little gasp, that was all, and the blaze of her presence went dim.

Summer's new king didn't understand her muted response, her failure to react. Dealla had stolen his lover and now his brother was *dead*. Didn't his mother care? Wouldn't she take vengeance even now? What kind of queen, what kind of Summer was she, that she could just stand there, silent?

Faelan tried to put his lover's body down, but even as he moved Tighe was dust. Horror and agony and love twisted Faelan's face. On his hands. On his clothes, on his *face*. Dust. All that was left.

Bran could only stare. He wanted to howl the way Macsen howled, but he was no wolf. His throat ached with tightness anyway. How much did he have to sacrifice?

His youth, his innocence, his love. His brother. The only real friend he'd had, the only one he had been able to trust. Even if that trust had cost him, it had only been a little. Barely enough to count. And now?

Even once he had found Macsen, brought him home again, that wouldn't bring Tighe back. "My. *Brother!*" His roar stunned the battlefield into silence.

In a moment, with one movement, Bran ripped through the nearest group of women as a hot wind then turned and faced them again. The sword in his hand slashed and thrust on its own, *flick-flick-flick*, one edge glutted with blood and the point aflame.

The corpses he left behind him smoldered in the field, and Bran heard Dealla calling for retreat.

Without her to lead them, the line she had organized fell apart. Wanting only her death now, Bran's blade hummed with killing intentions, but he couldn't see her through the red haze of his own wrath. Huntresses scattered at his approach, left the bodies of their dead behind and fled into the distance.

Bran sent fire after them, then returned to stand between his mother and Faelan. He could think of nothing to say in the face of so much grief. The subtle beauty of Faelan's features had all been dissolved and leached away.

"For me. Why would you? Tighe…" It was almost silent, a groan from some deep place so private Bran squeezed his eyes shut, as if that could block out the sound.

Tears came then, and a second echo of agony that Bran knew was his mother's. He couldn't lift his eyes to her, couldn't breathe.

"My son." She reached out as if she would touch what was left of his brother, then stopped. "Bran." Soft. An open wound, her expression, her voice. She was no longer his mother any more than the dust staining Faelan's arms was his brother. "It's enough, now. Go find your lover and go home. It is enough now. It is…enough."

Quiet, the fire inside her ash and embers, Bran felt her fading out of the mortal world, returning to the sacred gate. All she left behind was the sound of a soft summer rain on the charred autumn leaves.

Bran was very still, staring at the dust and the ground it had fallen upon, until the silence was broken by Faelan.

"Leave us."

'Us'. That the word was a lie was anguish all its own. Bran hesitated, and shards of fierceness gathered in Faelan's face.

"*Leave us!* Just—"

Bran turned away in silence and mounted his horse. In the distance, the forest was aflame. The change in the moon had painted everything bloody, darkened even the whitest, hottest fire to a visible shade of red.

While he stood there, Saoirse came up beside him, Aisling still in tow, and for a moment seemed as if she would question him. Had she not seen? Did she not *know*?

But Saoirse wanted answers from her sister, not from him. "Where now?"

He heard a little gasp as Aisling was shaken, and the answer came trembling out of the woman's throat. "S-south. You only need follow the road."

Bran gazed down at her, saw the light gone out of his own eyes as they reflected in hers, and turned away again. "We will go another way. It's time we made a deeper stir in the lands that have waited for our return."

"A deeper…stir?" Saoirse sounded only curious, but he couldn't bring himself to smile even for her benefit.

Instead he shouted loud enough for many to hear him. "Go to the wells. Lay the fire on the stones. Wake the trees, ride the bears out of the wood, the wolves into battle. Raise the tide with a charm of nine and call all those sleeping out of the sea. This isn't a game, this is *war*!" He bit his lip until he tasted blood. "What she wanted."

Bran sent his rage through the embers, the black, cracked soil, deep into the bare ashen ground. *Wake. Do you hear me? Wake. Wake up.*

They were all listening now, everything and everyone listening. There was stirring in the stones, in the hills, heads lifting and eyes opening as the ancient gateways swung wide. A rumble grew at the coast where the tide of Amergin had washed up on the shore, where Milesians had taken the beating heart of the land when they refused to retreat from it.

Come home. Here, come here. Come home, come here!

Home. Not a hidden kingdom, not a secret place, not another world. Here, in the land where the first of them had been born, where they had spent their days hallowing groves and pools and circles of stone. Here, where the fire had been waiting, all this time.

Wake. Up!

Bran felt the land and its spirits moving, searing and alive, but his own personal awareness of dark Summer's heart was deeper. It had been sleeping in him, waiting in him, as it had been a thousand years sleeping in his kingdom. Now it burned in his throat, in his hands, in his eyes, flowing out of him in steady pulses.

The rhythm of it drove his feelings to mad conflagration, every beat the same. Macsen and his brother, his brother and his lover. *Love. Fire. Lost.*

Speeding now, he hurtled across the wild to worn knees of sloping stone eroded by a thousand years of wilderness and weather. He knew them as dark Summer knew them — slow moving, slow thinking, with the sturdy loyalty of the earth's own bones.

Giants, asleep.

"*Awaken*. Your king is made new and comes to call on you again." There was a trembling in the silence, as he had felt at a distance. "*Awaken!*" This time he said it with fire in his breath.

The ground beneath his feet rose up, alive.

Flakes of shale and slate became wide, black-glinting pupils, large enough to fall into. Great eyes blinked with the sound of a stone door slamming shut. "My king."

"My king!" The rumble of their voices was deep as the sea, and when they bowed to him, went to one knee in unison, the Summer horde behind him shivered as the ground shook.

"What would you have of us, my king? This world is not as it was, and yet..."

Up, and up, and up he had to lift his gaze to meet their eyes. "You are awake, and Summer is once more at war with Milesians."

Their chuckles shook the ground, and the charcoal husks

of the trees Bran had left burning behind him toppled over. "So, the world is as it was even in its difference."

The Summer King ignored the giant's humor. "I would have you walk the wilderness once more. Take up your ancient residences—build again the circles of stone, the steadfast gateways."

Grumbling, growling, shaking the earth again, the first to wake peered at him closely. "And the mortals?"

Bran took a step toward his horse and shrugged. "Slay what you wish. Keep what you wish. The only one who matters to me, I will make sure is safe. The only one who must die for me, I will make certain is slain."

The isle rumbled beneath his feet as the giants rose to their full height and bowed to him once more, then moved off in the direction of the burning woods. Turning, Bran confronted the shadow of awe on Saoirse's face and terror on her sister's.

"Now. South. It will be midnight soon, and I won't leave Macsen even as long as that." He mounted his horse and galloped past them both, with such speed that it felt as though he was propelled by black and burning wings. He didn't know if they belonged to the horse beneath him or beat at his own back, but the distinction no longer mattered. His whole being had been reduced to one searing point of focus.

Macsen. I'm coming.

Chapter Eleven

Aisling was caught up in the screaming front line of the Summer host as they drove south from where the giants made the coast tremble. An inferno rushed with them, and beings she saw only as a hurricane of light.

Shattered shadows followed in the Summer King's train, as ash behind embers. Each howl framed new echoes of murderous intent. Aisling shivered at the sound of them. She had long before lost track of Cathán in the blaze, and beside her, Saoirse listened with her eyes closed and her head tilted, nodding slowly as if in time with music her sister could not hear.

They charged together, sometimes walking, sometimes riding, sometimes caught up in some other movement that was the flow of *sidhe* around them, but always at Bran Fionnan's side. Aisling's feet sped on their own through the mist, compelled — or maybe she was imagining it, losing track of her own reality as this tide of furious beings poured around her.

Too quickly, they came to the dark grounds of the church where she remembered it all beginning again. Here, more than anywhere else, their world had been broken, and for what? Pride? A promise to a dead man. If she met Vortigern in the world to come she'd slit his throat and pray for a dozen more chances to kill him.

But now...

Aisling searched for priests and found none. She wasn't eager to pass the gate of this place a second time, but the churchyard was deserted. The silence was less than reassuring.

"This is the place. This place…" Aisling glanced up, startled, but the Summer King said nothing else. She found herself falling in behind him as he strode across the open space inside the fences, toward the long tunnel that led beneath the earth.

She didn't ask how he knew where it was, or why Bran Fionnan had needed her guidance when he was so obviously familiar with where he was going. His expression kept her silent.

Saoirse laid the gold-capped tip of her staff near Aisling's throat as they came to the black chamber at the end of the tunnel. The princess brought a hand to her mouth and swallowed hard. The smell of rust stung her nose, more than metallic.

Intense nausea gripped her with sharp talons, clawed up out of her gut, into her throat, burned in the back of her mouth. It brought her almost to her knees. The last time she had been down here it had smelled of must and mud, damp wet odors brought up by the digging and the laying of bars. Now it smelled of nothing but blood.

Saoirse didn't seem to care. Her sister was stiff-bodied behind her, the staff at Aisling's throat not even trembling. Fire blazed into life then, not torchlight but the sourceless illumination of the Summer King's power. It threw the underground chamber into shadowed relief.

In the cell, strapped to the wall with chains that barely showed their gold beneath rusty stains, something with a red sheen lifted in their direction, a jerk of motion that was restrained.

There wasn't another.

Bran rushed forward the moment he saw Macsen and stopped as if struck. Summer's King or not, either the cell or the blessing or both were enough to repel him. He reached out for the bars but couldn't even grasp them.

He stared through the spaces between them at a bound and bloody shadow. "*Macsen.*"

There wasn't a clink or a rustle.

Bran intensified the fire but couldn't see the glint of Macsen's eyes or a gleam off the gold of his chains. All of it was covered over with blood. Again, he stepped forward. Again, he was stopped where he was.

He'd come so close, he was right here, and now he would be stopped by *this*? All of Summer at war behind him, the Red Kingdom run wild, stripping the world, and here he was, kept from his goal by a handful of slender bars.

Bran felt the low ebb of his power as midnight approached, and his hope with it. If he couldn't breach that barrier now… Perhaps there was one other option. He didn't trust the woman, but the girl had aided him before.

"Saoirse. Can you?"

She took a half dozen steps forward before she stopped just as he had, with the strangest expression on her face. Pleasure, and a glorying kind of joy…and aggravated distress. "I can't, I *can't*. I'm sorry, Bran."

"You've changed too much." Bran experienced a shift in his own power. The fire he'd summoned to the surface was fading, flickering out a little at a time, from blazing sun to dimness. It occurred to him then that he wasn't only *sidhe*.

His father was *fomoire*. Wild spirit, wild power. Could the god of these priests keep the moonlight out? He did not think so.

"Macsen. *I'm coming.*" He took a breath and let the sunlight go.

Behind him, Aisling cried out, but he ignored her. Saoirse squinted then covered her eyes with her hands and turned away from him.

The radiance grew to a blazing pressure that rebounded from the walls and heated his skin. It illuminated the horror of Macsen's broken body, the bloody chains and the walls of his cell, painted old crimson and peeling brown.

Reality rippled as Bran summoned the moonlight.

It intensified inside him until he was transparent with lunar glow. He took a step forward, then another, closed his hand first on the bars, then on the locked door. The metal made his fingers smoke, burning the cold, sharp way that ice could burn. He didn't care.

He rattled the door then scowled. *The key.* But he strained, pulled with inhuman strength, and the mechanism gave with a shriek of twisting metal. The barrier rippled behind the broken door, a soap-bubble surface that connected the bars with each other and the door as he pulled it open. But the barrier of that blessing wasn't enough to keep out the moonlight, just like he'd thought.

Bran passed through it as through a thin skin of water.

He rushed forward and the chains came open at just a touch, Summer gold obedient to Summer's King. Macsen fell into his arms and Bran let out a long, shuddering breath.

"Br..." It was only a hint of sound, but Bran went to his knees, cradling his lover against his chest.

The Red King wore neither a wolf's nor a man's shape. There was nothing of flesh left of him. It was blood Bran was holding, blood and feeling with a name, Winter's heart torn open and spilled into his arms.

"I'm here. *I'm here.* It's all right now. I'll get you out and — "

"*Bran.*" Shadow and bubbling blood whispered his name at him. "Bran..."

Something glistening with a shape that might once have been fingers reached for his cheek, then subsided.

"What did she do to you? What did she...? *Love. What did she do to you?*"

The fire began to flicker on his skin again. Only Macsen's eyes remained in the broken shadow of his face, but there was no glow in them and the vivid amethyst was blank and gray.

Careful of his burden, Bran stood and tried to step through the door again, but this time there was more than just resistance. The air dragged at him, tried to keep him in the cell. The barrier was all around him, pulsing at him, defying his intentions, but he refused to let it hold him. This place had been made to confine the *sidhe*, not what he was, more than and slightly other.

One step at a time, Bran forced his way out of the cell and into the dark chamber beyond. He didn't pause for Saoirse or her sister, but walked straight past them and up into the night.

* * * *

Something both less and more than sight let Macsen see the shift in Bran's features when he passed through the barrier. He trailed motes of moon-dust, his flesh a constellation with a coal-black heart of embers.

The flames returned to his lover as Bran carried him away from his blood-soaked cell, out of the dark of the underground and into the clean black of the night.

He had only two fragments of sensation that mattered. One was Bran, close to him, holding him, fire against his body, burning beneath the skin he no longer possessed. The other was hunger, greater than the first morning he'd woken into the world.

Macsen was *starving*. Every drop of blood that had been spilled useless on the ground or splashed on the walls had left its own void behind. It was agony like nothing he had ever known, but he didn't have the strength to lift his gaze, couldn't sharpen shadow into fangs to pierce Bran's gleaming skin.

"Saoirse. Your knife."

The girl was beside Bran in an instant, the blade in her hand, and Bran took it from her, tipped his head to the right and slit the thin skin of his own throat.

The pain of it showed on his face, and that hurt Macsen. How necessary it was hurt worse. To watch him, when Macsen couldn't even—but the rich flow beckoned him, pulled at him. He heard his own whimper and felt Bran's hands moving him, gathering him up and pressing him nearer.

The blood was everything then.

"Slowly. *Macsen*. Slow—*ah. Yes*. Everything you need, I'll give it to you. You know that. But slowly. *Ah*. Oh, love."

Macsen growled against his throat and sucked harder.

Bran didn't complain but he winced, ran his hands through Macsen's hair and tugged gently. "Slowly. *Love*. Please? For me."

Another growl. The dull *blip* of Bran's power intensified, filtered through the inner flood of shadow. It fed Macsen strength with every drop he consumed, and his lover's hot presence was more intense than ever.

He could almost sense Bran's thoughts, send his own along the intense thread of magic and feelings that connected them. Emotions sharpened until Macsen felt them as his own. *Waiting*. Fearless waiting, need and desire...love. *Love*. And behind those feelings...

Macsen. Bastard. Idiot.

He did not deny it. But he sent his own passion, the intensity of his own feelings, and heard Bran's voice close by his ear. "I know. I know everything you can't say, you don't have to—I know. Bastard, what you do to me. Oh, but I love you anyway. And I warned you—and I can't believe you—*bastard*. I love you. Just drink. As much as you want, as much as you need."

After a time, Macsen opened his eyes, and Bran's murmur filtered into his awareness. He wasn't asking him to stop, or for more, just muttering of love and Macsen's name. As if those two things alone were enough to keep him whole while the blood did its work within him.

When he finally pulled away from the narrow wound in Bran's throat, there was breath in him again, and strength enough to give himself shape. It was a struggle, but when he had form he rested his head on his lover's shoulder and closed his eyes. "You came for me."

Bran tightened both arms around him reflexively. "I shouldn't have, you bastard, you *bastard*. Do you know how much I...what I—?" He took a long, shuddering breath and blew it out. "What did she *do* to you?"

"Nothing I didn't ask for. She took me by surprise but she couldn't kill me. I think after a while it pained her more than me to try." But he had no strength for laughter, not yet. There was blood on his lips still and he knew it was his own, until Bran leaned forward and spilled another mouthful of fire across his tongue.

Macsen sucked at the lip Bran had bitten and felt another gasping trickle of strength flow into him. The taste of his lover was too hot, but the blood lost its fire soon enough, began to fill the well within him from which he could draw Winter power.

It gave him strength enough to sit up and kiss Bran properly. Enough to kiss him *thank you* and *I'm sorry*, but not yet enough for *when you want to kill you're so beautiful I could die*. When he leaned up, Bran turned his head and exposed the line of his throat again, that beautiful curve. This time Macsen bit deep and drank of the Summer flood.

Flowers…rich fruit…madness. If this much of Bran had made him drunk before, then this time it was madness.

One sip, one mouthful, one drop at a time, he swallowed back his thirst then stayed where he was, licking at the wound because it was there, because he couldn't help himself. Why waste it, even if it was too much for him to take, too much for Bran to give?

But maybe not. Maybe too much doesn't mean anything to him anymore.

The flavor grew to fire again, too scorching to leave a taste on Macsen's scalded tongue, but he needed it too much for that to matter. He felt himself on the verge of falling into ash, going to embers and disintegrating into the glory of it before the flavor went soft. Cool. Subtle on his tongue, trembling moonlight.

It was a weightless rush that put out the fire inside him. Macsen opened his eyes to see that Bran was pale as moon-dust, giving him the night.

"You should have said it was too much for you." There was the faintest hint of a pant in Bran's voice, a suggestion of strain at the corners of his eyes. He was restraining himself so well, *so well*, when he was usually begging by now.

Slowly, still licking at the stained, torn flesh of Bran's throat, Macsen lifted his mouth away. "Too much? Never too much, not of you. I'll never get enough, instead."

"You... Are you better already?"

Macsen smiled. Bran was so surprised, so worried, so pleased, he hated to disappoint him. "No. But I will be, and this is a better shape than what you found me in, isn't it?" He sucked at Bran's throat again, set him shivering, gasping.

"Love your shape."

Furious, hot as blood, sweet then bitter with fading terror, Bran's mouth was on his in a moment, kissing him breathless. He felt Bran's desire in his kiss, stronger now than it had been.

My Summer son is Summer's King. But he couldn't give Bran what he wanted, what he needed. Not yet. "Bran, I'm so tired. So empty. I'm sorry."

He felt Bran's effort, the way he restrained himself, how he shivered when Macsen bent for another, more gentle kiss. Suddenly the moonlight was outside him, as it was inside him, lulling as it urged him to rest.

"*Sleep.*" It was not the voice he knew, but it was Bran all the same. Everything he was, all sounds, all silences. "*Go on. I'll be here.*"

Macsen sank away from the memory of pain. Somewhere within him the wolf of Winter waited, its wail still locked in the cage of his throat. That howl... When it came to him, he would bleed the world.

But for now, the dark Winter sleep.

* * * *

The sight of the Red King filled Saoirse with both pain and wrath. He had saved her, but now he had suffered her fate. She knew from her own experience what Dealla's torture was like.

Immortal that he was, he wouldn't die. Perhaps he couldn't. But the soft, unformed curling of blood and darkness that Bran had carried out of that cell in his arms, shadow slick as oil, closed eyes dissolving to a fracture of blood...

Whatever he had suffered, whatever Dealla had done to him, it had drained him of a thousand years of power. Had left the Red King, Hunter that he was, without even the strength to bite Bran himself. Saoirse wanted vengeance. For herself, and for the pair of lovers who protected her. She owed them for saving her, for everything they had done for her.

"How do I help you both?" But the murmur went unnoticed, and she stepped away from Bran and his sleeping burden.

She knew things they did not. She could list them in her head. The ways a huntress was trained, the spells that were remembered, the magic she'd heard of and the weapons Dealla was proficient with. The secret places, the hiding places, the fighting places, all of them marked on maps in times when Saoirse had been trusted.

Where was close, that Dealla would think she could go to ground? She had left her prisoner behind in the only place he could be contained, and she had gone...where? Saoirse's skin tingled with the nearness of the truth. She was the handmaid of Winter, and she would wash away the stain of the blood she carried.

Breathe. In. Out. In. Through the still dark of the Irish night, she could track Dealla by her scent. *Near.* A thick, strong trail that began in the hallowed ground of the church behind her and wove into the trees.

The burned branches whispered in thin, throbbing voices that curled their way into her ears and stayed there. *This way. This way.* But she didn't need their guidance, and even when there was silence, Saoirse followed a pathless track.

The lessons she had learned served her well. As a shadow, she passed over the ground, disturbed no leaf, no twig, no bracken, made nothing but the nightly noises without which all calm was disturbed. She tightened her hands on the warm, smooth wood of her staff, and the gold was hot to the touch, breathing with her.

She felt Bran's power, moving with her but separate. Awake, as she was awake. Angry and seeking, as she was seeking. *There*. Human heartbeats. The sounds were loud in the stillness as she stalked through the trees, and the scent and sound together marked out her prey. *Dealla. I see you.*

The other mortals near her sister meant nothing. Summer fire and Winter hunters had done their work well, and whatever companions Dealla had kept would be no help to her now. Shadow to shadow, Saoirse slipped forward to the edge of a low, smokeless fire. Her sister was on her knees in the circle of light, binding strips of cloth around the wounds of one of her women.

Narrow gashes stood out on Dealla's arms. There were rents in her armor, made not by blades but by claws or talons. Some of the blood on her hands was red, and some of it black, and some of it glittering. Not human but *sidhe*.

The heat of the staff in Saoirse's hand increased, and she tightened her fist around it.

Would Dealla remember her, recognize her? Aisling's reactions said she would, even now that she was further changed.

She stepped into the firelight and Dealla's eye narrowed, then widened as they inspected each other. Saoirse smiled just to show off her pointed teeth. Dealla had been a pretty woman once, with features too sharp to be called beautiful. Now, more than the scars or the missing eye, madness and hate had made her ugly.

"Hello, *sister*. Which is it I'm seeing on your face? That you are surprised to see me alive, or surprised to see me *here*?"

There was a moment of silence that continued. The gazes

of dying women turned toward Saoirse and stayed focused on her while the scent of blood grew stronger and the muted lights of their eyes went out in pairs.

Dealla's mouth turned up, thin and red and wet—she'd bitten her lip. "I knew you weren't dead, but I did not expect you to dare show your face in Ireland again, or to me. And why have you come, hmm? Little traitor. Did I not teach you already that your youth does not protect you, nor your relation to me? Actions like yours have consequences, *sister.*"

The scars on Saoirse's back throbbed for a moment with remembered pain. "Consequences? Oh, yes, let's talk about consequences." An enormous bubble of laughter rose thick in Saoirse's throat, but she denied it.

"There is no Red King to protect you now. Isn't that why you're here?"

Saoirse shrugged and took another step forward. "I came because I am meant to have come. You won't understand. Don't try, and don't worry yet. I won't kill you. I could, but I can't, so instead I will bring you to them. Then you can worry." She leaned forward on her toes, as if confiding a secret. "He's already free, you know. The Red King. I will bring you to him...and to Bran."

Laughing at the expression on Dealla's face, Saoirse reached up a hand and patted her sister's unblemished cheek then slashed the skin with fingernails sharp as claws before she drew back.

"Are you going to fight me? Use your training against me, your magic?" Saoirse held out the staff in her hand and it pulled the campfire from its coals. The gold went brighter, the staff almost too hot for her to hold.

Dealla scowled down at her, reaching for her sword before she even answered. "Fight you? Why would I need to fight you? Do you think that little display frightens me, when I have spent my life hunting the real darkness?"

A slash of her blade cut off the end of her words, but Saoirse did not parry. She had seen her sister at practice a hundred, a thousand times. Instead she dodged, stepped through the darkness to Dealla's side and tapped her shoulder.

Her sister was dangerous as a cornered beast was dangerous, or any broken thing, but Saoirse had too much faith in the shadows to be afraid. "Is this how you took Macsen Cadoc? Did he hesitate at the scent of you, the sound of you? You aren't even prey anymore, Dealla." She smirked and knew it was the Red King's expression on her face. "A rabbit can run."

"You! I'll—"

Saoirse lifted her staff with a sigh and caught Dealla behind the ear with one gleaming, gold-capped end. Her sister dropped straight to the ground and there was a low outcry from Dealla's companions. Three out of eight were still breathing, and she narrowed her eyes.

"I will do you the kindness, though you don't deserve it." One at a time, Saoirse slit their throats, then dragged Dealla through the shadows the way she had come. She slipped to one side as she came to the clearing where Bran had brought the Red King.

He was himself again, at least in seeming, red hair and bright eyes and sharp fangs. But even for what she had brought, Saoirse knew better than to interrupt them when his teeth were buried in Bran. She watched the Summer King shift between the familiar golden features she knew and silver transparency, then peered down at Dealla, still unconscious, and settled on the ground to wait.

It was comfortable enough here, and she liked feeling the slow return of Winter power as the Red King drank.

* * * *

Macsen woke after only a few hours, as hungry as he had ever been, but everything he wanted was here with him. It would not, could not be enough—this flood he couldn't drink to its conclusion.

He didn't care.

With one hand, he reached up and pulled Bran's hair, pinned him to the tree he had sat them beneath and gorged on Summer. But the gnawing feeling inside him wouldn't abate no matter how much Bran submitted.

Macsen needed to hunt and to kill, but he already had the perfect prey. He had promised Bran a gift, and even if Midsummer was long past, Samhain was near. The delicate coolness of the autumn air murmured of its approach.

When he finally pulled his mouth away from Bran's throat, he relished the warm straining of his lover's body in his arms. "Do you know what I would like, *anwylyd*? To hunt and then to go home with you, to bed with you. To make up for the time we've lost."

Bran kissed him deep and slowly, held him against his mouth and shivered when Macsen licked away the blood from his lips. He relaxed his grip as he stood, but Bran rose with him anyway, kept hold of Macsen's waist and tugged him close enough to lay his cheek on Macsen's back.

"Are you not going to let me go?"

"No. Or hasn't the lesson sunk in yet? Do you know what it did to me, seeing you like that?" Bran's grip tightened. "And even now I can feel it. How much she took from you. You need more than my blood, Macsen."

"Would this help?" They turned together at the sound of Saoirse's voice, thin through the trees. "I found her. I *caught* her. But she isn't mine, so I saved her for you."

Macsen's confusion became a smirk as the girl dragged Dealla into the clearing by the length of her hair. He looked the woman over and detected the odor of power as well as her own blood. His people had found her, but they had heeded his mark on her, his claim of her life.

"Are you going to kill her, Bran?"

He laughed. "No, Saoirse. She's my present. Macsen will...ah, but is she a gift from you now, too?"

Macsen frowned over Bran's shoulder. "My *hunt*. My prey, but it would have been no contest, I suppose. Not without surprise on her side, and those chains."

The girl blinked at him. "Surprise?"

"Those priests she had with her." He turned his glance toward Bran, rubbed his cheek against the softness of golden hair. "I drank one, and the taste of him was not completely mortal. They have something of their god inside them, his blood in their blood. He was not pleased to have that power taken by me. It took time, to make it mine."

He scowled, shook his head and glared down at the woman. "Too much time. But what should I do, Bran?"

Fire. An eruption of heat crawled over him, held him quietly, a cocoon of searing radiance. The blaze of Bran's anger hadn't abated at all. "Drink her up. For me — for you — but do it. Kill her and be done with it."

Macsen stroked Bran's cheek with his knuckles. "You worried for me so, and it was my own fault. But you need not."

"No? But that's what you've said from the beginning, and it's the closest thing to a lie you've ever told me."

"Bran…"

There was no brightness in the blue of his eyes. Not even violent morning, only shades of night. "I'll do it if you don't. I'll even enjoy it, but I am not the one who needs her blood."

Macsen was amused. *Valravn.* "I only want to wait long enough for her to wake. For her to know."

Emotions shifted and flickered on Bran's face, then finally settled somewhere enticing, between rage and amusement. "I don't mind that. I *want* that. But, Macsen, I just remembered. You didn't like the taste of her father… What if she's worse?"

Frowning, the Red King considered this. It was true. Mac Briuin had tasted like rust and greed. "It doesn't matter." He turned his stare from Bran to Dealla and shrugged. "I'm *hungry.*"

Chapter Twelve

Pain.

There was throbbing in the back of Dealla's head, a lump when she lifted her hand to it. Soft voices murmured near her, lower than a whisper, and all the words blurred together. She opened her eyes slowly and squinted. Dark. No fire... No, there wouldn't be, would there?

The memory of her last conscious moment throbbed as much as her head. She clenched her teeth even though that intensified the pain. *Saoirse*. Worse than a traitor. Where had the little bitch brought her?

A power passed over her then that jerked her to her feet.

"Macsen Cadoc! So, you haven't had enough of me?" But there was no fear in his face when she turned and saw him already behind her. The too-pale skin was streaked with blood, but he was as she remembered him from her nightmares, not the ooze of broken flesh she'd left behind in that cell.

Scorching agony in the empty socket of her eye brought her once more to her knees. She screamed, but the Red King's chuckle was more piercing.

"Leave something for me, Bran, won't you? Didn't I tell you? I'm hungry."

The words meant almost nothing through Dealla's pain, but the answer the Red King received from Bran Fionnan made an impression. "I won't kill her, I'm only playing. Do what you want, love."

Dealla tried to breathe, but a coil of fire tightened around her throat like a molten steel thread.

"Bran..." In scolding tones, the Red King chastised his lover.

"I said I was only playing. I owe her more than this. For what she did to you there's no repayment." The Summer *sidhe* eyed her and Dealla was fixed into stillness by the weight of his stare.

On the edge of unconsciousness, fighting through a red haze, Dealla felt the stranglehold relax enough that she could suck in a coughing breath. The pain did not retreat. Her blisters had blistered, and still the fire circled the surface of her skin, more than a warning, less than a wound. Dealla thought of the thousands of deaths, the fire in gray fields that had once grown green and gold. All that, and the bastard said he was *playing*?

For the first time, she felt the fear that the Red King had promised her, nicking at the corners of her mind. Macsen Cadoc was an unnatural beast, it couldn't be denied. He rode at the head of the Wild Hunt, had slain mortals for centuries, maybe longer. Like the wild wolf, his was a ferocious hunger.

She would have thwarted him if she were able, killed him if she could. But the one they'd stolen—Bran Fionnan was the worse monster.

Silently, blind with agony, she cursed the day she'd first heard him say his name. She could have killed him then.

Could have. Then. His voice was still in her head, the smile still on his face, pure and untroubled. She shuddered. His glare was printed in her mind even when she closed her eyes, a floating blue stare that was another source of fire.

"*Wait.*" It was breathless, Bran Fionnan's voice directed not at her but at the Red King.

A certain strain of effort tightened his features, and she felt the flickering internal motion which she had grown to dread. It meant his power was approaching, the burning of his presence inside her brain.

"Wait, love. I want to give her to you." The smile on Bran Fionnan's face gained vindictive edges. The fire intensified until Dealla wondered why the blood in her veins wasn't boiling, breaking through her skin. The light in his eyes was cruel, so rich with killing desire she was trapped by it.

The Red King prowled behind her. "You can do that?"

"*Shh.* Watch."

Dealla had no doubts. She inhabited flesh that no longer belonged to her. There would be no escaping this.

"Bran." The Red King's voice was husky and she would have shuddered at the sound of it if she could. Instead a low, terrible noise squealed out of her before the bastard pinched it off and left her with only the knowledge of what was happening.

"Do you want her throat? Her wrist first?"

"*Wrist first.*" Hungry, barely words, Macsen Cadoc growled the sentence that damned her.

Dealla watched her arm lifting, watched as she was forced to make an offering of herself. Her heart pounded, speeding the flow of the blood he wanted from her. A blank nausea folded and unfolded in the pit of her stomach. She was made to press her own flesh taut against his mouth, and it was only then that he bit her.

Pain filtered out from the wound but it was secondary to the horror of the moment.

She had sought this death for herself, bought it and made full payment. She had fractured the world in pursuit of it, not seeing what she did. She swallowed the truth as the Red King swallowed her blood and hoped he found it as bitter.

When he lifted his mouth from her wrist, the sharp pain was reduced to a throbbing ache. Then she was made to lift her bitten wrist, bring her hand up and move the leather of her armor and the wool of her tunic away from her throat.

"There? Just there?" The Red King looked straight past her at Bran Fionnan. There was a hunger on the king's face that was reflected in the snapping of the fire around her.

Cold fingers closed deliberately around her throat, and for a moment it was relief. Then his teeth were icy needles in her throat. Mouthful after mouthful, he pulled the life from her. The thud of her heartbeat was loud in her ears, and louder—

It stopped. Dealla came out of her own death into a world that shone with a forgotten light. A layer of magic coated all things. The ground, the *sidhe* who had killed her, her own body and the charcoal husks of the trees.

The moon was rising and it pulled at her, summoned her toward the feeling of an open gate. But between her and the light there was a black silhouette with blacker eyes. It constrained her. The path of the moonlight was waiting, but the shadow shook his head and she knew that gate was closed for her.

A hand reached out and there was no escaping it. "I know you, woman. I have been waiting for you. You are the one who killed her, my wise-unwanted partner, my lover's daughter. *You* began the undoing of it all, began the end, though even now it is not over. A life is not enough, nor a death, but those are all you have, so I am taking them."

Those eyes, onyx, dark as the poured ink of all the words that might have come to her, told Dealla that denial would be meaningless. "It is not payment. It is not equal. But for my hawk, I am now and will always be *selfish*."

The dark hands were colder than the death that had taken her. His fingers were tight around her throat, like the talons of a bird of prey. Then she was cast aside, and a gleam of something silver snapped at her heels.

Shears with pearly edges cut the insubstantial boundaries of her soul apart. *Snip*. The noise was loud, as the moonlight was loud. *Snip*. A memory. What had it been?

Snip. Once, she had been…had been…

Snip.

* * * *

Bran was content to stay where he was now that Dealla was dead and the priests and huntresses who had served her were slain or had fled. The last remnants of her influence remained to be dealt with, but the time he had spent with Macsen sleeping in his arms had made him aware of a greater problem.

The weapons Dealla had used to forge her chains had been used in the war against Winter, made to fight the Red King. Now, having been fastened onto their enemy, the ghost of that power didn't want to let go.

Summer King or not, he wasn't yet sure how to make it do so, but for now Bran refused to go anywhere without his lover. He wouldn't leave Macsen behind, even under the watch of all his people. Instead he sent *them* out across Ireland, seeking Aisling – and, because Macsen had worried about it, the tunic that Dealla's women had stripped from him.

It was Saoirse who found her sister first, who brought the new Queen of Ireland to Summer's King. Aisling knelt before him while he stood with Macsen in his arms. Considering, Bran studied her for a long minute.

Then he turned and gestured with his head for her to stand. "Walk with me." He spoke very quietly.

There was questioning in her eyes, but she followed him in silence. Her gaze drifted again and again to Macsen's face.

Bran led Aisling all the way out of the wood, to the broken fence of the church grounds, but he didn't enter. "Go down into that – cell. Bring up those chains."

She sucked in a deep breath, but his glare was enough to keep her silent, and though she moved reluctantly, she obeyed. Four times she went down into the dark and came up with her arms straining under the weight of gold. The fifth time she brought up only a handful and put the last of the chains on the ground outside the fence with the rest.

Bran glared at those coils, glittering with seeming innocence as Macsen's blood burned under the sun. Then he turned away, laid his lover in the grass behind him and returned to the chains with empty hands.

"I have had *enough* of these." Bran made the links into light, undid the mortal shaping of so many days with a single touch of fire. The chains sharpened under his fingers, regained their original shapes and hummed with an eagerness that only sickened him. The blood they wanted was too precious to him.

But the silence of the weapons that had been remade under his hands was disobedient, and the echo of their true desires remained. He did not look at Aisling as he spoke. "Bury them. Bury *all* of them."

The young queen kept her gaze on the edges glinting up at them. "I'll see to it myself."

Bran turned to Macsen, still sleeping where he had set him in the grass, and left her standing alone before a pile of broken weapons. Then he paused. "Oh...and Aisling?"

"Yes, my lord?"

"Every weapon I ever made, all those things your sister did not include in her *chains*. Those, too, must be buried. They were never meant for mortals, but I don't want them."

There was only one answer she could give him, and Bran didn't wait to hear it. Instead he rushed away from her and imprinted his promise on the land beneath his feet as he departed.

It was time to go home.

* * * *

Kas watched the last piece of the woman's soul go to dust on the tongues of Autumn's people, as he had watched gleaming scissors taking the bits and pieces of her ever farther apart. Madness and identity. Knowledge and memory. It took longer than he had thought it would, such was the weight of loathing in her, the will to destroy.

But he sensed no change in the tide that was coming, unless it was an increase in momentum. That was not what he wanted, nor his hawk, either. Merlin was committed to finding a way out, but that was like him. To choose a fight that couldn't be won and stand his ground regardless.

Kas saw only his own reflection in the days to come. Nothing, no birth, no kingdom, that would last through the coming storm.

Only death.

"My king. You remain. Why?" The voice and the words it spoke were both equally unexpected.

"It is my choice to do so." He met beetle-black eyes as dark and glittering as his own and tilted his head to one side, contemplating. "Why ask questions of me?'

"They come from that woman. The many things she plotted were within her, and now they are within us. It is a bitter taste, and it was your choice to share it. Will you now be king of more than just the Rite of Spring and the silence after?"

Kas let his eyes drift shut as he considered, but he could think of no reason why that should be so. "No. I accepted a throne. A crown. A certain responsibility that was more than just my own duties. For him, I accepted it. For Merlin. Nothing else and nothing more."

Shadow bowed out of shadow. In a moment, Kas was alone as he had thought he wanted to be, but in the absence of other duties, other thoughts, he desired…

He waited, through long habit, for the twinge of pain at the thought of his lover. *Merlin.* But there was no reason for pain any longer. No reason for him to only think of the things he wanted when he could have them.

Where would his hawk be? Playing games in the world of real things, wasting time with humans still? Kas wandered the shadow of the mortal autumn and tasted Summer commingled with the harvest scents.

How strange, that even as it seemed like the dissolution of everything important was coming nearer, empty spaces were being filled.

The Wild Hunt had been freed. Summer had its dark king again. Kas had Merlin…and Merlin had him. Perhaps it was only that tendency of things to return to a semblance of their beginning at their end.

Perhaps it was hope.

Quickly now, motivated as much by his thoughts as by

desire, Kas passed through the autumn woods, over the narrow sea and into Britain.

He made his way north, toward the Avalon Gate. There, for the first time in more than five thousand years, Kas caught the scent of immortal apples coming from Spring, but there wasn't so much as a whisper of the one he was seeking.

That scent... Power was leeching into the world with it. The way had been open, recently, but now it was shut and still the Spring was leaking through. As if the gate they had built was beginning to fall apart.

And where was Merlin?

* * * *

Myrddin found a chill, quiet comfort as he ventured into dark Winter. It reminded him of his earliest years, before there had been eight kingdoms, or even a green land between the mortal world and Annwn.

Before Kas, when he had slept through the winter like the rest of the world's green things.

Perhaps it was wrong that he should find the Hunter's kingdom the most nostalgic, but he was in no danger here, even from Macsen. The Red King knew better than to hunt him, as Myrddin knew better than to test that with too much conviction. A slick, cold wind blasted his cheeks, and he turned in the direction it had come from.

"Not wanted, hmm? But I have a purpose and I won't be thwarted." Myrddin eyed the frozen glow of the sky as the dark between the stars intensified. The moon blinked, allowed a snapping moment of blackness, then brightened overhead, peering at him. He sensed amusement and a hint of irritation, and behind that, lust that had nothing to do with him.

It was very much dark Summer, and he shook his head, smiling a little while he passed through the wood. Neither Macsen nor his lover were waiting for him when he entered the Winter court, though he'd felt their awareness of his approach. If anything, they seemed ready to ignore him.

A slow, red trickle was visible through the white silk of the Summer King's tunic in half a dozen places. Blood flowed from his throat down to his shoulder, and from his wrist into Macsen's mouth. His thighs were parted over the Red King's lap, and the slow, eager rocking of his body gave away his pleasure more than the soft sounds he made.

Bran leaned forward and murmured something into his lover's ear. Myrddin couldn't hear what he said and didn't care. He was impatient with their love play. Had he not already told them he had come for a reason?

He climbed the steps to the dais, dropped himself into the empty seat that stood by Macsen's and rested his head on his hand. They still paid him no attention at all.

In a certain way, it interested him to watch the two of them together. Such a contrast, and yet the one was as much as a killer as the other. In their own way, each of them burned.

But he had only another moment to observe before Macsen lifted his mouth and Bran turned to meet Myrddin's eyes. "You're in my seat."

Myrddin shrugged and leaned back. "So? I won't trade with you, keep that one."

Bran laughed at him, a flash of white teeth as he dropped his head back onto his shoulders, and Macsen was on him in the next instant, teeth deep in the exposed curve of his throat. The Summer King only sighed, a low moan of exquisite pleasure.

"It's strange, watching that be enjoyable for you." Bran glanced at him again then closed his eyes. His lips were parted, his breathing languorous. Fire rolled away from his skin, wrapped over his lover and flowed down the steps.

Myrddin watched it moving, until a gleam of extra brightness caught his eye. For a moment, he was utterly still, staring at the hilt of a weapon he had seen a thousand times yet never before in waking life.

The Sword!

Then he took a breath and let it out slowly. One thing at a time — and it was not yet time for that. "I did not come here just to watch Macsen drink his dinner."

For some reason, that was enough to make both of them break into low chuckles, but it didn't shift Bran out of the Red King's lap. Instead he hitched himself forward again, as if to make a point of it, and Macsen settled both arms around his waist.

"If you have a reason to be here, make short work of it. I have better things to do, and to listen to." The Red King's voice was sharper than usual.

Myrddin sensed the sudden attention of the whole court on him and wondered what he'd entered into that he did not understand. Had there been some trouble that he'd missed?

He shrugged and smiled as openly as he could. "I thought it might interest you to know that there's a sweet sampler spread out near Dimilioc. The High King's army has surrounded a fort there, a lord who has rebelled against him. That lord, Gorlois…it occurred to me he's just your type. Hard and cold. The salt of the North Sea is in his blood."

Macsen seemed only a little interested, and slid his hands from Bran's hips up into his hair. "So? The hunt rides where it will, where *I* will, and it doesn't sound like there's much hunting to be done there. *An army*. Men jammed together, waiting in some old Roman fort." His voice was almost scornful. "And I suppose you came to tell me this out of the goodness of your heart."

Myrddin could not repress a fleeting grin, but he regretted it as Macsen's features shifted into angry, wolfish lines. "No. I did not say that. But it would make things easier if you —"

"I am not *here* to make things *easier*. Not for you."

Bran was laughing again, silently, his shoulders shaking, his lips turned up. A glint came to the corners of his eyes as he turned them in Myrddin's direction. He lifted an eyebrow. "Something, Summer King?"

"You've no idea how to tempt him, do you? I could do it for you…"

"Bran!"

"What?" A failure of innocence printed itself on Bran's face, a quirk of eyebrows and matching grin. "I want something more than racing around behind you this year. I have plans of my own, Hunter mine."

"Mmm…" Macsen hummed his disinterest—or Myrddin thought it was. But the Red King dropped his hands to Bran's hips, squeezed the soft curve of his buttocks then lifted his lover off his lap. "You want to watch me hunt this lord, this army?"

Bran shrugged as he stood. "That, specifically, doesn't matter." His eyes were focused on Myrddin. "But aren't you going to ask what our Green King is planning? I know what I want and why, and you know you'll give it to me anyway." Macsen growled at him, and Bran ignored it. "But *this* one…"

Myrddin frowned at him. 'Our Green King'. So mocking. He had forgotten what it was like to deal with a Summer King. Bran Fionnan's predecessor had been just like this. Perhaps not as bad, but then Bran was young and new to his power…and in love with the Red King. "You're just like him. Mac Gréine, the last Summer King."

"I wouldn't know." The fire burned brighter in Bran's face as he spoke, gold and white-hot,

Myrddin saw no change in his expression. Derisive. Amused. And yet…

"I have had very little to do with you. The most I've seen of you is at your Rite, but the more often I meet you, the more I think you dangerous. Why do you want Macsen to kill this lord for you? Why not go to your own lover?" As Bran's eyes narrowed, the lapping waves of fire that had run down the stairs returned to cling to his skin. "Well?"

Myrddin made an impatient noise. "Isn't it the Red King who should be—?" But he didn't even finish the question.

New layers of irritation were writ large on Macsen's face. "Very well. I've made a bargain for a boy, and so for a kingdom, though its current king does not yet know it. My half of the price requires a death. I could kill this mortal myself. One man, lord or not. But it's not in my nature, and the Red King rides soon, regardless."

Hard eyes blinked at Myrddin slowly from Bran's face, the blue turned steel-gray. His voice, too, was hard as he questioned. "And what else? The important part, the truth that's missing? Why not the Black King?"

Myrddin restrained his wince and shrugged. "Because I don't want him to know. He'll make more fuss than you have. And as to something else...there is. But I don't remember it. Not yet. Maybe I never saw it to remember. Either way, my only intention is a lasting peace."

"*Ha.*" The sound was breathless and bitter. "What you mean is, you are fool enough to believe mortals are capable of leaving well enough alone."

Myrddin considered the Red King, standing now with his back to them and gazing down at the dim, cool dance of his court. "Nothing to say, Macsen?"

"No. Perhaps I will go to this army, this lord. Perhaps I will cross the water to Ireland or the continent and ride, instead. I have no reason to listen to you." He glanced over his shoulder. "If that was all you came for, why are you still here?"

Myrddin shrugged. "I don't mind it here. It...reminds me of someone."

Neither of them asked who. Neither was paying attention to him anymore. Something intense had pulled them together, resuming whatever lustful play he had interrupted.

"You should go now." A girl, not more than twelve years old, pulled at his sleeve — but no. No, *girl* wasn't quite right. She was less than half human, and not by birth, though perhaps by blood.

"Should I? And who are you to tell me so?"

Shrugging, she looked him up and down. "Their handmaid. And Kas is my friend – that should mean something to you."

It did. Myrddin was surprised and didn't try to hide it. "Kas? A friend of my Kas." He chuckled and shook his head. "You're something strange then, aren't you?"

The girl only shrugged again. "You are more strange than I."

"Oh?"

"I've seen the way Kas loves you and then kills you. But you don't die." A curious smile crossed her face. "And you're here, aren't you? Trying to get the Red King to do what you want."

Myrddin found himself less than amused. "What I want. Yes, and what would you know about that?"

She eyed him with an equal lack of humor. "Everything you just said, and more of mortals than you. Did you know it was the High King of Britain who set the family I was born to against the Red King?"

"This is a new High King."

"There are always new kings. That doesn't mean anything is different." She was very serious, this handmaid, but Myrddin thought she understood very little of what he wanted, and perhaps less of peace.

"I have already made my bargain. Do you know what rebellion means to a king? And over a woman, no less." He allowed himself a flicker of a smile. "Or perhaps that is always the reason. A woman, a treasure...some lust."

"I was a princess, once." The girl took a step back from him. "All these things end badly enough on their own, but worse when there's interference from something *other*. Or is it only humans who tell those stories anymore?"

There was a hard edge in her face, something that reminded him of Macsen, but the moment Myrddin turned to the Red King to confirm his thought, the girl slipped away.

"You should listen to her."

Myrddin met Macsen's eyes as he spoke, but it was a dry, serious statement, without a hint of irony in it. "Is that all the answer I get?"

"What you get is whatever you decide. Even if I agreed now, in the end I would do whatever I pleased in the moment. I already said as much." He went down the steps to his court slowly, bringing Bran with him, and as easily as that the subject was dismissed.

Myrddin shook his head and turned away from the wild music as the Red King passed through its midst. He made his way out of Winter as swiftly and easily as he had come, more annoyed than he had any right to be.

His visit, his offer, *was* a manipulation, an imposition. It was for his sake, and not for Macsen's at all. And there was Bran Fionnan...dark Summer's King now. He paused for a moment at the edge of Winter and gazed over his shoulder. *The Sword*. He had been seeing it for so long, how could he fail to recognize it, even sheathed, only the hilt visible?

The pieces were beginning to come together, though slowly. Uther would have his woman. A boy would be born. The Summer King had forged a sword, and maybe...

But no. He wouldn't give his hopes words yet. Not even within himself.

Chapter Thirteen

Macsen relaxed as the aggravation of his unexpected guest vanished into the distance, but not completely. Bran was very still beside him, his smile faded. He was returning to the subdued version of himself he had been ever since they had come home.

The Red King's hunger had kept Bran distracted for a time, the play of lust and blood, but facing him now, Macsen knew he couldn't beguile him again. Myrddin had been too much of an interruption, had made Bran *think* too much, and those thoughts had turned dark again.

Macsen knew why.

Saoirse had told him what his rescue had cost, though Bran had said nothing. He seemed intent on keeping his brother's death to himself. Because Bran had kept quiet, Macsen, too, had not mentioned it, but now he thought that had been a mistake.

He touched Bran's shoulder and the blond shivered. "You've said nothing, but I know you feel the loss of your brother. How do I soothe you?"

"What? You—" He stopped, turned and leaned his forehead on Macsen's chest. "Saoirse told you, I suppose."

"Don't fault her." He drew his hands down Bran's back, then up again to hold his shoulders. "Haven't I told you I want to know if you are hurting? And you have been."

But Bran shook his head. "You're wrong, or not right, anyway. It's not that I feel loss, it's that I don't. I should be grieving for him, but I *can't.*" His eyes flashed with fury. "I keep wondering why he followed me, why he came into the mortal world when there was no need. And then I think he was a fool, and then I think…better him than you."

Something between a sob and a chuckle spilled out of his mouth, and Bran closed his eyes. "It's wrong. I know it's wrong, but he did it to himself! He could have just *stayed*—I would have kept track of Faelan if he'd asked. I would've…"

His anger was soft and tender, an open wound. Macsen stroked the curve of his cheek. "*Valravn*. My Summer king. Don't punish yourself. What do you gain by that? Is it wrong that you love me, that you would choose not to lose me?" Bran stayed silent.

Macsen embraced him tightly. "Your brother made that choice for his lover. Saoirse told me *everything*. He picked his own path, and that is not your fault."

There was the slightest relaxation in Bran's shoulders, and Macsen pressed his point. "The first time I saw him I knew he was one of those who would find death. He stood between your mother and me once, did you know that? If he was a fool, well…it had nothing to do with you. Perhaps he had always been one."

He pulled back enough to touch his fingers to Bran's lips. "It is *not* your fault."

Snow drifted over them in a sudden gust and clung to Bran's curls, to the pale thickness of his lashes. He blinked it away irritably and rubbed his cheek against Macsen's chest. "I know that. I know that, but I'm so angry! I should have hit him harder that time, maybe that would have knocked some sense into him."

He let out a shuddering breath, and Macsen saw a hot sheen in his eyes before he closed them again. "He was my brother, but I barely knew him. I barely… Why couldn't he just have *thrown* the damn sword?"

Macsen frowned and tugged at Bran's hair. The snow intensified, whipped up around them, aggravated by his distress. "Are you thinking mortal thoughts again, *Valravn*? Is that your trouble? If you want to yell at Tighe, go visit his shade. He was half-mortal, half of him should be left. I'll bring you myself across the black border of my brother's country."

"Mac...sen?"

He raised his eyebrows, curious. "You dreamed it with me, don't you remember? My brother's kingdom is Annwn. Mortals call it the Land of the Dead."

Bran blinked at him, sighed, then frowned. "This is like Talaith, isn't it? I could go there, but I can't bring him home with me."

"No. Not like Talaith. But it's true that you can't bring him out of Annwn. Not without giving up more than anyone can afford to lose, and I won't allow that." He tightened his grip on Bran's waist, bent over him and kissed the corner of his mouth. "I will do anything to comfort you. Anything, but I won't let you give yourself up."

Bran sighed and traced Macsen's spine with the tips of his fingers. The music behind them intensified, a rising thrill of flutes above panting drums. "I wouldn't do that anyway. I just have to accept it, that's all. I'm sorry I've been—"

But Macsen bent and kissed his apology away, then stood very straight and looked over his shoulder. For the second time since Myrddin had left, the weight of someone's heavy attention had fallen on him.

This time the sensation was accompanied by a glint of eyes in the green shadow of his daughter's trees, and he frowned toward them.

"Macsen?"

"I am being summoned again. All the way to the orchard." There was the faintest hint of an upturn in the corners of Bran's lips. He kissed Bran again and asked, "Will you do something for me, *anwylyd*?"

"And what is that?" The soft murmur of his answer was full of heat, and it was with the greatest reluctance that Macsen let him go.

"Help Saoirse choose my sacrifice. It's almost time." The dilation of Bran's pupils, the shift in his countenance from angry sadness to anticipation, the way he nodded and pressed his lips to Macsen's mouth were all an improvement.

He watched Bran cross the courtyard and reappear with the girl hanging on his arm, then cut across the snow to stand by his daughter. Morgan was very still, waiting under the leaves.

Though she watched him intently, she only spoke when he stopped. "Father."

Macsen wasn't sure whether to scowl or smirk at her. "You want something? I've felt your attention on me since Myrddin left."

"No, it is you who wants something. And if it is since the Green King departed, is it something you want of me that is to do with him?" Morgan fixed him with the fathomless black stare she had inherited from her mother. "You might be avoiding your other thoughts and desires in favor of your lover, but I can do no such thing."

Ah. Her words allowed him to settle on the smirk. "Is that so? You never mentioned that you had given me your allegiance in that way."

A thin sort of irritation spread across her face and he sensed the thought as if she had spoken it. *Idiot.* "You are my father, but you have never needed anything of me before now. Why would I have spoken?"

He leaned across and peered into her eyes as she reached up into the branches. "What will you do with the apples?"

Morgan shrugged as if the question made perfect sense. "Eat them. Put some aside for those who want them. Your lover, the girl he favors. Not even all your hunters like to live on blood alone."

"Their loss. But now that it comes to it…" He took a breath that was too heavy with sweet fragrances then stepped back into the snow. "There is something I want you to do. A task, a game, treat it as you will, but I am curious." He closed his eyes, then opened them slowly and focused on her. "Leave your orchard behind. Go into the mortal world, into Britain, to the court of the Pendragon king. Find out what's happening there, what Myrddin is *really* doing."

Macsen bared his teeth at the wind and licked his lips of strange flavors before he returned his gaze to his daughter. "I don't trust his motives. I don't trust *him*."

The line of her brow was smooth and untroubled, even as the corners of her mouth grew tight. "Do you have strength enough to challenge the Green King, Father?"

But he chuckled at her. Was she a fool? "I? Challenge him? To what purpose? I need nothing to do with Spring." He shook his head as he turned away. "No. I only want to know why he would seek to direct my hunt for his own purpose."

"What you ask will take much longer than for Samhain to come and go."

Macsen stopped where he was. "Oh, yes. But I want you there all the same. Myrddin said just enough about his plans to interest me."

She peered at him, a flicker of curiosity in her eyes. "What did he say?"

"That there was a lord of men with his warriors, just to my taste." Unease twitched down his spine. "And something… about the future."

She shook her head, and he sensed her amusement in the gesture. "A whole army, Father? Will that be enough to sate you?"

Macsen laughed, almost to himself. "Well…perhaps."

A soft, musing sigh escaped her. "And I am to go to the High King of Britain."

"Go, and watch, and wait. I have a feeling there will be something of interest there soon enough."

The rustle of her footsteps flowed away from him, then paused near the border of the orchard. "What if there isn't?"

Careless, Macsen shrugged, tilting his head to stare at the snow-clouded sky. "They're mortals, Morgan. I'm sure you can find some entertainment. Perhaps Myrddin will even enjoy the play."

She laughed to herself all the way across the court.

Macsen stayed where he was, scowling. "I will *not* be

used." Still. Salt and the sea. There weren't many hours left before Samhain, and despite his desire to deny Myrddin for the sake of being difficult, he could think of no better place to go.

He was as hungry now as he had been since the moment Bran had let him out of those chains.

Despite what Macsen had thought, the hours before the sacrifice passed slowly. Most years, he was not so restless for it, but he paced across the dais until Saoirse appeared with a girl in her hands that could have been her twin.

Bran stood with his arms folded, smirking up at him, and Macsen wondered what point he was missing, why this girl had been the one his lover had chosen. But his people were waiting, and he drank down the whole of the girl's life in one great draught that was not enough to make his thirst abate the slightest bit.

Not with the pulse of his court gone rabid with need. Not with Bran staring at him like that, desire mirrored in his eyes, and his whole flesh breathing lunar dust. He wanted to chase after the light that Bran could be, wanted to take the most precious — the most precious...

In a flash, he understood.

His sacrifice had been Saoirse's twin just to taunt him. The girl's life was another that he couldn't take, just like Bran's.

He darted down the stairs to stand at his lover's side. "I am going to hunt *you*. After everything else." The smooth, pale curve of Bran's throat beckoned to him, the ruby potential of the thick vein there hiding his lover's heartbeat and the promise of ecstasy.

"Because you can't kill me? Can only drink me up a little at a time? Never take it all. Never make the feast you want out of me." Bran tilted his head, and Macsen knew for certain he was doing it on purpose.

The ghost of a smirk haunted Bran's face for no more than a moment. "Don't you wish I was like Myrddin?"

"What? *No.*"

Bran leaned toward him. "But then you could kill me

again and again."

A rich groan slid out of Macsen's throat. He couldn't help it. It hurt to look at him and know he never could… oh, it hurt *so good*. "Brat." It was only a breath. "What a temptation. If I could only…ah, but I can't. You'll torture me forever instead."

"Yes." The smirk returned. "But don't you have a hunt to be leading, Red King?"

Macsen breathed in one slow, shuddering breath, rich with the embers of Bran's desire. His mouth watered for it, but he restrained himself, took a step away, and swept his gaze over the waiting Winter multitude, the dark Summer glitter here and there amidst the chill.

"Tonight, we run with guests. Shall we show them what the Wild Hunt means?"

A low, throbbing growl rolled out of every throat. Every mouth stretched in a smile that showed shining teeth.

"Then we run. Now. *Now*."

Macsen led the way over the river, across the snowy plain, through the spiral tunnel of the ancient barrow and out under the glare of mortal stars. The sky pulsed at him. The moon blinked in greeting and he felt Bran's power rising beside him, blinking back. "Come with me. All night long your eyes have been telling me you want to watch me kill."

He took Bran's hand and pulled him along the coast. There were little houses on the way, tiny villages, but the noise of a thousand heartbeats drew Macsen inland. The scent rising there was one that he knew well. Killing instinct, killing desire. The army of men Myrddin had told him about was just as tempting as Macsen had thought they would be.

Some of the scents were enough to make him thirst for them, even knowing that he would be bending to another's purpose. Not just one man, but many. So much rich warrior's blood, arrayed like a savory introduction.

He howled then heard Bran laughing beside him and the answer of his hunters wailing across the wind.

In the fracture of the moonlight a tide of screams was

rising. Doors opened out of nowhere, from darkness to blackness, shadow to utter night. The leaves and low grass rustling were footsteps and trailing ends of *sidhe* silk, soft as mist.

The wind was full of motes of power, the moonlight full of dust. The shades of hounds loped fanged and frothing then vanished into the grass. Dimilioc was encroached upon by gloom that pooled between the stars and dripped down to the ground.

Pulse quickening, Macsen shifted as he stalked forward, became fog and shadow, red as living blood. Bran moved with him, becoming elemental light that carried a primal hunger all its own. The sound of beating wings was beneath the luminance of it, and for the first time Macsen understood what the White Queen's word really meant.

Valravn.

Macsen raced the light. Now and then his shadow overlapped with the flicker of it, a sudden caress with the impact of a falling star.

Ahead of him was the flicker of mortal fire. The Red King slipped from single men, alone with their weapons at watch, into a fort that hummed with bloody promise. There were voices, frantic and harried beneath the noise of the hunt. The fortress was in chaos, men caught between the army behind them and the shrieks of their comrades giving up their lives to Winter's host.

But the curls of moonlight wrapped around Macsen urged him to the left now. He indulged Bran's desire and let his lover lead him into a narrow hut lit by guttering torchlight. Inside, there was a young man, barely bearded. He had brown eyes, black with fear, and he gripped the hilt of the sword at his waist as he turned, staring at the now-open door behind him.

Shadow poured in from outside, pushing densely at the firelight. The youth seemed mesmerized by it, but a scream from outside shook him back a full step.

"*A good choice, Bran. He will be a good first kill. Sweet before the salt.*" The whisper passed audibly out of the shadows and this new prey turned again, blade out, gaze probing the dark corners.

"Who's there? Show yourself!"

Macsen gave himself eyes and teeth and fingers. He stroked the boy's soft hair with tender touches, teased the beating of his warrior heart to a fever pitch. While he did so, the current of the moonlight gained fire. Hungry though Macsen was, Bran's desire enticed him to draw out the kill. He let shadow coalesce into something like the shape of himself, rolled forward on the fog and held the boy still with just a glance.

"A handsome thing, aren't you? But you are prey now, nothing more." Macsen reached one hand to the soft fuzz at the boy's chin, gripped his face and turned it slowly, until the tendons of his neck stood out.

The mortal took a deep breath then relaxed, as if unaware this was the end of his everything. Macsen nipped him once, enough to set the blood flowing. He licked it up with a lazy stroke of tongue then did it again.

The scent of Summer was as strong in the air as the scent of blood, and it was having its effect. "See what you've done, Bran? He *wants* me. Right now, I think he even wants his own death." Macsen leaned in again and bit deeper this time, sucked at the surface veins and stole bright mouthfuls that only inspired his hunger.

The mortal in his arms was dazed now, dizzy eyes staring at him, not without comprehension but without care. He lay back in Macsen's arms as if he were a lover. "Bran, can you make him beg me for it? Do you think...?" The hut grew full of the scent of green things, damp heat and dark Summer.

Lust.

Flames slipped along the floor and lit the canvas, adding a smoky crackle to the noise of screams from outside and the soft, panting breath of the youth in Macsen's grasp. He shivered, moaned. "What are you? What are you — *oh*, what are you *doing* to me?" He lifted his hips as he spoke, opened his mouth but no longer for words.

There was new tension in his muscles, a desperate flush of heat in the tips of his ears and the curve of his cheekbones, as if the life in him knew its time was up. His cock was rigid, hot with blood. He pressed closer to Macsen's body and rutted against him with hints of agony in the sweet motion.

Macsen admired his flush, the red on the boy's mouth from where he'd bitten his own lip, a scarlet smear of temptation. He would not *kiss* him, but he drew his tongue over the bloodstain, one delicate stroke.

It brought out a cry he'd never expected to hear from any prey of his but Bran.

The fire was at their feet now, licking up their calves. Macsen felt Summer power in it, an intensifying touch of lust. The youth in his arms let out another moan, then another, as if unaware he was being burned. His blood was sweeter and sweeter.

Everything smelled like Bran. The fire was hands, moving on Macsen's skin, teasing the tips of his nipples and the aching length of his cock. Moonglow lips pressed to his throat, and he almost turned to see if there was enough of Bran in the fire for him to kiss.

The boy groaned the moment Macsen lifted his mouth, then started to beg. "Please, please. Don't *stop*."

Macsen peered into his eyes, saw fire reflected there and dense moonlight. "We are killing you. I am going to drink you up. Did you not hear?" He knew the boy had heard, but nothing in him pulled away. The whole of his body was one pulse of desire.

"*Don't stop*."

The thirst roared up in him, alive, and before Macsen was aware of it he was drinking down the life in his arms, one aching mouthful after another. The boy shuddered through his release as the Red King swallowed, pressed his throbbing erection into Macsen's side and groaned out a breath. Then he shook while the fire started to burn him, one type of heat rushing away and the other smoldering ever hotter.

By then it was too late, and Macsen dropped him as the body turned to ash. His gaze was already focused on Bran. A craving was intensifying in the *presence* of him, until even the moonlight burned with a white-hot flame. "Soon, *Valravn*. I will give you everything you need."

But for now, he slid into the dark. Tonight was for blood, and he intended to gorge himself on men.

Midnight was nearly past, his teeth aching with the lives he'd taken, when Macsen found the one he knew Myrddin wanted dead. The smoke of flickering fires and the smells of leather and unwashed bodies were as strong in the air as the scents of blood and the wilderness.

None of those things were enough to distract him from the odor of this single man, which was to him as rich as a feast. What was his name? Myrddin had told him. *Gorlois*. Yes. The air around this Gorlois was savory, and the promise of it pulled Macsen along on an ever-shortening tether.

It had been a long time since he had feasted on a man like this one. Since the days before the long Summer war had turned to the embers of peace. Since before the Romans had come, and thinned out the blood of his prey. For a moment more, he considered the man, then came forward out of the shadow. He took on flesh and felt Bran still lingering around him, moonlight with the imprint of an embrace.

Before Macsen could move or speak, the mortal challenged him. "Stop there! Who are you?"

Macsen laughed and the man's features tightened.

"You are not one of my men."

"No, not one of your men."

Gorlois dropped his right hand to the hilt of his sword. "Name yourself and your allegiance!"

"Would you know me if I did?"

The hard eyes grew sterner and Macsen was amused to see such an attempt at a glare. "You will answer to me or to my sword!"

The Red King stepped forward into the full of the moon and firelight. He knew what the man would see now. Skin too pale against the night, hair too red under a silver crown of fangs – eyes too lively, too violet.

Inhuman.

The acknowledgment crossed Gorlois' face with a fleeting moment of terror that he seemed to extinguish through sheer force of will. Macsen caught hold of its fleeing edges with his smile. "What do you know, mortal? I am Macsen Cadoc, but that is meaningless to you. Now that I am here all that will pass between us is the simplest of nature's transactions."

Wary now, Gorlois tightened his hand on the hilt of his sword. "What transaction is that?"

"Blood, spilled for a hunter."

Awareness flickered in the man's eyes, but Macsen's hands were already at his throat. He sank in his teeth and sucked up the truth of his own words with hungry satisfaction.

* * * *

Myrddin found Uther outside his camp, listening to the wild noises of Winter's hunt with trepidation on his face. He might be a Christian king, but his fear of the old powers was obvious. Myrddin stood silent beside him for nearly two full minutes before he turned and noticed.

"You –"

"Me. Yes. If you are ready, it is time." Myrddin was impatient. The night was dark, and there was a deadly weight at the edge of the horizon. Already howls encircled the fort where Gorlois and his men sat at arms.

"I have been hearing –" Uncertainty had thinned out Uther's voice.

"Better not to hear. As it is better not to think of it."

For once, Uther surprised him. "Fool boy! I know the Wild Hunt, I know what it means that tonight is Samhain, and what the price might be for me to leave my men here. I am no pagan, but I know. *Fool*. My men—"

"Will sleep. And so not be harmed, unless I find some reason to change my mind. The Red King rides at my will this year, Pendragon." It was a lie, and a terrible one, but he saw no way that it could hurt him.

Uther drew back. "At *your* will. More and more I wonder if I should ever have sought you out. Son of no man. Whose child are you, then?"

Myrddin allowed a grin on his face, let it spread wider than it should have. "You may wonder. But it is too late for questions, Pendragon. Is now the time to be second guessing your desire? Or is that desire less now than it was?" He said it only because he knew it wasn't so. The fact of Uther's presence, here on this most dangerous night, proved it to him.

The High King could have stepped away from this Ygraine before there was blood spilled over her. Not a war, he'd said. Not over a woman. Yet there she was in her tower, and here Uther was with his army, waiting for whatever magic he expected Myrddin to work on his behalf. Something that would slip him up Tintagel's narrow stair and into Ygraine's bed.

Restless agitation was in Uther's eyes behind the scowl he had chosen as his answer to Myrddin's questions. Myrddin only listened to the howls coming from the distance.

More than just the Red Kingdom's hunters were on the move tonight. It was as if the seasons were bleeding one into another. Winter and Summer power were no longer separate, but Myrddin couldn't tell if that was a new symptom of the trouble he feared or just an inevitable thing, considering the way Macsen was with his lover.

He turned and held out a hand. "Come with me."

Starlight and torchlight flickered over the lines of Uther's face. The eagerness of his lust, once deferred, coursed into the foreground. Suddenly it seemed as though there was too much red in the curve of his cheeks. Too much skeletal promise beneath that florid touch of heat.

Death, or death? The thought came to Myrddin abruptly, stuck in his brain somewhere between his hopes for the future and his awareness of the mortality of the man in front of him.

"You are taking me to her?"

"Yes. Come with me." He did not intend to say it again.

Uther took an impatient step and Myrddin took his arm in an iron grip. The man opened his mouth to protest, then shut it as the ground spun beneath them, too fast for him to process. His face grew gray, and he squeezed his eyes shut while Myrddin laughed.

Uther shook when they stopped, and let out a startled breath as he gaped at their new surroundings. "How...?"

Myrddin had brought them to the coast. The sea was a sheet of shale in the darkness, and Tintagel stood tall and threatening beside them, a bastion of stone throwing its shadow onto the water. No army could have crossed the narrow bridge that led from the castle rim on the mainland to the tower proper. No legion could have penetrated the guarded doors, the narrow stairs, to bring Uther to his woman...but Myrddin could do it.

"You will ask that question too many times, if you allow yourself the wonder. Now, be still." The Green King had made sure to see Gorlois for himself, and now he built the illusion of the man's image over the body of the High King. Uther's red hair grew darker now, gray marked with white as with streaks of salt.

Myrddin gave him thinner cheeks, thinner lips, firmed his cheekbones and the lines of his eyes. When he was finished, Myrddin saw the High King with doubled vision. There was the appearance he had given the man, and beneath it the king's own features.

Myrddin turned to lead him toward the tower, but Uther stayed, as if something was keeping him where he was. "You will come with me, or I will bring you back to meet the teeth of Winter." The High King glared at him sharply, but Myrddin felt each moment that passed now like the sting of a bee. "Winter has gone wilder than usual. It is the fault of mortals, and mortals will suffer for it."

The lines of Gorlois' forehead reflected the depth of Uther's irritation, and his fear. "None of this matters to me, boy. If the Wild Hunt will leave my men and take traitors instead, I have no complaints. If the Red King desires to drink up nations, what does it matter, as long as they aren't mine?"

His eyes glinted as he gazed up toward the tower, and for the first time since Myrddin had shadowed his shape with his rival's, Uther took a step forward. "What does it matter, so long as the woman *is*?"

In the guise of a nameless guard, Myrddin accompanied the High King through the layers of security around the base of the tower. A half dozen men in one place, and three in another. One, watching the narrow door that led to the spiral stair curling its way toward the tower chamber.

Past that door, up the stairs, they met no one. Myrddin stepped back, allowed Uther to walk in front of him and stopped when the man heaved open the door at the top of the tower. It slammed against the inner wall, and there was a shallow gasp from inside the room. Only the woman was waiting, and a single matron with her, a servant tending the hearth.

Uther was still then, drinking in the whole of the circular chamber and the women inside it. Myrddin stepped in ahead of him, contemplating from close at hand the lady he had studied from the tower window all those months before.

With the special arrogance of a royal woman, Ygraine greeted him. "You dare disturb me?" But her gaze drifted immediately to the man standing behind him, and her eyes widened. "My lord? I did not expect to see you tonight."

She took half a step forward. Before she could complete the movement, Myrddin pulled a thread of power and undid the magic. He blew away the glamor with a single breath, and the illusion dispersed like leaves in a strong wind.

The bedclothes were almost blown into the fire with the force of it. The curtains were torn from their rod and sucked out of the open space of the narrow window. Ygraine stood still, her mouth open wide. Her servant shrieked then fainted as Myrddin resolved into the boy he chose to be most often, and Gorlois became Uther.

The silk of Ygraine's dress whipped around her but settled finally into limp lines that reflected the supine drag of her features. "My...my lord..."

"Am I? I do not think your husband would agree." There was a playful humor in Uther's words that Myrddin had never suspected in the man. Desire wrought such strange changes on mortals. *Perhaps on all of us.* Was it not desire that had brought him *here*?

Desire and love.

The silence on Ygraine's face, the stillness of feature and feeling, lasted a moment longer. Then she completed her step forward and smiled with a challenge in her eyes, and a promise – many things. "My lord." She repeated herself without a quaver, and Uther took a step of his own, reached out and caught her by the waist.

"*So.* Here we are, with your bed and the night, both before us."

She did not flush, but her gaze darted away from Uther's, coy and collected. "So we are."

The High King bent to kiss her, and Myrddin shut the door behind him as he departed. He heard Ygraine's questions while he slipped down the stairs. *Who was that? How did you...?* Her voice gave way to surprised laughter and soft moans.

The night outside was full of darker iterations of the same noises that filled the tower. A long wail came out of the dark, followed by the echo of inhuman chuckling, but he closed his eyes and did his best to ignore it.

He was done with killing.

In the back of his mind, regardless, his own conscience laughed in time with the wild.

Done with it? Fool. You have always chosen Death. Fool, fool! He couldn't even argue with himself. Instead, he turned his thoughts to the tower behind him. The vision the spring had thrust on him had showed him much of this, and much that was to come, but not all.

A boy. "*A beautiful baby.*" Had he remembered that before? Who had said that? He closed his eyes, but the image was beyond his reach. "*A new name, but I...*" The same voice! "*A new name, but I need to finish becoming, first.*" It was the voice of a girl, who would become a perilous creature. "*Arawn said he would give me a new name, but...*"

Something more dangerous would come of those words, and he had heard that voice before, in waking life. But he could not make himself remember when that had been.

Not for the first time, he wished he had never decided to prevent the spring. What had it gained for him? Kas would never have left him to be overrun by it, if only... But what was done was done. Now he owed in guilt and had to pay for it.

Now he knew what was coming and how few paths there really were for him to choose.

Chapter Fourteen

Myrddin passed through the Avalon Gate and wandered through the sweet green of his own kingdom. He wanted just a moment before he continued into the empty silence of *between* and on to Autumn. A chance to put his thoughts in order.

Macsen would probably kill Gorlois. Probably. There was a chance that he wouldn't, just to spite him, but Myrddin thought that the Summer King's influence might be enough. Bran Fionnan had seemed…at least not hostile to his purpose. Had questioned, but that was only wise, if inconvenient.

At any rate, the Red King and his wild hunt were in Britain. The nature of the beast would work in Myrddin's favor. He had not told the whole truth, given all his own reasons, but he had not lied, either. The man who had been Ygraine's husband was just the type Macsen most liked to take. A perfect image of lordship among men. And the rest—there was bloodlust in the waiting tension of them, and that waiting only for the permission of their lord.

He was almost certain of the outcome of his intervention, but almost equally certain he would pay some kind of price. What was it the girl had said? *'Old stories.'* Well. The words had a certain kind of truth, but he would avoid those pitfalls. Was that not what the vision had taught him?

Even if the world was changing rapidly. Unease flitted along his spine. Not only was the Wyrdwood bleeding into the mortal forest, but the gray space of *between* that separated Spring from the other seasons was vanishing day by day.

It had been nearly five thousand years since he and Kas had laid the foundations that had become eight hidden kingdoms, but now they seemed to be coming apart. *Why* remained beyond him, unknown to him, but it couldn't only be Spring—no, he knew it wasn't. He had *seen* it, in the overwhelming vision...a world coming undone.

Having met with Uther, brought him to his woman, Myrddin's choices going forward were a little less clear. The path the vision had shown him, at first so obvious, was beginning to diverge. Two roads, each with their own consequences, waited before him. The road of the city and the road through the wood. Neither road led to safety. One road led to...

Death.

Sound-scent-taste of it, overwhelming, powerful...even in the memory of a vision, even only being recalled, the intensity restored the immersion that had accompanied his original experience. *One road leads to death. Or Death?* Which was it? The difference was important, so important, and he couldn't tell which he was seeing, couldn't—

"Merlin?"

"*Kas.*" He pushed himself to his feet, but Kas was already behind him, bending over him, and Myrddin turned into his arms. It was nothing to complain about, but he was surprised. He lifted himself up on his toes enough to press his lips against Kas' mouth. "I wasn't expecting you. You sent no word, nothing."

"I came when I was done with my work. I was so far behind after spending all that time with you, and then... But I do not regret it."

Myrddin kissed him again. "Does that mean you can't stay?"

"Not for long, but long enough."

"*Never.*" Kas laughed at him, the old, soft laughter, and Myrddin restrained himself from just leaning up to lick it off his lips. "What?"

"The way you say that. I could almost believe you mean

it."

Agitated, scowling now, Myrddin took a half-step forward and pressed his whole body against Kas, ran his hands up his arms to his shoulders then slid them into his hair. "Should I go with you when you leave? Follow you? Would you believe me then?"

Darkness accumulated in Kas' expression and resolved to some emotion Myrddin couldn't name. "You have never liked to spend time in Autumn. Not even with me."

"I don't care about that now."

"*You should*. You chased me down once already this summer." The words, like Kas' smile and his laughter, were gentle, but there was something hovering behind them that promised more than what he was saying, more than the softness…almost a reprimand.

Something that brought back the thoughts he'd been thinking just before he'd noticed Kas' arrival. *Death or death?* Spring was moving into spring. Soon, as it used to be, there would be no dividing line, no difference. If only it didn't matter, but it did. "Should or not, I don't care. *I don't care*. I don't have duties, just…half a game. It's not the same for me as for you. You know that. It never has been, not since we made —"

"I know."

Again, that flutter of *something* and he frowned, rested his forehead on Kas' chest. "Kas…it sounds like even if I did go with you, it wouldn't matter. Would you ignore me, turn me away?"

"*No*. I have my task but still, there is always time for you, will always be time for you, now that you are mine again. What has gotten into you? It has not been so long that we have been apart, but you are clinging to me now like I might disappear. Like I will push you away and let you go."

"Wouldn't you? Couldn't you? Don't act like it's a foolish thing to fear. It wasn't that long ago that I thought I wasn't ever going to have you again. Not even to kiss." He wrapped his arms around Kas' neck and pulled him down against his mouth, as if to prove that he *could* kiss him, really, that Kas wasn't going to move away.

Instead he drew Myrddin closer, tasting his mouth, teasing his tongue, until they were exchanging breaths, leaning into each other, pressing close and closer. Myrddin grinned at Kas' eagerness, equal to his own and reassuring because of that, if nothing else. He couldn't, wouldn't forget, even for a minute, that there was something coming, waiting to pull them apart—*something*.

But *now* had its own presence. The moment had its own demands and its own pleasures, none of which he was willing to deny. He ran his hands through Kas' hair, the dark strands tangling with his fingers and smoothing under his touch, until he pulled lightly, a rich black handful, and felt Kas laughing, silent but shaking in that certain way.

"What *now*, you—" He pressed his mouth to Kas' lips again. "Never mind. I'd almost forgotten that you could be like this. Laughing Death. My Death, Kas."

"Yours? No. Once, maybe. Before I understood what it meant to love you."

"But I thought…"

"You were talking about death, Merlin." The use of the love name soothed his suddenly splintered feelings. "There was a time when I would have killed you before losing you, giving you up. It was over long ago. Not when I first loved you, but when I learned what loving you meant." He brushed his fingers along the line of Myrddin's lips.

"I walked away from you then. I do not think I could kill you now, any more than when you…" The words tangled with each other, stopped the pain they carried at the tip of his tongue. "But if not now, why in some future time? When what I want is this, unlikely as it seems? These moments, when they are allowed. Quiet, and alone with you. In the green of Spring or blackest Autumn—or even the mortal world you linger in so long. I would care not at all which you chose, if only…"

"I would choose it?"

"If only you *could*." Kas touched his cheek then his lips. "But you are the son of the wood's wild god, and I am Death, even desperate. I am yours, but not your *death*." This time he chuckled, breathless as he was sometimes breathless from pleasure. But this, Myrddin thought, this was not pleasure he was hearing but pain.

"Kas, your ending — the *terrible thing* that's coming. I want to turn it away. I want to…" But he stopped, knowing that he had to start at the beginning if he was going to start anywhere, and that…that meant he couldn't start at all.

"Merlin?"

To begin at the beginning would mean to go on to the end. And he couldn't do that. Not now. Not yet. Maybe not ever…hopefully not ever. To mention it might be to make it real, and if he were to say it — *something. Tearing us apart again. Kas.* Wouldn't he run now? Wouldn't Kas leave now, rather than risk some stupidity of his renewing the old, cold trauma?

"What is it you want, Merlin?"

One road leads to failure. The other must lead to Death.

He would keep the secret. The truth of the vision — he would keep it to himself, at least until he learned what it was that he needed to do, how he could make it unreal. Just a dream.

"I want you, Kas. I want you to make me forget everything that isn't you. For a little while." He temporized, seeing the amusement in Kas' eyes, the humor there that he didn't, couldn't share. Not now.

"Even words, Merlin?" A black bolt slammed into him without warning, Kas' power coruscating, a dragon of desires and promises as undeniable as anything in the world. He gasped, infused and overcome by it, then settled dazed into Kas' arms as a hot mouth descended over his lips and kissed the breath out of him.

He felt the ground tipping out from under his feet, the grass suddenly cool on the nape of his neck. Kas held him still, but he arched up until Kas slid his hands from

Myrddin's back, over his chest to his throat.

Off-balance. Too much. Night-Autumn-Death-Kas-Perfect. Some things were feeling and some things were reality and some, like this moment, were too much of both. "How was it you wanted me? How is it you need me? Is it already too much for you, Merlin?"

Cool, teasing, he passed a thumb along the curve of Myrddin's lips. Myrddin reached up and caught hold of his wrist, held Kas' fingers to his mouth. Kas leaned closer, pressed one slender digit over Myrddin's tongue and let him draw the finger out of his mouth again, lap it once.

Still almost panting, he grinned. Kas shook his head, laughing, bent over his mouth and kissed him deep and fully as Myrddin entwined their fingers and pulled him down over him, down to the ground. He didn't even have his clothes off and he was already rocking against Kas for more. If his eagerness surprised his lover, he didn't show it.

Kas was equally eager, too much even to overpower the living magic of Myrddin's clothes and dissolve them away. "Merlin...*hmm*."

"*Ka* –" But Kas kissed him again, hands tracing the dip in his back just above his buttocks, pulling him into Kas' lap, off the ground, then slipping under his tunic. Cold, his hands. Hot, then freezing again. *Kas...touch me.* But he couldn't say anything with Kas' mouth sealed to his, couldn't say anything even once he lifted his lips, because...

"*Merlin*. You should know better by now." Fabric finally melted away between his fingers.

Myrddin looked up into his eyes, so black, glittering with desire.

Kas stroked the peaks of his nipples, then pinched them gently, tugged and let go.

"*Oh...*"

"Yes. Sounds, not words."

It had only been weeks since the last time he'd had Kas' hands on him, his cock in him, the heat of his mouth at his throat like it was now. Like so many other things, that didn't matter. It could have been another five thousand years.

Kas knew just where to touch him, always had. The heat of his fist wrapped around Myrddin's cock, stroked in time with his pounding heartbeat. The fingers of his other hand were splayed by Myrddin's head, browning the grass by his ear even in Spring.

"K – mmm…*ahhh, n-no – ohhh*. K…K…ah…*ah!*" Asking was beyond him, but his lover wouldn't let him and he didn't need to anyway, didn't need to say anything. Kas pressed two fingers past his lips, letting him wet them, suck on them, tease them. Myrddin wanted Kas' cock in his mouth instead, the silky heat of him on his tongue, but he knew what Kas was doing, knew what he wanted.

Moaning, he lifted his hips to Kas' touch as Kas drew his hand away from Myrddin's mouth and reached between his buttocks instead. His lover slid wet fingers inside him, stretching, enough to leave him gasping as Kas worked them deeper and curled them, stroking.

"*There!* Oh, there, right there. Don't stop, it's – "

"I will do what I want to you. That is all, now as before. But I am going to be careful with you, careful how I touch you. I will open you up for me, make sure you can take me without pain. I do not want to hurt you again."

"*Ahh…*"

"And you enjoy it, do you not? *Being mine.* Giving in. Every time, every time just like the first, like our rite – you like to fight me just so you can give in, is that it?" His fingers crooked, teasing, stroking.

"Yes. I know. I know your secret. Just like I know how much you love to take me in your mouth, so I will let you. Come here." He sat back on his legs with his thighs parted. Myrddin was still, panting, empty, missing Kas' fingers inside him and his hand on his cock and…everything. "Spoiled you, did I not? When we were last together. But now it is *my* turn to have what I want."

Myrddin sat up and shoved a hand through his hair. Licking his lips, he sprawled on the ground between Kas' thighs, held his cock at the base and started to lick it over without any hesitation.

So good. He'd always loved the taste of his lover, tingling on his lips, hot and chill at the same time. And Kas was eager now, wanted it as much as he did, thrust into his mouth, pulling Myrddin's hair as he sucked, hollowed his cheeks and tried to take it all.

He moaned around the thickness of it, felt Kas' hands dragging him down, until he swallowed the whole length of Kas' cock and his thighs twitched under Myrddin's hands.

The taste of him filled Myrddin's awareness, salt and sweet and Kas, *Kas*, driving into his mouth, all but choking him with his cock. His own erection throbbed against his thigh, so hard it hurt, but he enjoyed the ache of it, the promise. He was going to suck until Kas made him stop, and he was going to —

"Kas." He licked up from the base, curled his tongue around the head and moaned. Dripping for him. *This taste...* "Kas, you're going to take me, aren't you?" He sucked on the tip, then more, lifted his mouth off to breathe and turned his gaze to meet Kas' slitted eyes. "After. *After I...*won't you? *Take me.*"

Kas tugged at his hair, pulled him down onto his cock and kept him there. "Yes. *Yes.* I said as much before. But not now. Now I want you to — *yes.*"

"*Mmm.*" He couldn't say anything else, not with Kas keeping his mouth on his cock, forcing him down and hauling him up. Harder. Thicker. Myrddin moaned, sucked and tasted bitter heat as Kas started coming on his tongue, tightened his fists in Myrddin's hair and kept him where he was, swallowing around his cock, choking and groaning and trying to take more.

Finally, Kas tugged him up and off, watched him licking his lips, his fingers, and got to his feet. His cock stood out red and wet in front of him, tempting, so tempting, but Kas smirked and stepped away when Myrddin licked his lips again and got onto his knees.

"No more now. On your back." Kas stayed over him as Myrddin obeyed, grabbed him by the hips and bent him almost in half. Hot fingers circled his entrance, teasing him, slipped inside, one, then two — *three*. "Does it hurt?"

"*No*. No, you...-"

Kas tightened the hand holding Myrddin's buttocks apart, spread him open more and twisted the fingers buried in him. Myrddin sucked in a breath, gasped it out and did it again. So rough. Kas was being so *rough*. Slender fingers worked him open, teased inside him, even through the roughness, even when he needed no teasing.

A heavy, impatient tension swept through his body, a tight heat in his belly coiling tighter. Something hot and wet dripped onto his cheek, and Myrddin brushed at it with his knuckles. It smeared over his lips, and only when he tasted *himself* did he realize his cock was leaking all over him, dripping onto his chest, his cheek.

He licked his lips again, tried to lift his hips toward Kas' hands and moaned a little louder every time his fingers surged past the right place inside him. All his attempts at begging came out as a cry, a sound that was nowhere near Kas' name. Once he'd opened his mouth he couldn't *stop* crying out, every time Kas pushed his fingers in, curled them, stroked inside him.

By the time he stopped Myrddin was out of breath, had no idea why he hadn't come yet, but Kas pressed the head of his cock into him, then another inch, and he bucked *up*, wobbled and almost fell over until Kas' hands steadied his hips. Their grip kept him still for his lover to thrust down into him, filling him up and filling him up and —

"How long has it been since I had you this way? Not even at the rite. Did you think I did not notice? When I have always liked you this way best of all, ever since the first time I took you. Did you not want them all to see you so vulnerable? Giving in to me completely? Look at you. My hawk."

So slow. So deep, and so slow. Myrddin tightened his whole body, reaching for his release, but it was hovering in front of him, always one stroke, one inch away. The way Kas was staring down at him, tightening his hands on Myrddin's thighs again and again—he was doing it on purpose. On *purpose*. He squeezed around Kas' cock, clenched and gasped

"Kas. Going to. Kill me. *Ohhh*—"

But Kas laughed at him and pressed deeper. "Not today, Merlin. Not until spring."

"Going to *kill* me." But he was laughing, too, laughing as he moaned.

Kas' cock stretched him more and more, until he sank all the way inside and stayed there, bent over him, staring down at him. His eyes were gleaming behind the black fall of his hair.

"*Tight for me*. I love you like this." He spread Myrddin's thighs a little more, drew back and thrust deep, then again. Faster. "*Love* you like this. Bent over for me, all mine, all open. Dripping for me. And you want your pleasure, yes?" Long, slow thrusts. "You want it so much." The whole length of Kas' cock hammered into him, sparking starbursts inside him, white fire behind his eyelids.

"*No*. Look at me. *Look at me*."

"Ka…*ahhh*. Ahh…ah!" He forced his eyes open, fisted his hands in the grass and gazed up through his own splayed legs, his parted thighs, into Kas' hungry stare.

"*Yes*. Like that. Stay like that and fall in love with me again. Fall apart for me again. Give it all to me, *all to me*. This time I will not be denied, will not be…" He stopped, unbent Myrddin's legs and drove deep as he came down over him, pinning him to the grass with his whole body.

"*Kas*. I never *stopped* loving you. I…I…I…Kas!" He moaned again, so close, *so close*, canted his hips *up* and cried out when he got that last inch, perfect and just enough when Kas slammed into him again. With one hand, he reached over his head and rooted himself to the ground, lifted his hips and clenched tightly as the pleasure reached its peak and rolled through him in waves.

He heard himself crying out, almost screaming, except that Kas had made him cry out too many times and his voice was hoarse with it. In counterpoint, he felt the throbbing flush of heat inside him that was Kas' release.

His lover was still for just an instant, clutching him close, breathing out one long exhalation that held maybe the shadow of his name, that sweetest word. *Merlin.*

Then Kas was shifting with him, bringing him up and rolling them over together. "On top of me. Take it for yourself now, take it all, Merlin."

Myrddin obeyed without a murmur of complaint, sinuous, wanting, oversensitive and not caring in the least. Something moved him, curved his back as he took Kas' cock all the way down then lifted up and dropped onto it again. He bent over Kas' chest, rocking, taking it all easily, slick with heat now, so wet inside.

It dripped out of him around Kas' cock, sticky on his thighs as he braced himself and took his lover deeper.

Fall.

In love.

With me.

Again.

It passed between them in silences, then in moans. Myrddin kissed him and Kas slid both hands into his hair, holding him there, kept him against his mouth until they had only the sweet, scalding air of each other's breath to breathe.

"*Kas.*" He gasped, clung to Kas even though he was almost too hot to touch, and Kas clung back, dug his nails into Myrddin's skin and drew blood that spilled wet down his spine. It was pain. It was pleasure. Everything he wanted, everything he needed. *Just to keep him. Forever.* "Kas…"

"Yes. More. I know."

Epilogue

Alone with his thoughts and the matching whispers of his companions, Marcus Pontius contemplated the fall of mortal power in Ireland. The creak of the oars and the low splash of dark water against the hull of their ship were no comfort.

Neither were the madness and death of the queen to whom he had been in service.

He had watched from his hiding place in the church as the Summer King had passed through all barriers of holy power and hallowed ground. He had seen Aisling, the new queen, return the chains her sister had worked so hard to forge.

It had been enough to convince him to leave Ireland. More clearly than ever he saw the reason for their failure. Despite all his attempts at freeing the Milesians from their pagan beliefs, the old powers and the old gods were still too strong among them. Rather than giving ground, the *sidhe* had been restored to their place as masters of the isle.

Marcus glanced over his shoulder once more then fixed his attention on the approaching British shore. Perhaps here, in a more civilized land, he could manage to do more, and better.

It was the end of the year, and the Red King had already run roughshod over the wild with his hunt. There would be a safe space. Time for a deep breath, and then? Once more the plunge.

The work of God was not to be halted by the sabotage of lesser spirits.

"When we land..." He paused to make sure the others

were listening. "You must say nothing to anyone of where we have come from or what has happened there. Instead, ask after the new High King, this Pendragon who rejected Dealla. Ask after his influences, his desires, his most important councilors."

One pale youth, his hair and eyes washed out to shades of gray in the dimness, gazed at him with a mixture of exhaustion and dedication. "Is there something specific we—?"

"Nothing specific. Too many questions with sharp purposes close mouths. Move among the people and listen. Minister to their needs. Make a place for yourselves in the churches, and share with those you find there what we have learned about how to protect ourselves from darkness."

His stare passed from one to another of his priests and their acolytes—a score of men were left, no more, though his mission had started with more than a hundred. "I had heard that there was trouble here, Saxon raiders at the coast, a rebel lord in an inconvenient position…and this Uther is said to be a Christian king."

That was enough, he was sure. They were intelligent, loyal men. Men of faith. They would understand his intentions, all that he had left unsaid. Trouble always offered inroads to power.

To stand by such authority was the one thing of this world that Marcus coveted for himself. Enough so that he had followed the lure of it away from the Mediterranean and the glory of Rome. To convert a king, to baptize a kingdom—that would be to engrave his name in the annals of history.

His thoughts drifted again to Dealla. Poor queen. If only she had not been driven mad. If only she had seen the truth and given up the beliefs that had betrayed her. It was… unfortunate. She had been a woman who had understood the danger civilized man was facing.

Ah, well. Too late for her now. And perhaps in the end it had been her methods, more than her madness, that had caused trouble.

He would have to think on that.

Wolf of the West

Excerpt

Chapter One

Marcas stared upward at the sound of an imperative caw, and knew he must move faster. Four legs paced under him, swift as the wind, but he could see even from a distance that what had been a battlefield had now become a scavenger's rout. Above him, black crows crossed the sky, first in twos and threes, then a streaming murder.

It is coming.

The twilight darkened into premature night under the shadow of their wings, and from the gore that littered the field came crawling shadows, stick-figures unbending against the light.

Darkness made flesh.

Once, twice, Marcas howled, but the moon was not yet risen and he could summon no light into his service. From the top of a low rise, he could only look down and watch more carnage in the making. Warriors, bloodstained, wounded — waylaid in victory or defeat, they had survived the battle only to suffer something more terrible.

His gaze focused on their widened eyes, the glaring darkness in each overburdened pupil, teeth visible behind lips thinned with fear in each face — yet in none of them did he see what he had come for. A spark of light — *the mark of brightness* that told him the one so marked was meant to survive. That one, he would protect. But where was he?

Wraiths absent of flesh unfolded across the carnage, seeking their prey. The survivors who could move stumbled away from them with all the speed their broken limbs could muster. Marcas' gaze caught on three that moved together, two older, one younger, perhaps a son or nephew of one of the others. The elder two held him back, their hands across his chest at what they must have believed was a final moment of fear — and yet that youth stood forward, his face all confrontation, nothing of terror in the glare of his eyes.

The shadow moved to confront him, the youth painted with blazing light in the dark field of Marcas' mind, and the truth flamed in him, sudden and precise.

This one! This one — now, now!

In a flash, Marcas leaped down the hillside, crossed the blooded grass and buried his teeth in the shadow nearest the youth. Black blood spurted around his fangs, and he felt dark fingers clutching at the fur of his back. Marcas whipped around and lunged at them. He caught sight of the three men behind him, their eyes wider now, if that was possible — watching him, wondering — but there was no way for him to explain.

Like many men before them, they would have to come to their own conclusions.

Growling, spitting, pacing back and forth, Marcas marked a circle with his steps, with his body, with his flashing fangs. He leaped across to threaten any reaching hand, any open mouth, rattle-breathed, foaming.

Three of them, but I can't protect just that one. The boy. The boy wouldn't let me, and it wouldn't be right.

But three men were two more than he had expected. A battle like this one, wounds like theirs—the older men should probably be dead, but there was no accounting for the strength of a heart, a spirit or a warrior. Marcas' quick eyes took in the wound on the younger one—the thigh, wrapped tight, blood soaked but older blood now, not fresh flowing... *Not so bad, boy.* It would be easier to protect him than the other two—closer to death, closer to the enemy.

The crawling multitude of bloodthirsty spirits reached out first for the men, not the boy. For a moment he felt a vain desire to take the boy and leave these fools to their fate. One wounded young man was no match for a wolf of the *faoladh,* no matter what his desires.

But across his mind's eye flashed that first glimpse again—blazing light and eyes with no terror in them at all.

Black energies tore at his back again, gripped his tail and pulled him. He whirled, ears laid back, snapping, tasted darkness and congealed death, but it was neither blood nor anything real. Shadow screeched, a sound like the caw of the crows, but deepened, twisted, broken. He sought the matte jet throats, tore open wounds that spilled nothing, but it was nothing with the taste of ash. Marcas pushed them back with the weight of his body, with his claws and fangs that snapped with supernatural swiftness. Tireless, intent, he fought against the circling foes that increased in number even as he engaged them. They flowed back and receded, then returned to wash around him, a new and stronger tide—

Until the moon rose. The moonlight fell on Marcas' back and his fur shone with a pale light, every hair illuminated. He lifted his head and those of his foes closest to him took a step back. His mouth opened, and out of his throat came an illuminated noise, more than a howl—the true song of the night, safety from all shadow in that one note, even as it was many.

The wolf song shattered the shadow, broke it apart into

bits as the moonlight spread and painted the black of the hills and the gore of the field with light. Panting now, feeling the pain of many wounds, Marcas fell silent and stepped back, looked around with wary eyes to see if the night might choose to rebirth its horrors.

There was only silence and stillness. The natural shadows of the night, death in coherent slumber. What the violence had awakened was restful now. *Quiet.*

Satisfied, Marcas turned to face the trio of men he had protected. They, too, were silent, all but unmoving, until he turned to leave.

"*Wait.*"

It was a young voice, the voice of the one he'd been called to protect, but Marcas didn't look back. He turned away despite that call, and vanished into the cloak of the night.

* * * *

The dawn came early, yellow and heavy, sunlight spreading like spilled yolk across the horizon. It was welcome light, which scattered shadow and imprisoned the fears of the night behind walls of memory. The shapes of dark and crooked power that had spilled from what had once been the bodies of friends and foe — the tide of dark within the night — those things were faded, but the memory of that which had conquered them was not.

The wolf.

"Still well, Connor?"

Startled from the thoughts that had distracted him, the throbbing of the wound in Connor's thigh returned full force at the sound of his father's voice. He almost brought up the image that lingered in his mind's eye. *Moonstruck wolf.* But he hesitated, and only answered the question his father had asked.

"Well enough. I'll make it."

They lapsed into silence after that. As Connor limped forward beside the single horse they'd found wandering at the edge of the battlefield, he drew himself out of his thoughts and watched his father over the horse's neck. Silent, craggy, a mountain in motion, he stomped forward as if nothing could—or would—stop him, as if he felt neither the pain of his wounds nor the pain of their journey. How far now? Since the wolf had left them in the blazing moonlight—since they'd found the horse and his father had forced Lord Aran to mount? *Too long.*

There had been an apology on his father's face, as he'd shoved Aran up on the beast, but despite the agony of this stumble through the dark, there'd been no other way to keep Aran moving.

Again, Connor looked into his father's face. His dark eyes were crowded under the clenching of his brow and the poor bandage that was bound there. His father nodded once, approval or encouragement, and Connor set his eyes on the road again, a dusty band that cinched the green hills before them like a poorly tightened belt.

It was good that he hadn't said anything, hadn't brought up the questions that burned in him. When he had asked in the dark after the wolf had left them, his father had shushed him right away, warned of bad luck and spurned blessings. *Some things we should not speak of, even amongst ourselves.* He heard the echo of his father's voice, the only answer he'd gotten, and knew that now wasn't a time to add to his worries—but despite his outer silence, the questions remained inside him, loud and urgent.

What had those things been? Shadow had risen from their comrades and from the enemy warriors both. Was it the power of their foe? *But then, what of the wolf?* Where had he come from? He had never seen anyone fight the way that wolf fought. Focusing on those moments, those memories, he shuddered, stumbled, caught himself and forced himself not to look at his father again. *Some things weren't meant to be faced by mortal men.* He had seen training injuries enough and the wounds on returning warriors — he'd thought he'd known what there was to know of battle and death.

He knew better now.

Battle was not wounds and weapons and warriors. Battle was blood-smoke, a mist of red in the air, so fine the taste of it was in every breath. Battle was stepping forward and slipping and not looking down to see if what was under your boots was mud or the blood-slick guts of someone who didn't know he was dead yet. Connor had learned that the arm could grow so tired it couldn't stop swinging, that a blade new-sharpened could clot in a glut of flesh, chip on a sternum and still shatter a skull. Battle was heaving breath, every muscle burning and nerves dead ended or on fire — no in-between, no pause, no breathing space... And in the lulls, everything too quiet. Every crow's cawing, every breath of wind became a thing that stirred alertness out of impossible fatigue.

He'd thought the end was just another one of those lulls. That there would be another charge, another rush — something else, because it couldn't be over. It would never be over... But it was.

Until night came.

His leg had been long-bound by then and he had done what he could for his father, limping, reaching across the broad shoulders to bind a wound that streamed new flow over the rusty stains of old blood. But it had been Aran who was the worst wounded, by the loss of his sons. Connor had found him, bent over the bodies. Perhaps it had been Aran's cries that had woken shadows out of the dead. *They were loud enough. They went on forever.*

Not that he could blame him. There would be no honored burial, no pyre for those boys, not after this battle. Not when no one survived, no one but them — who would carry the bodies? Who would return to this plain and bring away the crow's feast that remained? They had come to the very edge of his father's kingdom to fight, two hundred warriors seeking to spill blood in the name of an ancient feud long abated. Fifty years of the High King's peace had been broken there, and for what?

Nothing had been won, nothing gained, nothing threatened—a field in the middle of pastureland, and no herds in sight, and now his father's men and the men who had rebelled both were dead.

Connor sighed, licked dry lips and looked up across the endless rolling of the hills and into the sunlight. *How much farther?* He took another step, and another, and another…

"Connor? Stop, Connor."

He heard his father's voice, but it seemed to come from a distance. Why would that be? His father was…right there. He turned his head to the left, and the motion unbalanced some precarious state he hadn't even been aware of. His head was light, and his leg was numb. Thigh to foot, he couldn't feel a thing.

"That isn't right…"

"Connor!"

Darkness.

It reached out to envelop him, and for an instant, his heart sped up in fear.

But no.

No worries.

The thought came to him of itself, soothing, silken.

Wolf will protect me.

There was no need to fear the night.

More books from
Pride Publishing

*When a prince finds his soul mate in an enemy soldier, he
must fight everyone around him to keep his love.*

Book one in the Keepers of the Gods series

When Seth, a Keeper of the Gods, finds the two men he is destined to live eternity with, he must defy the very Gods themselves to save his mates and preserve the existence of man and love.

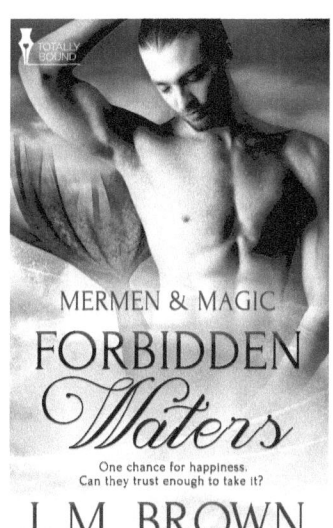

MERMEN & MAGIC

FORBIDDEN
Waters

One chance for happiness.
Can they trust enough to take it?

L.M. BROWN

Book one in the Mermen & Magic series

*For the dying race of mer people, homosexual relationships
are prohibited. When Kyle falls for Prince Finn he knows
he is navigating forbidden waters.*

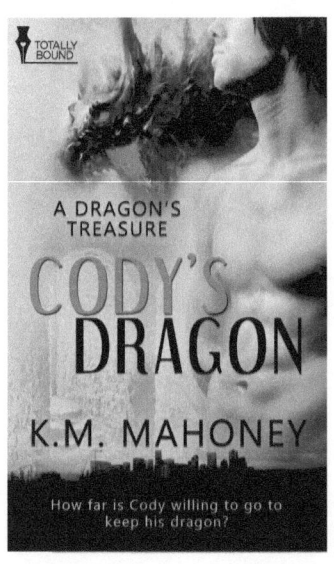

Book one in the A Dragon's Treasure series

How far is Cody willing to go to keep his dragon?

About the Author

Belinda Burke

Belinda currently lives on the New England coast with her fiancée, their room mate and her cat. When she's not writing, she's working toward degrees in Philosophy and English, embroidering or reading.

Belinda writes in several genres, but a little lust and love always work their way into her stories.

Belinda Burke loves to hear from readers. You can find contact information, website details and an author profile page at https://www.pride-publishing.com/

www.ingramcontent.com/pod-product-compliance
Lightning Source LLC
Chambersburg PA
CBHW030140180626
46812CB00002B/772